Books by Alysha Ellis

Bodices and Boudoirs

A Boudoir for Three

Lust Bites

Her Lord's Table
The Devil Made Me Do It
Lone Wolf

Sexy Snax

Downunder Heat

Sweet Sensations

The Kissing Bough

Anthologies

At Your Service
Boots, Chaps and Cowboy Hats

Single Titles

Sharing the Billionaire
Submitting to Him
The Gardener's Sins
Lasso Lovin'
Claiming the Cowboys
Send Me An Angel
The Cowboy Takeover

I0680779

Books by BA Tortuga

Roughstock

Blind Ride
And a Smile
File Gumbo
Coke's Clown
Back to Back

Roughstock Sweethearts

City Country
Picking Roses

Top of the Leader Board

Ace and Kitty

One Horse Town

Mr. Unlucky

Anthologies

Boots, Chaps and Cowboy Hats

Single Titles

What She Wants
Tied and Taken

Books by Nan Comargue

Wanton Witches

Sudden Storm

Sexy Snax

Rock Star
Captive Angel
The Gamble
Snow Fire

Anthologies

At Your Service
Wild After Dark
Boots, Chaps and Cowboy Hats

Single Titles

All Together Now
Country Hearts
A Lady for Two
Lasso Lovin'
Hard Luck Ranch
Darker Nights
Three to Feud

Books by Wendi Zwaduk

Heart Attack

Over My Head

Haunted By You

Miss Me Baby

Immortal Love

Until the Night

Wanton Witches

Candlelit Magic

Jolly Rogered

Ruined by the Pirate

Clandestine Classics

The Phantom of the Opera

Lust Bites

Must Be Doing Something Right
Love Remembers

Sexy Snax

Firelit Magic
Sunshine of Your Love

Books by Molly Ann Wishlade

The Duggans of Montana

Harlot at the Homestead
A Rancher for Rosie
Her Montana Cowboy

Sexy Snax

Desire in Deadwood

Anthologies

Racing Hearts
Boots, Chaps and Cowboy Hats

Single Titles

Healing Her Cowboy

Books by Beth D. Carter

Red Wolves Motorcycle Club

Along Came Merrie
True North
When Dove Cries
Lily Roar

Anthologies

Boots, Chaps and Cowboy Hats

Single Titles

Mad Delights
Madness Ends
Cadence Falls

BOOTS, CHAPS & COWBOY HATS ANTHOLOGY

THE COWBOY TAKEOVER
ALYSHA ELLIS

TIED AND TAKEN
BA TORTUGA

THREE TO FEUD
NAN COMARGUE

BETWEEN US
WENDI ZWADUK

HEALING HER COWBOY
MOLLY ANN WISHLADE

CADENCE FALLS
BETH D. CARTER

Boots, Chaps and Cowboy Hats

ISBN # 978-1-78651-342-7

The Cowboy Takeover ©Copyright Alysha Ellis 2016

Tied and Taken ©Copyright BA Tortuga 2016

Three to Feud ©Copyright Nan Comargue 2016

Between Us ©Copyright Wendi Zwaduk 2016

Healing Her Cowboy ©Copyright Molly Ann Wishlade 2016

Cadence Falls ©Copyright Beth D. Carter 2016

Cover Art by Posh Gosh ©Copyright May 2016

Interior text design by Claire Siemaszkiewicz

Totally Bound Publishing

This is a work of fiction. All characters, places and events are from the author's imagination and should not be confused with fact. Any resemblance to persons, living or dead, events or places is purely coincidental.

All rights reserved. No part of this publication may be reproduced in any material form, whether by printing, photocopying, scanning or otherwise without the written permission of the publisher, Totally Bound Publishing.

Applications should be addressed in the first instance, in writing, to Totally Bound Publishing. Unauthorised or restricted acts in relation to this publication may result in civil proceedings and/or criminal prosecution.

The author and illustrator have asserted their respective rights under the Copyright Designs and Patents Acts 1988 (as amended) to be identified as the author of this book and illustrator of the artwork.

Published in 2016 by Totally Bound Publishing, Newland House, The Point, Weaver Road, Lincoln, LN6 3QN, United Kingdom.

No part of this book may be reproduced, scanned, or distributed in any printed or electronic form without permission. Please do not participate in or encourage piracy of copyrighted materials in violation of the authors' rights. Purchase only authorised copies.

Totally Bound Publishing is a subsidiary of Totally Entwined Group Limited.

If you purchased this book without a cover you should be aware that this book is stolen property. It was reported as "unsold and destroyed" to the publisher and neither the author nor the publisher has received any payment for this "stripped book".

THE COWBOY
TAKEOVER

ALYSHA ELLIS

Chapter One

Sweat trickled down Maddie's neck, gathered in the hollow at the base of her throat then poured into the valley between her breasts. She'd already dialed the air conditioner down to its lowest setting, fan running at full speed. For a fleeting moment, she thought about opening the window to let in a blast of fresh air, but outside, where the sun beat down on the dry grass plains, the temperature was close to forty degrees.

According to the GPS, there were twenty minutes left in a journey that should never have been necessary. If Kyson Brown, manager of Harwood Downs, had returned her phone calls, answered his email or acknowledged any of the numerous attempts the legal firm she worked for had made to contact him, she wouldn't be driving in this outrageous heat.

A small part of her winced at the thought of this beautiful scenery stripped and scarred by the ugliness of open-cut coal mining, but progress was progress, and profit the bottom line.

An orange warning light flashed ominously on the dashboard, and her lips tightened. She'd told her boss she needed the bigger, newer company car, but John O'Kane had shrugged and said, "Someone else has it booked."

It hadn't mattered that the other lawyer was using the car to drive from one part of the city to another, and Maddie had been making a five-hundred-kilometer trip. Maddie was the most junior member of the practice, and the job she'd been given was little more than a courier's run. The badly maintained vehicle she'd been allocated matched her humble task. She had to deliver a set of documents into Kyson Brown's hands, then head back to the blessed cool of the city.

Assuming, of course, that Kyson Brown was still working and living on Harwood Downs. The company that owned the cattle station, having acquired it in a takeover and appointed Brown as a manager, had taken no further interest in it. Maddie's well-regulated legal mind had been horrified to discover there had been no audits, no perusal of expenses, not even the most basic of inspections to make sure the property and its buildings were properly maintained.

She looked again at the high temperature warning light. Her mechanical ability didn't extend much beyond finding the petrol cap, so other than pulling over and letting the car cool down, she had no idea what to do.

Her mobile phone, cradled in the hands-free device, showed no signal. Harwood Downs was only a few minutes away. Better to try to make it there than stop on the side of the road and wait for roadside assistance, which out here, could take hours to arrive. She hoped Kyson Brown *was* still in residence and had maintained the homestead, because she needed a cold drink and somewhere shady to wait for the car to get back to normal operating levels.

Jaw clenched, knuckles white, she drove on.

When the generic female voice intoned, "In five hundred meters, you have reached your destination," Maddie almost kissed the console. She put on her indicator, in spite of not having seen another car for the last sixty minutes, and made the turn.

Something in the engine clanged ominously when she bounced across the cattle grid, but Maddie pretended she hadn't heard it. She kept her foot down and headed toward the buildings at the end of the driveway.

In spite of the heat, the place looked green and well maintained. Cattle, clustered together in the shade cast by overhanging pepper trees, turned their heads to look at her.

Even to a complete city girl, it was obvious they were in good condition. Kyson Brown might have been a negligent correspondent, but he knew his job.

Not that his competence would make any difference to the outcome. The decision had been made. All she had to do was make sure he was aware of it.

She switched off the engine, grabbed the yellow envelope from the seat beside her and stepped out into a wall of fiery air. Her sweat-dampened silk shirt dried instantly.

"Who the hell are you?" The deep voice came from behind her. She gasped, choked on a mouthful of dust and succumbed to an uncontrollable fit of coughing.

When she finally caught her breath, her head swam and tears blurred her vision. She turned around to see a long, blue shape that resolved itself into a man. Maddie gasped again. This was not just *any* man. This was an escapee from her most private dreams.

From the top of his cowboy hat clad head, to his chiseled, handsome face, wide shoulders, narrow hips and powerful legs, he was the epitome of male perfection.

His bad-tempered rasp fractured the illusion. "I asked you who you are and why in the hell you're on my property." He waved a hand dismissively. "Doesn't matter. Bugger off back to whatever city you came from."

"My name is Madeline Nelmes," Maddie said, taken aback by his aggressive tone. If he was this annoyed before he knew who she was or why she was there, it was going to get very unpleasant once she told him. "My firm, O'Kane Legal Services, is acting on behalf of the owners. Lyall Holdings—"

"I know who owns the bloody property," he interrupted. "And I know why you're here."

Maddie's fists clenched involuntarily. "Then asking me was a waste of time, wasn't it?" She knew she sounded snarky. Tough. She was hot and tired and it was his fault.

If her attitude offended him, he didn't show it. One broad shoulder lifted. "Less of a waste than your trip out here.

There'll be no open-cut mine on Harwood Downs."

Maddie blew out an exasperated breath and stepped around the back of the car toward him. All she was supposed to do was hand over the documentation, person to person. She wasn't here to argue about the inevitable.

"Regardless of what you might believe, this mine is going ahead. I've driven five hundred kilometers in this rotten, awful, stinking heat because you couldn't be bothered to acknowledge receipt of the notifications we've sent you. The surveyor arrives tomorrow. Please see he has whatever access and accommodation he needs."

He folded his arms across his chest. "The surveyor can turn around and go straight back. This land will be mined over my dead body."

Maddie looked him up and down. It was a damn fine body, but the stubborn mind that controlled it was reflected in the hard line of his lips, and the blue eyes, that even in these absurd temperatures, were icy enough to send a chill up her spine.

"You don't own the property." She tried for a conciliatory tone. She looked around at the neat buildings, the sturdy fences and the well-fed animals. "Lyall Holdings has already signed an agreement with BRX Mining. That won't change, but maybe I can negotiate some compensation for—"

"I don't want compensation. I want..."

Maddie didn't hear the rest of the sentence. She knew he was speaking, because his lips moved, but a wavy, clear wall suddenly appeared in front of him, distorting everything. She dragged her hand across her eyes, but the blurriness increased. The heat bore down on her. Her stomach churned and she tried to call out, but the sound, like her vision, was lost in the encroaching darkness.

Chapter Two

The cool trickle of water down the side of her neck brought Maddie back to awareness. Her hand, lifted to her forehead, encountered the lumpy contours of ice blocks wrapped in some kind of textured cloth.

"Leave it there." The rough voice came from somewhere out of sight. She struggled to push herself up on her elbows.

"You passed out," the voice continued. "I suck at tender, loving care, so if you don't want to attempt another face plant, stay down."

The owner of the voice moved into view and memory flooded back. Kyson Brown. At least she assumed that's who it was, because he'd never introduced himself.

"Thanks for the rescue and the ice-pack," she said, pleased her voice didn't sound as woozy as she felt.

She lay on a comfortable leather sofa in a large, darkened room. A chilly wash of air, combined with a low level hum, indicated an effective air-conditioning system. A hard wooden chair was pulled up near the sofa. The yellow envelope was lying, opened, on the floor beside it. "Thank you for bringing me inside." She was no lightweight, so it couldn't have been easy, even for someone who looked as fit as he did.

The sound he made was little more than a grunt, but it didn't sound angry, more a reluctant acknowledgment.

"I don't usually faint," she muttered into the awkwardness. "The heat must have got to me."

"That's not all it got to," he said.

"What?" She furrowed her brow, trying to understand. Under the ice pack, pain throbbed dully.

"Your car. The radiator hose is ruptured."

The headache intensified, moved down to tighten her shoulders and stiffen her neck.

"Can I drive it?"

"Nope. You need a replacement part."

She squeezed her eyes shut, but it didn't help the pain, so she opened them again. "Is there somewhere I can get one?"

"Not around here."

Did she have to drag every word out of him? She'd heard about the strong, silent type, but she hadn't realized, until she met one, how frustrating they could be.

"Where can I get one then?"

"Town."

Very calmly and quietly she asked, "Could I trouble you for a lift into town then?"

He shook his head. "I've got too much work to do to be making unscheduled breaks. You'll have to wait."

"Wait?" She sat up sharply and the pain ratcheted up a notch. She ignored it. "I can't do that. I have work." She glared at him. "I have to get back to the city. I have an important job."

His lips lifted into what might have been a smile but was too dangerous to make her feel comfortable. "Can't be too important if they can spare the time to send you all this way just to deliver a message. And frankly, I have no interest in doing anything to make life easier for bloody O'Kane Legal Services." He said the name with a sneer, as if they were filthy words. "You got yourself into this situation and you're going to have to make the best of it. The next delivery of goods to Harwood Downs is tomorrow..."

"Well, okay then," she said with relief. Spending the night here wasn't something she wanted to do, and Kyson Brown didn't sound as if he'd be too happy about it, but at least she had a timeline to work on. "If you ring someone and order the part for me, I could be on my way tomorrow afternoon. If you know how to fit it?" He appeared to be a man who could do all those sorts of jobs. He lived way out here—he'd have to be independent and capable.

"Maybe you could shut up for a minute and let me finish," he said dryly. "Last week, while I was out riding the fences, a lightning storm hit. A strike near the homestead took out the wireless network router and the phone base station. The delivery on Wednesday is bringing the replacement appliances. Once they're installed, there'll be phone service again. Then we can order the radiator hose. If you're really lucky, the garage in town will have one in stock. If not..." He gave a dismissive shrug.

"You don't have a phone?"

"Or Internet."

"Oh." Maddie thought for a moment. "So you weren't just ignoring the messages we sent. You couldn't respond."

A faint stroke of red highlighted his cheekbones. "I may have read a couple of your emails before the storm hit."

"And the letters? They were sent weeks ago."

"I got those." If he'd seemed embarrassed a moment ago, all traces of it were gone now. His face was a study in grim. "They're in the hands of my lawyer."

"I don't understand," she said.

"You don't have to. My beef is with the mining company and the legal firm that represents them." His hard mouth softened a little. "Your name wasn't on any of the papers I've received."

Her name wasn't on *anything* important at O'Kane's. No matter how hard she tried, she never seemed to get noticed or rewarded. Not that she was going to let Kyson Brown know how low in the pecking order she was. "I'm not one of the principals in the case."

His gaze locked with hers. "You work for the enemy. I don't know whether that makes you the enemy or not. In either case, we appear to be stuck with each other for the next few days. How about we call a truce?"

A different kind of heat sparked in his eyes. Tension thrummed between them. Maddie drew a deep breath. His

19

scent, heat, raw male and something musky and alluring, came with it.

His pupils dilated, making his eyes dark. He leaned forward…

"Hey. Is anyone home? I knocked." A male voice crashed in on them. Kyson leapt to his feet and turned toward the sound.

"Three years without a damn visitor, now they're all over the bloody place," he grumbled as he strode out of the room.

Maddie tried to stand, but her knees were wobbly and her heart raced. "It's the heat," she told herself. And if it was also the after effects of Kyson Brown, she wasn't going to admit it, not even to herself.

She plopped back down onto the sofa.

The rumble of male voices grew louder, and Kyson shouted, "Like hell you will."

Her breathing steadied and her brain kicked in. The newcomer was most likely the surveyor, but he appeared to be a day early. She'd better stiffen her spine and her recalcitrant knees and get out there and find out.

She followed Kyson's path into the homestead kitchen. He stood, legs planted apart, fists clenched by his sides, weight balanced on the balls of his feet, confronting a tall, slender man who stood half a step inside the open French doors.

The newcomer wore a suit, yet he looked cool and elegant. The only sign of the long journey was the shadow of stubble on the clean lines of his cheeks and jaw. His arms were folded, his head tilted slightly to one side, his eyebrows raised.

"What's going on here?" Maddie demanded.

The newcomer lifted his head, brown-eyed gaze focusing on Maddie, taking her in from head to toe. "You're Maddie from O'Kane's? They told me you'd be here today." He smiled and held out his hand. "I'm Connor Benton."

"The surveyor, right? I thought you were arriving

tomorrow, but it's nice to meet you." Maddie took Connor's outstretched hand. Instead of the cool touch she'd expected, an electric buzz sizzled across her palm.

She wasn't the only one who felt it. Connor's deep brown eyes opened wider. His fingers tightened for a moment, then he slowly released them. His lips curled wickedly. "I'm glad *someone* is happy I'm here. Our cowboy friend just ordered me off the property."

Maddie took a deep breath. How could Kyson be so considerate one minute and such a jerk the next?

"He does that." She frowned over her shoulder at Kyson. "He doesn't have any right to make you leave."

"Try me." Kyson glared at Connor.

Maddie sighed. "I was trying to explain this to you before. The deal is done. BRX has applied for a mining lease. Lyall Holdings, who I shouldn't have to remind you, *own* Harwood Downs, has abandoned the property to BRX and their employees. You are no longer needed as a caretaker or manager. You need a new job and a new place to live."

Kyson shook his head. "I know what you said. You think that's how it is, but you're wrong."

"Is she?" Connor Benton unfolded his arms. "You seem pretty certain."

At the same time, Maddie said, "That's ridiculous. You don't have the power to stop this."

Kyson rocked back on his heels. "Don't bet." Muscles flexed under the rolled up sleeves of his shirt as he folded his arms.

"You two can argue that out," Connor said. "I'm just here to do my job. O'Kane offered to pay well over my usual fee to get the survey done quickly."

Kyson's eyes narrowed. "BRX is an international company. They should have their own surveyors."

"Yeah." Connor nodded. "It seemed odd to me. But I'm not in a position to turn down work. And since I got paid in advance, I'd really like to get the job done." He half-turned to peer out at the landscape. "Pity to see this place ripped up for mining, though. Looks like good grazing land."

"It is," Kyson replied. "And it's in a water catchment area."

"I'm surprised the mine application was approved." Connor stopped and turned back to face Kyson. "Seems a bit dodgy to me."

A look passed between the two men that Maddie couldn't interpret.

"Too dodgy," Kyson said.

"Coal's not the way of the future anyway," Connor said. "They'd do better to invest in renewables."

Kyson nodded. Two sets of shoulders relaxed and the aggression in the air subsided.

Connor gestured to the table. "Can we sit down?"

"Sure," Kyson replied. "I'll get us a drink. Beer?"

"Love one," Connor said. "You having one, Maddie?"

Maddie thought for a second. Hell, why not? She desperately needed to rehydrate, and something that might help her relax was a bonus. "Yes, please."

When Kyson returned, three frosty bottles dangled from his fingers.

He put them on the table and pulled out a chair.

Connor picked up his beer and held it to his mouth. His lips wrapped around the bottle. Maybe it was the heat, or the long sexual dry spell, during which all her energy and time had been devoted, however futilely, to advancing her prospects at O'Kane's. Maybe it was the unique circumstance of being a woman in the presence of two gorgeous men, or maybe it was all those things, but Maddie's imagination took flight. What would Connor's lips feel like on her mouth, her breasts, the suddenly damp place between her legs? What kind of lover would Kyson be? Strong and forceful but with a hidden softness he revealed only in tender moments?

What were the chances of her wildest, most secret fantasies ever happening in real life?

The plain truth, judging by her past history, was—not

good.

But right now, awareness danced across her skin and fizzled in her blood. Kyson's speculative gaze fixed on her and her heart beat faster.

"How long have you worked for O'Kane's?" he asked.

"About a year." She frowned. She'd been indulging in wicked thoughts, and Kyson had been considering the conditions of her employment. Hardly flattering. "Why does that matter?"

"It matters because I'm trying to work out if you're just a messenger and pretty much in the dark, or if you've been actively engaged in the negotiations."

Familiar anger churned in her gut. She was not going to let another male dismiss her as irrelevant. "I'm as competent as any other lawyer working at O'Kane's. I'm capable of negotiating high-level transactions."

"So you worked on the case," Connor said. "You know what's in these documents."

She didn't. She'd been handed a sealed package when she left O'Kane's, and told to deliver it. Kyson had called her a messenger, and in truth that was what she was, but her pride baulked at admitting it.

"I am a fully qualified lawyer," she said. "What I know or don't know is confidential. I told you, I'm not the principal legal advisor. That's John O'Kane." She pushed to her feet. "Have you got coverage on your mobile phone?" she asked Connor abruptly.

He pulled his phone out of his pocket and looked at it. "Yeah. Why?"

"There's no coverage for my network out here. Kyson's landline won't be operative again until tomorrow and I need to order a part or hire a car so I can get out of here." She turned to Kyson. "You've got the documents I was sent to deliver. It's up to you to conform to their requirements."

"You can't do anything today," Kyson said. "It's too late. The nearest garage is a forty-minute drive away and it closes at five. O'Kane should know better than to send you out in a dud car."

Connor nodded toward his phone, still clasped in her hand. "Send O'Kane a text. Tell him you're stuck here and you expect to be paid for the inconvenience." He grinned. "I'm sure we can find a way to make the time pass pleasantly."

"Might as well accept it," Kyson added. "While you're here, you can take a look at Harwood Downs. See what would be lost if this ridiculous proposal went ahead."

It wasn't as if she had a lot of choice. Blue and brown eyes focused on her. Waiting for her consent. She couldn't help feeling that she was agreeing to more than taking an unexpected couple of days' leave. She breathed heavily, trying to dispel the tightness in her chest. For all the efficiency of the air conditioning, the heat was rising again. This time she welcomed it.

She punched out a quick message, then pushed the phone back to Connor. "I told them I'm stuck here without proper phone or Internet access." She gave a halfhearted laugh. "They can't fire me for that. And if they do, I won't know about it."

Connor grinned. "If they try, you can take them to court for unfair dismissal... We know a good lawyer who can fight it, don't we?"

This time her laugh was more genuine. "I guess we do at that." Somehow, three people who a short time ago had never met, had moved quickly to become 'we'.

Kyson stood, stretching his arms above his head. Maddie didn't think he did it in order to show off his work-hardened muscles, but where his shirt rode up, she caught a glimpse of washboard abs, bisected by a thin line of hair that pointed like Apollo's golden arrow to the enticing bulge in those worn jeans.

"I'll feed the animals, then I guess I'd better feed you two." When the gruff aggression disappeared from Kyson's voice, it left a surprisingly sexy huskiness.

"If you point me toward the supplies, I'd be happy to

get dinner going," Connor said. "Unless you want to do it, Maddie?"

Maddie squirmed and developed a sudden fascination with the toe of her shoe. "Er, no. I don't."

Connor held up his hands, palms out. "I wasn't suggesting you do the cooking because you're the lone female amongst us, honest! I like to cook. I'm happy to cook..."

"It's not that," Maddie said, cutting short his embarrassed apologies. "I don't... I *can't* cook. *At all.*"

Kyson's eyebrows shot up. "You must cook something. Toast? Boiled eggs?"

She shook her head. "No." Her cheeks heated. "I'm not positive I can boil water."

Connor opened his mouth then shut it again. "How do you survive?"

Maddie grimaced. "I live in the city. I get my breakfast coffee and bagel on the way to work. Lunch and dinner — there are hundreds of options." She shrugged. "I've never had to turn my hand to cooking."

Connor reached out and covered her palm with his own. "No wonder your skin is so soft." He rubbed his thumb against her wrist.

The light pressure set off a trail of sparks. His fingers curled around hers.

Her heart raced. Connor's gaze dropped to where the wild beat fluttered her silk shirt, and his breath caught in an audible hitch.

Maddie licked her lips.

"You could help with the evening chores," Kyson growled. "You don't need cooking skills to fling grain to the chooks." He held out his hand. "Coming?" He glared at Connor as if daring him to intervene.

Maddie looked from one man to other. A delicious flare sizzled along her spine. Two of the most gorgeous men she'd ever seen and they were vying for her attention. Her groin tightened. She crossed her legs and clenched her inner muscles. The throbbing increased.

In the city, she avoided anything that could interfere with her drive for professional advancement. She had no time to go out socializing, no time to spare in a search for relationships or even casual sexual encounters. But here, she and Kyson and Connor were alone, isolated every bit as much as if they were on a desert island. A strange kind of fate had thrown them together. This once, the strict rules she adhered to didn't apply.

She tugged her hand free of Connor's and stood up. She leaned over him, knowing her shirt gaped, giving him the view he obviously craved, nipped him lightly on the earlobe and whispered, "Later."

The ambitious, disciplined, do-what-it-takes-to-be-partner part of her brain protested. This wasn't like her, she didn't do this. But her body was humming, driven by a desire too strong to be ignored.

She sauntered over to Kyson, letting her hips sway as much as they could in her sensible, two-inch heels. She held out her hand. "I'm ready for whatever you have in mind."

Kyson blinked, then, taking her hand in his, led her out the door.

Cocooned in the air-conditioned homestead, she'd forgotten the outside temperature. A blast of hot air hit her face and she staggered back a few steps.

Kyson's lips tightened and his focus sharpened. "Dammit. You shouldn't be out here. You fainted a couple of hours ago. I wasn't thinking."

She could feel herself wilting in the searing wind. Kyson gave her a gentle push. "Go back inside."

"I was going to help with the chores," she protested.

"No need," he said. "I do this every day." He looked into her eyes.

His pupils were wide and dark, and she saw herself reflected in them. Felt herself falling into them.

"Take another rest." He ran his hand down her arm, from shoulder to elbow. "Use my bed."

"Your bed?" Her voice was breathy, soft with newfound

sultriness. In a secret part of her mind the dream was building. If there was any chance of making it reality, she'd need all the energy she could muster.

"If that's what you want," he said. "*Do* you want that, Maddie?"

More than he could know. And more than she was capable of saying at the moment. She simply nodded and scurried inside.

She shut the door and leaned against it, waiting for her pounding heart to steady. Finding Kyson's room in the one level homestead shouldn't present a challenge.

The first door she opened revealed Kyson's office. The currently useless phone, a computer, a printer and a stack of papers sat on top of a huge, antique desk.

On to the next room.

This had to be Kyson's room. The air vibrated with the memory of his presence.

She made her way to the bed and pulled back the covers. She kicked off her shoes, wriggled out of her business skirt and shrugged off her silk shirt. Then she sank onto the bed.

A faint, masculine scent wafted around her. Clean, fresh but carrying soft hints of horse, soap and sun-baked cotton. Closing her eyes, she let herself sleep.

When she awoke, she immediately sensed a change. The perfume that filled her nostrils was stronger, more immediate. She rolled over. Kyson sat in the room's single chair, his ice-blue gaze focused on the lacy bra and pants she'd slept in.

A blush heated her skin and for a moment she considered grabbing the sheet she'd kicked to the bottom of the bed. Then she stopped herself. What was the point in being coy? Let him look. She didn't have a perfect body, but who did? Kyson's heavy lids and his flushed cheeks suggested he was happy with what he saw.

She stretched, raising her arms above her head. Light burned in Kyson's eyes.

She smiled in satisfaction and slowly dropped her hands

back to her sides and swung her feet out of the bed. "Your bed is very inviting."

"It's an open-ended invitation," Kyson drawled. "But dinner is ready."

"There are more important things than food," she whispered, moving toward him.

A sudden rumble, clearly audible, shattered the sultry atmosphere. She clutched her stomach, her face burning with embarrassment.

Kyson laughed. "Apparently not at the moment."

She smiled back at him. "Can't pretend I'm not hungry after that, can I?" She reached down to grab her skirt and her hand made contact with her overnight bag. "How did this get here?"

Kyson lifted one shoulder. "I saw it in your car and thought you might need it."

She pulled the bag onto her lap and sat back down on the bed. "Thank you."

Kyson pushed to his feet. "I'll leave you to get dressed." A smile lightened his stern mouth. "Not that I'd mind if you came to dinner looking like that, but Connor's gone to a bit of trouble and we ought to pay some attention to the food." He turned away, then threw over his shoulder, "But whatever you wear, I'm going to be picturing what's underneath the whole time."

Chapter Three

"Hey, there," Connor said when she walked into the kitchen. "Perfect timing." He swung his hand widely to indicate the food-laden table. "I even found a couple of bottles of wine."

Kyson pulled out a chair for her and she sat.

The first bite of tender roast beef melted in her mouth. "This is delicious," she murmured after she'd swallowed.

"The beef was fresh," Kyson added. "One of mine."

Maddie's city-bred stomach gave a little lurch. "One of yours?" She held up her fork, with a small square of meat on it. "Did this used to be...? Did you...?"

Kyson's expression hardened. "Was it once one of those cows you saw happily grazing out there? Yes. Did I slaughter it? Again, yes."

Maddie swallowed a rush of cold saliva and dropped her fork with a clatter.

"You shouldn't eat meat if you can't accept where it comes from," Kyson said through gritted teeth.

"You're right, of course." She lifted her fork to her mouth and washed the morsel of beef down with a swallow of the surprisingly good red wine Connor had opened.

The hard lines of Kyson's face relaxed and he smiled.

Connor leaned forward. "Eating should be more than just loading up on fuel. It should be a sensual experience." He lifted one of his elegant, long fingers and trailed it down her cheek. "You should enjoy every experience on offer."

"Every experience," Kyson echoed. He put his hard, work-toughened hand on top of hers. "Your car won't be fixed for a day or two. You can't use the Internet to do any work. For this short time, forget why you're here, forget that we're on different sides and simply enjoy the break. Do whatever you want and only what you want."

Maddie's brain whirled. When was the last time she had done something purely because *she* wanted to? When she went back to the city, she would resume her single-minded, ambition-driven path. No one would thank her for coming out here. No one would remember her contribution at all. Why not, this one time, take what she wanted?

"And if I want to be greedy..." She turned her head from one man to the other. "And have everything at once?"

This time, when the two men exchanged glances, she didn't have to wonder what it meant. She didn't need anyone to explain Kyson's terse nod or Connor's whispered, "Yes."

But she wasn't going to rush this. A once in a lifetime experience needed to be savored.

The meal became an extended flirtation. Every time she put her fork into her mouth, she was conscious of her lips closing around it. Every time her tongue slipped out to lick away a stray crumb, she rejoiced in the restless movements the men made, the quickened breath, the high patches of color on their cheekbones.

Connor opened a second bottle of wine. She wasn't drunk, far from it, but her inhibitions were lowered. The table they ate at was small. Connor's foot stretched across and rested on hers.

Her thighs nudged Kyson's. There were constant small touches, a brush of her cheek, her finger rasping across Connor's stubbled chin. The tension rose until she could no longer sit still. She rocked involuntarily on the hard wooden seat to try to ease the delicious, building pressure.

Kyson surged to his feet. His thighs crashed against the side of the table and china rattled, but he ignored it. "I can't wait," he growled. "I want you. *Now*."

"Is this what you want, Maddie?" Connor's warm, wine-perfumed breath wafted across her cheek.

"Oh yes," she sighed.

"Both of us?" Connor asked.

"Both of you." Her heart pounded with the knowledge she was about to take a giant step in the unknown. But if she didn't do it now, when would she? In spite of the many, many men she might have encountered in the city, not one of them had ever affected her like this. And here, entirely by chance, there were two. And she could have both. Wanted *both*. She'd never been more certain of anything in her life.

Kyson spun her around, his head lowering to hers, his lips closing over hers, shaping them. He licked into her mouth, exploring. Her blood pounded in her ears and her knees went weak.

When he lifted his head, his lids were heavy

"Where?" Maddie asked.

"My room." Kyson's husky reply was accompanied by a low growl from Connor. "Now. God, right now."

In an unexpected display of male strength, Kyson swept her up into his arms and strode out of the kitchen and into his bedroom. He lowered her to her feet.

For a brief moment, panic fluttered in Maddie's chest. She had no idea how this was going to be managed. She'd secretly watched a video or two in the past to fuel her fantasies, but they usually started with everyone set up for whatever they were into. In real life she'd have to deal with the awkward, get-your-clothes-off-and-get-into-position stuff. Not that she knew what position she wanted.

For a moment she considered taking a passive role. Perhaps she should stand there and let Kyson and Connor do what they wanted.

No.

This was *her* adventure. *Her* life, *her* fantasy and she was in charge of it.

She straightened her spine and pushed her splayed palm against Kyson's chest. "Get your clothes off, cowboy."

He grinned, a wicked curve of the lips. "Yes, ma'am."

She nodded at Connor. "You too, mister."

Connor blinked, but ripped his shirt free with no

consideration for its obvious expense. The sound of buttons popping off and bouncing and rolling on the floor gave Maddie a gratifying sense of power.

Her mouth went dry at the sight of his tanned chest, but she forgot all about it when he unbuckled his belt, flicked open the button, slid down the zip, hooked his thumbs into the waistband and pushed down his tailored silk pants and boxers together in one swift movement.

His cock sprang free. The thick head was already swollen, a bead of moisture sparkling at the tip, the girth greater than she'd expected from his lithe elegance.

She crooked her finger. "I want that."

Connor moved to stand beside Kyson, who stood, his mouth slightly open, watching the scene unfold.

"I think I gave you an order, cowboy," Maddie snapped. Kyson blinked, then unbuttoned his shirt so quickly Maddie had to stifle an urge to giggle. But the sight of Kyson's naked body dispelled any desire to laugh. Damn. The man was magnificent.

Maddie licked her lips. Then she dropped to her knees between the men.

She wrapped her hands around the two erect cocks. In the videos she'd seen, there appeared to be a lot of tapping of male members on the woman's cheeks. She didn't quite get it, but perhaps that was the way it ought to be done. She moved her fists tentatively, pressing the iron-hard, silk-covered flesh against her skin. But that was as far as she got. She rubbed her cheeks against first Connor, then Kyson, more like an affectionate kitten than a cock-slapping porn star.

Kyson groaned when she squeezed her hand into a fist and slid it up, turning her head, opening her mouth and closing it around the shaft. She added to the suction with a flick of her tongue over the slit, tasting Kyson's sweet saltiness.

She hummed in appreciation and Kyson gripped her shoulders. "God, that's so good," he grated out.

In her other hand, Connor thrust his cock hard into her encircling fingers. Maddie pulled free of Kyson, letting him go with a soft pop, and looked at Connor. Twin streaks of color painted his cheekbones and his breath escaped in irregular puffs through his parted lips.

She licked her way down his shaft, pushing her fist down toward his balls, loving the breathy sounds he made. But when those balls tightened and pulled up, she let both men go and stood. No way was she going to allow them to come before she'd done everything she wanted. And she'd had everything she wanted done to her!

Now it was Connor's turn to drop to his knees. He buried his face in her groin, taking a deep sniff. He clasped her buttocks and he brought her forward and licked his way into her damp folds. When his tongue circled her clit, she gave a little moan and would have collapsed if Kyson had not stood behind her and held her up. He pulled her back against his chest. With his knees slightly bent, he supported her on his thighs as he eased them down onto the bed.

And all the time, Connor licked and sucked and sent Maddie swirling into a paroxysm of pleasure.

She had no resistance. No ability to delay or extend the experience. Her body convulsed, her thighs clamped tightly around Connor's head and she arched off the bed. Wild and incoherent sounds issued from her throat, but she could no more stop them than she could stop breathing.

Her legs dropped open and with a last, lingering kiss, Connor leaned back. Her eyes were closed, her body still pulsing with tingling aftershocks. Kyson nibbled on the acutely sensitive hollow between her shoulder and her neck, when she felt the gentle intrusion of Connor's cock. She reached back and felt the silky slickness of the condom he had already donned.

"I'll always take care of you, Maddie," he whispered.

She nodded and relaxed into him.

She'd thought his mouth had felt good. The rigid thickness stretching and filling her took her to another level. He moved slowly, in, out, almost withdrawing then sinking back, the delicious friction making her catch her breath.

Kyson said something, but the words didn't register. Connor pulled back again, and this time he withdrew completely. She whimpered and begged, "Come back." Connor ignored her plea. He grabbed her by the waist, lifted and rolled her, and Maddie realized what was happening. Sitting on his haunches, Kyson waited for her, a pearl of moisture winking at the tip of his erect cock.

She needed no instructions. As Connor pulled her onto her knees and eased his way back into her dripping pussy, she opened her mouth and took Kyson in.

She twirled her tongue around the thick head, probing the slit and letting every thrust from behind push Kyson deeper into her mouth.

In spite of the orgasm she'd had, her body reacted with renewed desire. Connor's balls slapped against her buttocks. He stroked her clit as he drove into her over and over.

She opened her mouth wide, taking Kyson in.

He groaned, "Fuck yes," and his fists gripped the sheets. His balls drew up tight again and with a guttural groan, he came. She swallowed greedily, wanting it all.

Connor flicked her clit harder and faster. She erupted in a blaze of white-hot orgasm.

With his other arm, Connor hauled her in tightly against him. He came with a great surging thrust. He collapsed onto her back, and lay there a moment, catching his breath, then he rolled to his side, taking Maddie with him.

Kyson, rolled too, so that they faced each other. He leaned forward and kissed her, a sweet tribute. "Maddie. You were magnificent."

Connor rose from the bed and disposed of the condom, then slid back in and snuggled up to her back, planting a kiss on her nape. "Thank you."

"There's another bed in the spare room, if anyone wants to go there," Kyson said sleepily. "But this one is pretty big, and we'll all fit well enough."

"Sounds good to me, "Connor murmured.

"Mmm," Maddie agreed, and fell asleep, cradled between two of the sexiest men to ever rock her world.

Chapter Four

Maddie opened her eyes then slammed them shut again. The sun shining in through the window hit like a bomb blast. She slapped her hands over her face and peered between her fingers. Wooden floor, sparse furniture. She rolled over, and the soreness in places she was unaccustomed to feeling soreness brought all the memories hurtling back. Kyson! Connor! And the things they'd done last night.

Neither man was in the bed, nor in the room.

She swung her feet to the floor and stood. A navy cotton robe lay draped across the bed, and she shrugged into it, then went to the bathroom to take care of the most pressing matters. Once she'd showered and dried herself, she put the robe back on and headed for the kitchen. There was no sign of Kyson or Connor.

Although she was nervous about seeing them—she'd never had a morning after like this because she'd never, ever had a night before like *that*, she found their absence disturbing.

She slumped down at the table and dropped her head into her hands. She sat that way for a moment, but the fierce longing for a cup of coffee drove her to her feet again.

She checked all the upper cupboards and was bent over to look in the lower shelves, when a pair of hands encircled her waist.

"Very nice," Connor's laughing voice said, "But as much as I'd like to take you up against the counter, I have things I have to get done today."

She swatted him lightly on the arm. "I was trying to find coffee."

Kyson laughed. "Oh Maddie, Maddie. You really weren't joking when you said you never cooked anything, were you?"

He pointed to a silver-sided contraption on the countertop. "Coffee machine."

Maddie felt her face redden. It was a huge thing and she couldn't believe she hadn't seen it...or the hopper full of coffee beans on top of it.

Kyson opened the refrigerator and pulled out several packages. "You made dinner last night, Connor, so I'll do breakfast. We can tell Maddie the plans for today while I'm working."

Maddie leaned back, feeling smug. She could get used to having two men provide her with some of her most basic needs. Not that there was anything *basic* about what she was getting from Kyson and Connor. Great sex with good food thrown in as well.

What a pity it was only for a day or two.

Her smile faltered. Returning to the city wasn't as appealing as it had been yesterday.

"Kyson thought we might like to take a look around the property," Connor said. "So you can see exactly what would be lost if an open-cut mine started operation." He held out a chair for Maddie. Once she was seated, he grabbed three cups from the cupboard and used the shiny monster on the counter to fill them. Maddie held hers in a death grip and did her best to absorb the coffee straight into her bloodstream.

Connor sat opposite her. "Do you ride?"

She swallowed a large mouthful of the fragrant brew. "Ride? On horses, do you mean?"

When he nodded, she lifted one shoulder. "When I was a kid, I nagged Mum until she let me have riding lessons. I haven't been on a horse for a long time, though."

"You'll remember," Kyson said, from his post at the stove. "And we'll take it slow."

"Kyson and I have been out this morning to bring in some

horses from the paddock," Connor continued. "They're down in the barn now, waiting to be saddled."

Maddie smiled. "I'm willing to give it another go."

"It's a good day for a ride," Kyson said. "A southerly change blew in overnight, so this morning it's about twenty degrees cooler than it was yesterday. It won't last, so we'd best eat up and go."

The aroma of sizzling bacon wafted through the air and Maddie's mouth watered. When Kyson slid a full plate in front of her, she devoured it as though she hadn't eaten in a week. "This is delicious. Thank you."

"Worked up an appetite overnight, huh?" Kyson ruffled her hair. "It's nice to have my cooking appreciated." He looked down at his own plate. "It can get a bit lonely cooking for one. And I'd feel downright silly telling myself how good it tastes."

The three of them were soon dropping plates and cutlery into the sink. Maddie felt another twinge of her conscience when she saw the dishes from last night stacked in the drainer. "Someone washed up?"

"Did that first thing this morning," Kyson said. "But we can leave the breakfast dishes until later. It's more important to take advantage of the cooler air."

"I don't have jeans...or riding boots," Maddie said.

"You could have a spare pair of mine," Kyson offered. "They should stay up if we put a few extra holes in the belt. There's no way my shoes would fit, though."

"I have a pair of runners," she said. "If we're not out all day, and won't be moving too fast, that should do."

She looked at the two men, already dressed in jeans and elastic-sided riding boots, the de facto uniform of most men who worked on the land.

Maddie followed Kyson into his room. He grabbed some things out of the chest of drawers and dropped them on the bed.

"These should do." He gave the belt a quick flick with the utility knife he'd pulled from his pocket. "I'll meet you back in the kitchen." He sauntered out.

The jeans he gave her fit her curvy figure better than she'd hoped. Once she cinched them in with the worn leather belt, she was reasonably confident they'd stay up. She dressed quickly and went out to join Connor and Kyson.

"Looking good, Maddie," Connor said, when he saw her.

She shook her head. "Nice of you to say so, but I don't think this is quite what the well-dressed equestrienne is wearing this season."

"You look fine," Kyson said. "There's no place out here for fancy clothes and top hats. Speaking of hats…" He reached out and dropped a broad-brimmed felt hat onto her head. "You'll need this. It's cooler today, but the sun is still fierce and we don't want you sunburned."

When they reached the stable, Maddie insisted on saddling her own horse. Being pampered was one thing, but she wasn't about to sacrifice her independence. The sturdy brown mare stood patiently while Maddie fumbled with buckles and straps. She led the horse out, put her foot into the stirrup and pushed up. She landed in the saddle with an oomph, but at least she hadn't fallen in an unceremonious heap on the ground.

She settled herself and looked around for Kyson and Connor. Her breath froze. Kyson sat astride a beautiful, golden stallion. The animal danced and sidestepped, but Kyson's jeans-clad thighs gripped the horse's flanks, holding him in check. Beside him, Connor was mounted on a black gelding that patiently nuzzled at a clump of grass.

"Ready?" Kyson asked.

Maddie took a deep breath. "As I'll ever be."

"You'll be fine," Connor said. "It all comes back pretty quickly. Like riding a bike." His horse lifted its head and took a few rapid steps toward the paddock gate. "A bike with a mind of its own," he called over his shoulder.

Maddie bounced her heels into her horse's side and followed.

Kyson rode past her and in one fluid motion, reached the

gate and leaned down to release the latch. He waited until they'd ridden through, then swung it closed behind him.

Although Maddie had seen some of Harwood Downs when she'd arrived the day before, she hadn't realized how varied the terrain was. Kyson led them toward a line of rolling, tree-covered hills.

"Look." She pointed to a mob of kangaroos sleeping under the shade of a towering gumtree. "There's so many of them. And, oh, they have joeys. Can we stop and take pictures?"

"City folk," Kyson said with a smile. "If you lived out here you'd see so many 'roos you wouldn't look twice."

But, nevertheless, he took her horse's reins for her and held them while she slid off, pulled her phone out and snapped a few shots.

"If you think that's worth taking a photo of, wait until you see where we're heading."

"Where? What are we going to see?" she asked.

Kyson just shook his head. "I don't have the words to describe it adequately. You'll have to see for yourself."

"Connor?" Maddie asked. "Do you know what he means?"

"Not exactly," he said. "But given the nature of the land, I'd guess there are limestone caves around here."

"There are," Kyson agreed. "But there's more than that. Come on. We've got about another forty minutes' ride to get there."

The ride passed pleasantly. Maddie moved easily in remembered rhythms. As Kyson had predicted, they passed several more mobs of kangaroos. Maddie didn't care if it confirmed her city dweller status, she watched transfixed as a joey scrambled into its mother's pouch and the two of them bounded across the open field. The path they followed narrowed as more trees crowded in from either side. They were moving uphill, but her horse seemed to handle the gentle slope. They reached a tight turn and Kyson called out, "Ready?"

When she nodded, he waited for her to come closer, then set his horse in motion again. Connor and Maddie followed him around the bend.

She pulled the horse to a halt, and stared, awestruck.

A chasm split the earth in front of them. It was about twenty meters wide and plunged down, deeper than she could see from her position atop the horse. The rock walls were weathered to a deep gray, and on the far side, a waterfall spilled over the edge and cascaded downwards in a silvery ribbon. Native ferns grew in clumps and small orchid-like flowers sparkled in the spray.

"It's beautiful," she breathed.

"This land is ancient," Connor murmured. "It takes thousands of years for formations like this to develop. Open-cut mining will destroy them in a day."

"But this isn't where they'll mine, is it?" Maddie asked.

"No," Kyson agreed. "The land they intend to mine is on the other side of the property. But the river that feeds these falls runs through there, and by the time they build a tailings dam, the falls will either stop flowing altogether or be so polluted that the animals and vegetation that depend on fresh, clean water will die."

"But there will be restrictions in place. They won't let that happen," Maddie protested.

"Who won't let it happen?" Connor asked. "BRX? They're in it for the money. O'Kane? You might work for him, Maddie, but there's something dishonest going on here. This whole area west of the mountains is part of a catchment area. More importantly, the water flows into the Artesian Basin. Do you really think the Environmental Protection Agency would agree to something that poses such a risk to our scarcest resource?"

Maddie shook her head bemusedly. "That can't be right. There must be some mistake somewhere."

"Oh, there's a mistake, all right," Kyson said. "But it *will* be rectified."

He swung the horse away and rode down the path.

The ride back to the homestead was carried out in silence. Maddie didn't mind. She had a lot to think about.

They unsaddled together, brushed the horses down and took them back to the paddock. Kyson checked to make sure the water trough was full and they strolled back to the house. At the front door a cardboard box awaited, with a delivery voucher on top.

"The replacement phone and router," Kyson said with satisfaction. "You two can get cleaned up while I get it all put together."

Maddie's heart fell. Once the phone was working, she could make arrangements to have the company car repaired and be on her way. The thought of leaving Connor, Kyson and the beautiful land he'd showed them settled like a stone in her chest.

She couldn't stay, but there was something she could do for him. Back in her city office, she'd check the plans, make sure that the right protections and permissions had been gained. That proper steps had been taken to preserve Harwood Downs' unique landscape.

The protocols would have been followed, she assured herself. John O'Kane was a reputable lawyer who would never proceed without a valid Environmental Impact Statement. Connor's surprise at O'Kane commissioning his one-man firm for such a major task, and offering him so much more than the usual fee, didn't mean anything was wrong. Once she got back to work, she could prove everything was above board and be certain the gorge and the native animals were safe.

She pulled off her borrowed jeans and reached for her skirt. Her lips tightened. It felt as if she were shucking off the country and being reclaimed by her city life.

She trudged out of the room and made her way to the empty office. Maybe she should wait and ask Kyson if she could use the phone, but he wasn't around, and she didn't think he'd object.

She picked up the phone and dialed.

John O'Kane growled in her ear. "Maddie. What the hell's going on? You were supposed deliver the documents, then get back here."

"Didn't you get my text?"

"I got one that said the car broke down. Why the hell haven't you fixed it? I'm taking the cost of the repairs and the wasted time out of your pay."

"The breakdown is your responsibility," she snapped. "You sent me out here in a car that wasn't reliable. And it's a good thing I stayed longer than expected. I found out something important."

There was silence from the other end of the phone, then John said, slowly, "What do you know?"

"There might be a mistake with the EIS." The words tumbled out in a rush. "The mine shouldn't have been given the green light without a ton of protection strategies in place, and even then, it probably still shouldn't have got the go ahead. Kyson Brown seems to think the study might not have been done at all. He's determined to fight. He mentioned the Land and Environment Court."

"What the fuck did you tell him?" John snapped.

Maddie rubbed her forehead. "I didn't tell him anything. He'd already consulted with his lawyers before I got here."

"Fuck him then. I'll draw up the eviction notice now... and make sure it's executable within three days. He had his official warning, and he chose to ignore it."

"You can't do that," Maddie gasped.

"I bloody well can. The State Government passed a change to the law last year. Only people immediately affected by a development can object to it. Once Brown is off the property, it won't affect him any longer and he'll have no legal right to say or do a damn thing."

Maddie reeled. "You don't understand how special this land is. And you don't understand a man like Kyson Brown." Kyson was honest and strong and worth twenty times a man like John O'Kane. "He won't give up without a fight. When I tell him—"

"You bloody well better not tell him anything. I don't want him to have time to think, or to organize."

"That's not fair!"

"Fuck fairness. He had his warning. The land doesn't belong to him. He has to go."

"I need to tell him."

"You tell him anything and you'll never work for me or any other law firm again. I'll make certain of it." The menace in his voice traveled clearly across the hundreds of kilometers. "Lawyers can't breach confidentiality. If you even *hint* to Brown that something is in the wind, your job is gone. You want to keep your job, keep your mouth shut. I'll sort you out when I get there."

Maddie clutched the phone so hard her knuckles whitened. "You're coming to Harwood Downs?"

"I'm not sending another incompetent underling to fuck up a simple job. I want Brown out of there and you've shown you're not up to it."

"You need to find the record of the EIS," she protested. "It has to be on file somewhere. Bring it with you."

There was no reply. John O'Kane had said what he wanted to and ended the call.

She stared at the wall for a long moment. The urge to go to Kyson and tell him about the disaster that was about to eventuate was strong. John O'Kane wasn't a man to make idle threats. But telling Kyson wouldn't stop it from happening. He couldn't fight the law. She'd be throwing away her job for no reason. Throwing away any prospect of a career.

She hated the thought of deceiving Kyson, but maybe it was for the best. By keeping the phone call to herself, she would be sparing him hours of anger and despair, all of it futile because the end result was inevitable.

She nodded to herself and walked back to the living room, taking a seat on the sofa. She was staring moodily into space when Kyson walked in.

"The phone's fixed," he said. "I guess you want to order

that radiator hose."

She sighed heavily. The car was the least of her worries.

"I'll make the call, if you'd like," Kyson offered. "I know the guy who runs the garage and I can make sure he gets the spare part out to us quickly."

The lump in Maddie's throat made swallowing difficult. In three days, Kyson would be gone from Harwood Downs, whether the car was fixed or not.

Kyson strode into the office and picked up the phone. Maddie held her breath, irrationally afraid he'd know she'd already been in there, already made a phone call.

Instead, he held out his hand beckoning her closer, dropping his arm around her shoulders when she stood beside him, holding the phone between them so she could hear the conversation.

"Don't have one of those in stock," came the laconic reply to Kyson's request. "I'll ring the supplier and see what I can do. Let me call you back."

"Cheers, mate," Kyson replied and hung up.

"Looks like you're stuck here for the next little while." He squeezed her shoulders. "Which is good, because I'm damn sure not done with you yet." His eyebrows drew together and he peered more closely at her. "But only if you want. You look a little stressed. If Connor and I are too much, or this situation is making you uncomfortable, you only have to say. I wouldn't—"

"No, no, it's fine. Good. Great." She rushed to cut him off. How could he think she wouldn't want more of the amazing sex they'd had last night? How could any woman not want that? "It's just I'm a bit tired. I've been working really hard lately…" Her face heated. "And I um, didn't get much sleep last night. And the ride…"

He pulled her close. "You're exhausted, and now that you've got a forced break, it's catching up with you."

She blew out a long breath. No matter how physically exhausted she became, she doubted if her conscience would let her sleep easily tonight. She could try to rationalize it, but she was lying by omission.

The phone rang again, cutting off her internal debate. Kyson picked it up.

He listened for a moment, then said, "No, that's okay. I know what it's like. Thanks."

He put the phone back in its cradle. "They can't get the part for a week. Have to order it in from the distributor, then wait for it to be shipped out here." He ran his hand through his hair. "Is that going to be a problem?"

"Is what going to be a problem?" Connor appeared in the doorway.

"The part for Maddie's car won't be here for a week. I was asking if she minded having to stay here for that length of time." He dropped his hands onto her shoulders. "You know I want you to stay, but if you absolutely have to go back to work, I'll drive you to the station."

Now would be the time to tell him that her boss, who would be here tomorrow, could take her back to the city. But that would involve an explanation she'd already decided she wouldn't risk making. Instead she murmured, "I can't leave the car here."

"You can come back with me when I'm done," Connor said.

"You can always come back," Kyson said. "It's not that long a trip, really."

She knew she wouldn't be coming back. She wouldn't be seeing Kyson again. After tomorrow, he wouldn't want her anywhere near him. Even if he never found out she had advance knowledge of what was about to happen, she worked for O'Kane. That would be enough to place her firmly on the side of the enemy.

Today she would take what she could, and enjoy her last night with Kyson and Connor.

Your last chance at happiness, a sad voice in her head insisted.

She turned away, guilt and regret lodged like a heavy weight in her chest. "I…I think I'd like to lie down for a while."

Instantly, Connor and Kyson rushed to her side.

"I should have realized the ride was too draining when you haven't been out for years." Kyson bent and swept her off her feet. "Take a quick rest," he urged. "I'll crank the air conditioner up."

Ignoring her protests, he strode into his bedroom and placed her gently onto the bed. Connor appeared beside him a moment later. "I brought you a cool drink, and I have some aspirin if being out in the sun has given you a headache." He put the glass beside the bed and ran the back of his hand over her forehead.

"I'll be fine," she whispered, as they both turned and tiptoed out of the room. She knew she lied. Nothing was going to be fine and she had no idea how to fix it.

Chapter Five

An hour later she woke up, her eyes gritty and her head feeling as if it weren't attached to her shoulders. She staggered through the empty living room and into the kitchen. Connor and Kyson sat at the table, their heads bent over some sheets of paper.

"Ah, Maddie," Kyson said, sweeping the papers up. He spun around and shoved them into the dresser drawer behind him. "Do you feel better?"

Connor moved to lean against the dresser, almost as if he were protecting whatever Kyson had put there.

Her heart felt as if a giant fist was squeezing it. Kyson and Connor were hiding something from *her*. Because they didn't trust her.

A small part of her knew they were right. She was keeping secrets from them too. But she was hurt. She'd thought they'd formed some sort of bond, but it seemed Kyson and Connor were able to separate their sexual desires from the rest of their lives.

She stood there, dressed once again in Kyson's jeans, and felt like an outsider, bereft and isolated.

Kyson stood. "I have to feed the animals." On Harwood Downs, the welfare of the animals came first. Kyson had a cowboy's love of the creatures he raised and cared for. "If you're feeling better, perhaps you'd like to help."

Did he really want her help, or did he want to get her out of the homestead so Connor could finish up whatever they'd been doing? It didn't matter. The future was set. She nodded. "Sure."

Kyson took her hand. The familiar tingling warmth

flooded her, from her palms to her toes. No matter what secrets they held, the sexual connection between the three of them was strong.

"Dinner will be ready when you get back." Connor pushed away from the dresser and scooped Maddie into his arms for a kiss that made her toes curl.

"Hold that thought." Kyson laughed, then led Maddie out the door.

In the stable, Kyson showed her where the feed for the horses was kept. She carried it into the grassy paddock behind the barn. The scent of fresh hay and well cared for horses filled her nostrils. She gave an extra handful of oats to the horse that had carried her around the property. In return, the horse nuzzled her shoulder.

Dusting the last bits of feed off her hands, she returned to the barn. Kyson glanced up from the feed sacks he was putting away. His gaze, through the dust motes sparkling in the last rays of evening sunshine, was heavy with lust and heat.

No, Kyson and Connor didn't trust her, but they wanted her. If all they wanted was the pleasure their bodies could bring them, fine. That worked for her. She'd *make* it work. When it was over, she'd walk away without ever looking back.

The barn door squeaked open and Connor stepped inside. "We're only having salad and cold meats for dinner, so I came to see if you needed help." His gaze flashed from one to the other, his eyes narrowed. "You've been gone a long time and I wouldn't want to think you were doing anything — interesting — without me."

His lithe form, advancing slowly, was suddenly dangerous. He wouldn't hurt her, she knew that instinctively, but he wouldn't allow himself to be ignored either.

Kyson began to prowl toward her from the other side of the barn. Last night, Maddie had been in control, issuing instructions. They didn't look as if they were prepared to take orders this time. She shivered in anticipation.

"Take your clothes off, Maddie." Connor's voice was level, but that didn't disguise the command.

Hay covered the floor of the barn. They meant to take her here? Now? Her heart raced, but she lifted her head defiantly. "What if I don't?"

"Oh, Maddie, Maddie. Do you really want to find out what happens to disobedient girls?" Connor moved closer.

Out of the corner of her eye, she saw Kyson reach out to grab something off the wall. She ignored him, focusing on Connor. An explosive crack inches from her cheek made her jump and spin.

"You're not going to defy us, are you, Maddie?" Kyson held the plaited handle of a stock whip, the long leather thong trailing along the floor.

"You're going to whip me?" she gasped, outraged.

Kyson's hand flashed again, and the top button of her shirt spun away into the dark corner of the barn.

"No. But if you don't take those clothes off, I'll use it to strip them from you." Another crack of the whip and a second button joined the first. "Don't think I can't."

She touched the third button on her shirt, but pulled away. Kyson's unerring accuracy turned her to hot, molten jelly. He wanted her naked? Let him work for it.

His face remained grave, but his eyes sparked with amused acknowledgment of her ploy. *Crack! Crack!* The last two buttons were gone. A final crack and the shirt fell from her shoulders.

She stood in her bra and Kyson's jeans, waiting for his next move.

"Ah, a little help here?" Kyson asked, nodding at Connor. "I *could* rip the jeans from her body, but..." He paused and grinned. "They *are* my jeans and they're quite new." Then he looked her up and down. "And I really, really wouldn't want to risk damaging that beautiful skin."

Behind her, Connor unclipped her bra and tossed it aside. The whip lifted again, but instead of cracking it, Kyson moved closer, caressing her shoulders and the top of her breasts with the supple leather.

While she trembled under the touch, Connor undid her jeans and slipped his hands inside her pants, pushing them down her legs. "Step out," he whispered. She did as she was told with no thought of defiance.

Connor pushed her feet farther apart and pulled her back to lean against him. One hand slid down into her slick wetness, opening her, stroking across the wet flesh, his thumb finding the hard nub of her clitoris.

Her knees sagged and she would have fallen, but Kyson was there to hold her up, the whip abandoned, his hands spanning her waist, his head bent forward to claim her mouth.

Connor's fingers moved faster and faster. Kyson moved from her lips to her nipples, sucking and stroking.

Their combined attention drove her higher and higher, until she gasped and panted and came in a shuddering climax.

Kyson dropped to his knees on the hay behind her and Connor lowered her, so that her head rested in Kyson's lap, his now outstretched legs serving as a cradle to both lift her and protect her.

Connor wrenched his clothes off, somehow managing to grab a condom from his pocket before he hurled his jeans aside.

He drove into her, hard and fast and frantic.

The bulge of Kyson's cock, constrained by his clothing, was full and powerful at her back. He stroked her breasts and leaned forward, pressing kisses to her forehead and eyes.

Connor's thrusts grew more powerful, faster and the breath rushed in and out of his lungs. "Can't stop it," he rasped, his head flung back, his mouth a rictus of pleasure.

His cock pulsed deep inside her and a shudder passed over his skin. "Maddie. Fuck. I wanted to wait, but I..."

Maddie smoothed his sweat-soaked hair. "It's ok," she said. "You took care of me first."

"And *I'll* take care of you now," a rough voice growled in her ear. Kyson's big hands pushed at Connor's shoulders. "Move it. Let a man who's up to the job take over."

As Connor rolled away and to the side, Kyson turned Maddie so she faced him. He arched his hips up while he unzipped his jeans and tugged them down his thighs. After grabbing a condom from his pocket, then tearing it open with his teeth, he rolled it on. His hands returned to Maddie's waist and he lifted her into the position he wanted, kneeling astride him, his heavy fullness nudging her entrance

"Ride, Maddie."

She hovered there, feeling his heat, teasing them both, until he groaned and slammed her down. She ground her clit against the hard bone at the base of his cock, her back arched, head tossed back.

Then she rode, taking what she wanted. Sliding, letting his thickness fill her, lifting herself up until he almost slipped free, then lowering herself again. Slow then fast, she concentrated on her own pleasure, her own need and all the while he panted, "Yes. Yes. God. You're beautiful, Maddie."

She barely heard him through the pounding of her own heart, the rush of blood in her veins.

She slapped her hands behind her, on his thighs, gripping the bunched jeans, holding on while she drove herself higher and higher until she shattered.

She slumped forward. The waves of her orgasm pulsed through her, each one causing her muscles to twitch and contract.

Kyson waited until she'd caught her breath, then nodded to Connor. "Pick her up."

Connor's arms came around Maddie and he lifted her gently away.

She eyed Kyson's erection, standing proud. "But you haven't…"

"Oh, I'm going to," Kyson murmured. "I want to come so

bad. But not here. I'm going to slam into you so hard you'll need something soft at your back." He pulled his jeans up and made a futile attempt to tuck himself in. He shrugged and left the pants sagging open.

Connor strode with her back to the house and dumped her onto the bed. He kissed her, then moved downward, taking tiny bites of her flesh, sucking them into his mouth, then moving on.

Until, suddenly, he wasn't there.

"Later," growled Kyson. "I want her and no one is getting in my way."

While Connor had been kissing her, Kyson had undressed. His cock was ramrod stiff, coated in another condom, or maybe the same one. Maddie didn't know or care.

Kyson knelt between her thighs, hooked her knees over his elbows. With one hard thrust, he planted himself deep. He shuddered, gave a guttural moan and his control broke. He pounded into her, deep, wild and savage.

Maddie gasped. He held her open, leaving her defenseless against the power of his possession. With anyone else it would have been frightening, but this was Kyson and she gladly took everything he could give her. The force of his hips pistoning over and over drove her back against the headboard of the bed, but Connor was there, bracing her, cradling her head on his lap, his cock, as rigid as Kyson's, standing to attention beside her left cheek.

With a wordless shout and a final, powerful thrust, Kyson came. The deep pulsing triggered Maddie's own orgasm and she arched up, throwing her head back, grinding it into Connor's groin.

His fist, wrapped around his own cock, pumped up and down, once, twice, and a thick white rope of cum spurted out and splashed onto Maddie's chest. "Fuck," he groaned. "That was so hot."

Maddie was too exhausted to answer. She lay there in a sex-induced haze, only vaguely aware of Kyson stirring and pulling back. Her eyes drifted shut. The soft touch of a warm washcloth felt wonderful and she smiled softly. Above her she heard the murmur of male voices, but she had drifted too far into sleep to listen.

Chapter Six

The morning was cool and fresh. Kyson had woken them when he'd slid out of bed to tend to the animals. Connor had showered and headed to the kitchen, and now all three of them lingered over a lazy breakfast. The sudden sound of tires crunching on gravel traveled clearly in the still air. Maddie dropped her spoon.

"What the—?" Kyson began, but his words were cut short by the blast of a car horn, shockingly loud in the country quiet.

Kyson shoved his chair backward and stormed out. Connor followed in his wake.

Maddie walked slowly to the door, her heart racing and her breath short. Her time here was over.

"Which one of you bastards is Brown?" John O'Kane yelled.

Kyson stood with his feet a shoulder's width apart, fists lightly clenched by his side. "I am."

"Think you're tough, don't you?" O'Kane said. "Think you're going to use the law to beat me. You've got another think coming, smart arse. You're done here." O'Kane reached into the car and pulled out an A4-sized envelope.

"Fuck you," Kyson snarled.

"You're the one who's fucked." O'Kane waved the envelope in the air. "This is an eviction notice, executable immediately. You have an hour to pack your personal belongings and get the hell out."

"You said he had three days," Maddie gasped.

Kyson swung toward her. His face was stone hard, his eyes icy. "You knew about this? And you didn't tell me?"

"I couldn't, I..."

"You can't do that." Connor moved and stood shoulder to shoulder with Kyson. "He needs time..."

"He's had warnings and he ignored them. He gambled and he lost." O'Kane tossed the envelope onto the ground at Kyson's feet.

Kyson ignored it. His mouth was a thin white line.

"I didn't know he was going to do this." Maddie picked up the envelope. "He told me he'd give you three days."

Kyson plucked the documents from her hand and dropped them back on the dirt.

"I don't give a damn if you read them or not," O'Kane snarled. "Your time is up. Get out."

"And if I don't. What do you think you could do about it?" Kyson asked.

O'Kane was silent for a moment. Next to Kyson's stocky strength and Connor's lean athleticism, he looked like the overfed, under-exercised bundle of flab he was.

"I'll call the cops," he said at last.

"Good luck with that," Kyson replied. "Most of the local cops hate the thought of open-cut mining in this area as much as I do." The smile that stretched his mouth didn't reach his eyes. "I don't think a call from you is going to be a high priority. The crime rate in this part of the country is simply unbelievable. Keeps the poor, overworked police really busy. Could take weeks before they get here."

O'Kane's face grew red. "Think you're so damn smart. You're nothing!"

"I'm here," Kyson said. "And I'm staying."

"Maybe the local cops won't toss you out, but that won't stop me," O'Kane replied. "BRX has more power than you'll ever have. They've got politicians in their pocket. They can do anything they damn well like. How do you think they get permits for all these mining leases? Buying a cop or two is nothing."

"You won't buy me," Connor said. "Or Kyson. Or the Land and Environment Court."

O'Kane laughed. "You're not real smart, are you, boy? I've already bought you. Didn't check exactly whose account your suspiciously inflated fee got paid from, did you? It might surprise you to learn that for some time you've been taking bribes to fudge survey boundaries."

"You bastard," Connor shouted. "I've never accepted a bribe in my life. And I don't falsify data."

"The records show otherwise," O'Kane sneered. "I've got you by the short and curlies. You keep your mouth shut or I'll ruin you."

"Leave Benton out of this," Kyson said. "You and I both know no EIS was ever conducted."

"What you think you know doesn't matter a damn." The smug look on O'Kane's face made Maddie want to hit him. "Records can be created. Computers can be hacked. Give the right people enough money and you'd be surprised what can happen. The EIS will be found just where it should be, and it will say just what we want it to. Mining this coal is in everyone's interest. Everyone's but yours, Brown."

"Why?' Maddie asked. "Why would you do this?"

O'Kane licked his lips. "The coal under this property is worth billions. And my share, for making sure the whole thing goes through under the radar, is a nice percentage."

Maddie shook her head. "I can't believe you'd do that. *You* lectured *me* about trust."

"You're an idiot," the lawyer sneered. "An ambitious, gullible idiot. I only sent you out here because your nauseating naivety would keep Brown from getting suspicious. Apparently you couldn't even get that right." His lip curled. "You're too fucking stupid to live."

Kyson moved so quickly that Maddie barely saw it. He grasped O'Kane's collar. "Speak to Maddie like that again, and I'll grind your face into the dirt."

"And when he's finished with you, I'll take a swing or two," Connor added.

"Fuck you," O'Kane spat out. Kyson tightened his fists. O'Kane's face grew bright red and his mouth opened and closed like a stranded fish.

Kyson relaxed his hands, stepped back and rubbed his palms together, as if trying to remove something disgusting.

O'Kane fell to his knees in the dirt.

"Get out of here," Kyson snarled. "Before I really hurt you."

O'Kane drew in a few gasping breaths, then struggled to his feet. "I don't need to be here to make this happen," O'Kane said. "You might be physically stronger than me, but it won't make any difference. It's over."

"You still think you can get away with this?" Connor's eyebrows rose. "The Independent Commission Against Corruption is going to have a field day."

"ICAC won't be able to do a thing. The evidence is buried too deep. You don't have enough to get them to start looking for it."

"There's your confession here today," Connor said. "That should get them interested."

"What confession?" O'Kane asked. "I'll deny I came here. It'll be my word against a disgruntled, failed squatter and surveyor who has been proven to take bribes."

Maddie stepped forward. "Not quite." She held up her phone. "I may not get mobile coverage out here, but the recording function still works. I've got every word."

O'Kane launched himself at her. "You bitch."

Before he'd covered half the distance, Kyson felled him with one hard punch. O'Kane tumbled backward and sprawled in an ungainly heap. Connor placed one foot on O'Kane's heaving chest and held him down.

"You're pretty free with the insults, O'Kane, so here's a few for you. You're not only a criminal, you're an ignorant one." Kyson stood over him. "They won't need Maddie's recording to convict you. BRX has been under investigation for months. Everything I've done has been with the help and advice of ICAC. The politician you've got in your pocket? The Independent Commission Against Corruption is about to charge him. You, your cronies, your firm and everyone connected with this project are stuffed. Your little confession here today will make a nice addition to the television news."

Connor tossed Kyson his phone. "You wanna call the police now?"

"My pleasure." Kyson dialed and spoke briefly.

"I thought you said the police won't come," O'Kane sputtered.

"They wouldn't come for you, but they will for me," Kyson replied. "You sit there and wait."

Connor removed his foot, and for a moment it looked as if O'Kane might try to make a run for it, but the two men squared their shoulders and he subsided into a sitting position.

Kyson and Connor stood guard. No one spoke.

Both men looked grim and kept their attention firmly focused on O'Kane.

Thirty minutes later a cloud of dust heralded the arrival of the police.

A lanky, uniformed officer slid out of the white and blue four-wheel drive. "John O'Kane? I have a warrant for your arrest. Come on, let's be having you." He hauled O'Kane to his feet.

"Get your hands off me," O'Kane snarled. "You won't make this stick. When I get out I'll…"

The policeman shifted his feet and O'Kane took a sudden tumble back onto the ground.

"Oh, dear. How did that happen?" the cop said innocently as he pulled O'Kane back up and snapped a pair of handcuffs on him. A sly grin crossed his face. "This is all too complicated for a country cop like me. I'm afraid you'll have a bit of a long wait in the lock-up until someone senior comes up from the city to take charge of the situation. I'll apologize in advance. Our cells are very uncomfortable. And hot. Such a pity."

He loaded O'Kane, still cursing, into the back of the vehicle and, with a wave, drove off.

Chapter Seven

Maddie slumped onto the floor, trying to make sense of all that had happened. "You knew all along the project was illegal?"

"Yeah." Kyson walked toward her. "The Environmental Protection Agency and ICAC were already onto BRX."

"Connor, did you know?"

"Not before I got here, but Kyson filled me in."

She'd kept John O'Kane's proposed arrival from him, but Kyson and Connor's secrecy still stung. "You didn't tell me?"

"We couldn't. You worked for O'Kane. We *knew* how corrupt he was. We didn't know how far your loyalty to him went."

She drew a deep breath. "I thought he was honest. You have to believe me when I say I never knew what was happening."

Kyson looked at her steadily. "You didn't tell me O'Kane was on his way here."

"I should have. I know that now. But I wanted you – us – to have one more night." She winced. "I don't mean that to sound as selfish as it does. By the time I found out he was coming, it was too late to do anything and I thought twelve hours wouldn't make any difference. I was trying to spare you worry."

"Maddie. I'm a grown-up. I can handle my own problems."

He'd proven that. He'd done a better job handling his problems than she had done of handling hers. Her legal career was unlikely to survive the taint of this scandal.

"What do you think will happen?" she asked.

"O'Kane will be charged with fraud, the politician who accepted the bribe will be expelled from government and charged," Connor said. "I'm not sure what will happen to BRX, but at the minimum they'll lose their license to operate in Australia."

"What about you?" she asked Kyson. "Will you stay here?"

"Harwood Downs' owners don't seem to have any part in the corrupt behavior. They simply negotiated the sale." He ran his fingers through his hair. "After the news of all this breaks, they might be keen to get shot of the place. If I can negotiate them down to a decent price, I'd like to purchase the property. Assuming I can convince the bank to give me a loan. I'm not going to be able to raise much of a deposit."

"I think I might be able to help with that." Connor smiled. "An open-cut mine on this place would be an abomination, but how would you feel about renewable energy? A solar and wind farm?"

"That's not a bad idea," Kyson agreed.

"I've wanted to get into that for a while." Connor made a wide sweep with his arm. "It wouldn't interfere with your grazing activities. There'd be a nice irony in using the fee I got from O'Kane to contribute towards the start-up."

"We'd need..." Kyson and Connor spoke rapidly to each other, tossing around ideas and figures.

Maddie leaned her head against the veranda rail and let the buzz of their voices pass over her. The idea Connor had come up with was excellent, and she predicted they would soon have an agreement. Everything would be settled — for everyone except her. She felt sick. And afraid. The thought of leaving here, knowing Connor and Kyson were forging a new life for themselves, a life they might eventually share with someone else, made her feel like someone had driven a spike deep into her chest.

"Will that be okay with you, Maddie...? Maddie? Maddie!"

It took a moment for her to realize Connor was calling her

name.

"What?"

"If we set up a partnership, Kyson handling the grazing, me the renewable energy and you handling all the business and legal issues, will that be okay?"

Maddie shook her head, trying to clear it, to be sure she'd heard right. "Me? A partner? Here?"

Kyson frowned. "If you don't want to... I — we — assumed you'd be part of this." The light in his blue eyes faded. His shoulders fell. "We thought we'd found the perfect solution. So we could be together."

"We thought you'd want that," Connor added. "Because we do. So much."

She could stay. They wanted her.

Who knew what the future would bring, but if they were together, she had high hopes for it.

"Yes," she whispered. Then she yelled, "Yes. Yes. Yes."

She ran to the two men and flung her arms around them both. "We can do this. We'll make it work."

"You bet we will," Kyson said. "Now come inside and let's do some celebrating."

A stray thought made Maddie falter. "The car. It belongs to John O'Kane's legal practice. What should I do with it?"

"Stuff him," Connor replied. "If he wants it, he can come and get it."

Kyson laughed. "I don't think O'Kane is going to have the opportunity to come anywhere near Harwood Downs or anywhere else for a long stretch of time."

He bent to kiss Maddie and all thoughts of the car, John O'Kane and anything other than the two men beside her fled.

Together they turned and went inside. To the start of a new life.

TIED AND TAKEN

BA TORTUGA

Dedication

In memory of my stepmother, Terrie. Cowgirl up and
we'll see you on the other side.

Chapter One

Kase Jakoby did like roughing it.

Okay, so roughing it wasn't really rough at the KOA, where he had showers and electrical hookups and a pizza and beer with the guys. Still, he liked it better than some of the swanky host hotels at the big events. Kase wasn't a Vegas man, though he was happy enough to place at the NFR and make money.

His cowboy heart was in the down and dirty little events around the Fourth of July, what cowboy folks called Christmas. He loved the sweat, the sun pounding down on him and the cold shock of beer on his throat after he made a good ride and had the money to buy a round.

'Course, now it was pretty late and he must have been the only roughstock rider not driving out first thing in the morning, because his buddies had all abandoned him and his well-stocked cooler.

Maybe he ought to go take advantage of that shower. With his luck, the next stopover would have a pit toilet. Even worse, the next campground would have a swimming pool near the bathroom and thirty thousand screaming kids wiping out in the communal showers. Right now he could handle some cool water, a little quiet time and enough light to check the shower stall for snakes.

He headed back to his truck from the common area, wheeling his cooler behind him, to grab some shorts and a towel. His eyebrow went up when he saw the little red pickup truck with PRCHD8R vanity plates parked next to his big old duallie as if they were fixin' to have a snuggle, and Kase dropped his cooler handle like he'd been poleaxed.

Ainsley Preacher. The one that got away. That damn girl had had him thinking about things like rings and ranch houses and fences, for fuck's sake.

He'd be God damned.

Kase wandered over to Ainsley's area, noticing the bright purple horse trailer hitched to the pickup. Yeah, Ainsley never traveled without her bitch mare Lilith. Lord, that nag was vicious, but there'd never been a barrel horse who knew her rider as well. Together they'd won, what? Damn near half a million dollars.

Enough that she had obviously moved up in life. Hell, he didn't think she was riding down in Texas no more. She'd hied off somewhere up north like a startled snowbird, without a single word. Not a text, a phone call, a fuck you very much. Nothing.

Rumor from the other cowboys was that she'd been crying when she left, but he'd not even been there at the arena. He'd had his fucking truck broken into and he'd been at the bank, trying to convince them to let him into his own damn bank account so he could buy boots.

The powers that be frowned on riding in stocking feet. That whole fucking event had sucked. He'd been robbed. He'd fallen and snapped his damn femur and had been out for six weeks, living on the relief fund and his folks' good humor.

Sucked because Ainsley had turned his soul inside out, then left him broke dick and moaning the blues. He'd never met a gal who had wanted the same things he did, never met a woman who had wanted him to…

Kase shook his head and damn near jumped out of his skin when the old bitch mare kicked the side of her trailer as if she knew he was thinking thoughts about her rider that he oughtn't.

"Smell me, Lil? You used to eat sugar out of my hand well enough." Sorta like her momma had. He'd seen Ainsley on her knees, over his knees, straddling his cock as if she was circling barrels.

The huge mare snorted, nodded at him then bared her teeth in a clear warning. *Back off, Mister.*

"Where's your momma, lady?" Ainsley couldn't be in the wee living compartment of the trailer or she'd be out there telling him off for upsetting her horse.

Was she out here? Camping with the yokels? Her Majesty deigning to stay with the little people?

He shook his head. She had to be having a drink with someone then moving on. Ainsley wasn't stuck up, but she was classy. Too classy for a roughstock bronc rider like him.

Sure, they'd tied their wagons together a couple three years ago, but things had gotten too hot and heavy, too far outside her comfortable white bread life, and she'd run like a startled calf.

Shame, too, because she'd been hotter than a two dollar pistol, with her hands above her head, her beautiful body stretched out for his touch, her breasts heavy and firm, her thighs glistening with her juices.

The memory made his mouth dry.

All he could reckon was that she'd been caught slumming with him, testing the East Texas ranch water. God knew her daddy was rodeo royalty and could shut a man's career down with a phone call. Stood to reason. Still, he'd been caught through the balls, just fishhooked by her near-black laughing eyes and long, dark curls that smelled like strawberries.

He slapped the bed of the truck, making Lilith kick again. What was this bullshit? Mooning like some calf over a stuck-up little girl who got scared because he could make her come harder than any of those straight-laced boys that her daddy paraded in front of her?

A man didn't have time for that shit, even if Ainsley was the one who got away. Shower. Then a bag of Cheetos and *Tombstone* on the DVD player.

Kase grabbed his go-bag and tugged it onto his shoulder. There were a second set of showers in the back, older, but quieter, less likely to be full with anyone, especially so late at night.

The piney woods made it look even later than it was, even with the full moon trying its best to push through, the lights flickering and buzzing along the trail, making everything glow.

He chuckled at himself, shook his head. God damn, he was getting fucking poetic in his old age.

The restrooms had men and women signs, but the showers were unisex back here, which gave him all sorts of pleasant fantasies about Miss Ainsley joining him and telling him how wrong she'd been to leave him without a word. Heh. Right. He hit the head before going to bathe, and damned if he didn't come out the door to the men's room to the sight of Ainsley walking right into the showers. Her back was to him, her long hair like an inky swath as she swooped it up, tying it into a lazy bun.

Oh damn.

Kase blinked, mouth opened to call out, because he was a lot of things, but he wasn't no Peeping Tom. About the time he went to say something, though, she tugged off the dark button-down shirt that was her signature look, leaving her in a tiny, white, skin-tight tank top that was damn near see-through with sweat.

See-through enough that when she stepped under the lemon yellow light of the naked bulb that swung over her head, he could see it.

A tattoo.

Not a tiny little filigreed cross or a butterfly tramp stamp.

No. This was a pin-up, inked from her right shoulder to somewhere past where he could see under those cut-off jeans.

Not just a pin-up, but a dark-haired cowgirl straddling a saddle, wearing next to nothing. A full back piece. He stepped closer, drawn to her, and he read the spiky words above the picture, *Tied and Taken.*

Jesus Christ on a crutch. That was—

His cock went hard, his mouth went dry, and Kase's

feet began to move toward the showers, his brain utterly disengaged from his body.

Ainsley stepped into a stall and pulled the curtain closed behind her. The button-down appeared over the top of the curtain rod, so did the cut-offs, but the tank top and a pair of tiny, lacy panties were dropped to the top of her bag.

He leaned against the wall, his brain a blank, filled with the sound of water and the scent of strawberry shampoo.

That was when he finally managed to speak, voice pitched low so he didn't scare her too badly.

"Christ, woman. You have been naughty."

"Christ, woman. You have been naughty."

Ainsley damned near jumped out of her skin, and she grabbed the K-Bar blade she kept in her go-bag with one shampoo-slippery hand. "Who the fuck is there? I will beat you down."

"Language! I thought you were a good girl. Too good for my likes."

She looked out the curtain, scowling at a certain blue-eyed, blond-haired asshole who she had left the Texas circuit for. She was on a roll for the finals, though, and she needed to ride where the money was plentiful, so here she was.

Kase Jakoby. At least he wasn't dangerous, right? Well, not in a criminal way. To her senses he was deadly.

"Go away," Ainsley said.

"Oh, honey, I can't do that. Now, you know I won't peek over the stall, but damn, I want to see your tattoo."

"I don't know what you're talking about." Oh, God *damn* it. Her ink was no secret on the Turquoise circuit, the Mountain States either, but here?

Here, her daddy was a big deal and he didn't know his only daughter had a tattoo at all, much less a back piece with a cowgirl lashed to the horn of a saddle.

Some things were meant to be secrets.

"No? Did you have your back with you all year? Because that thing took weeks, I bet."

He ought to know, she guessed. Ainsley had some seriously fond memories of the Chisholm Trail thigh piece Kase had, complete with longhorns skulls and prickly pear. He wore a bucking bronc on his upper arm, too, stylized and perfectly placed.

The memory of it as he held her arms above her head, fingers playing her like a guitar, made her belly go tight.

"Go away. I'm taking a shower." *Dammit, girl! Don't get all husky and shit. Don't let him know how much you want him even now.*

"I know. I wish I was your soap. You still use Ivory in the bar? I could help you lather up." His voice got deeper, his drawl lengthening, scraping her nerve endings.

"Shut up, you bastard." She backed into the spray, the water just warm enough not to make her gasp. He'd turned her inside out, then. Before the tiny marks on her breast, on her shoulder, the inside of her thigh were even faded, he'd been making out with Sheri Ballard, the stick-skinny little blonde. Right behind the arena.

The utterly stupid, vapid stick-skinny blonde. Ainsley could handle being dumped, but for Sheri? Lord.

"Now, now, my momma is a lady, honey." She could still hear him. Rats.

Ainsley started washing, using the body wash that went with her shampoo. She loved the feel of her skin with the bubbles, and she wasn't going to get to enjoy it now, not with him right there.

Damn Texas anyway.

"Just shoo, Jakoby. We got nothing to discuss."

"No? I think bondage cowgirls are a great place to start a conversation. Gives a man thoughts. And a hard-on."

"I know I have no idea what you're on about." She went for icy, but she was damn worried it came out needy and sad. "A gentleman wouldn't stand there and talk at a girl when she's showering."

"Nope. I am not a gentleman. Not a creep, either. It's a delicate balance." He could still laugh at her, at himself.

"Uh-huh." She surprised herself by chuckling softly. "What do you want, Kase?"

"Well, I was gonna take a shower. Then I saw you take your shirt off and I lost my mind. Only excuse for it."

"You're a dipshit, cowboy." And she *had* been crazy for him, for the way he'd made her need when he'd touched her, his fingers all callused from holding the bareback rigging. "Go take your bath and be good."

"Oh, honey. You know what I'd pay to see you in a big old claw foot bathtub, bubbles letting me play peekaboo with all your bits? Although, I'm thinking there might be something to seeing you in a shower, all slick and ready to play."

She was going to lose her mind. Ainsley could feel heat between her legs, warmer than the water. She should just finish up her shower and walk away, but she found herself leaning into the spray and imagining the wall disappearing between them.

"I never eat strawberries without thinking of you, girl." His voice went all honey pouring over open flame.

"Oh, God." She swallowed hard, her breath coming faster with every second. She pushed her hand against her belly, needing relief. "You don't fool me, cowboy. You never think about me."

His laugh was more a bark than a chuckle. "Shit, I wish. My balls ache from not ever thinking on your sweet ass. Every other fucking memory."

"You have plenty of relief opportunities." Not that she was still bitter, but the thought was better than turning on the cold water for a second or two.

"None of them are you, baby girl."

Yeah, right. Baby girl. Fuck that shit. She turned off the water and grabbed her shorts and tugged them and her shirt on so fast she broke a nail. "You didn't have a single fucking problem dipping your wick, asshole, when your prick was still smelling like strawberries."

She whirled out of the shower, grabbing her bag, her

panties flying off the top. "Go find another girl to chat up. I ain't interested, asshole."

God, he made her get her redneck on. Her daddy would be appalled.

"Hey—" Kase wasn't right outside her shower stall, but he stood between her and the main door.

"Look. Don't. You don't know me. I don't know you. Let's keep it that way."

That wasn't exactly true, was it? He'd started her down a road that didn't lead to Heaven and he'd seen that in her before anyone else. Didn't matter. What mattered was that she was in Texas and she needed to ride.

Barrels.

Not cowboys.

Barrels.

"Damn it, Ainsley." Kase reached for her, but she spun away, sliding through the door before he could touch her. She might melt clean away if he did that.

She ached for him, for the things he could do to her, and that was dangerous at best, because everyone in East Texas knew her daddy and folks talked. She intended to go back to the mountains in Colorado, but not with her tail between her legs.

Better to let him have his—hopefully cold—shower while she went to feed Lilith. She'd ride the three more events she had in Texas and hit the road back to her world as soon as she could.

Once she got back where no one knew her as Danny Preacher's daughter, but just as Ainsley Lynn, she was going to nail her boots to the ground and damn Kase Jakoby as she did.

* * * *

Kase spent a restless, miserable night thinking of Ainsley, tossing and turning in the bed of his truck, the damned bugs driving him nuts. The only thing that kept him from going completely crazy was jacking off and the fact that Ainsley's truck was still right there. She hadn't jumped right into it and driven off.

Damn that girl anyway.

He woke up early, his balls heavy, his hand just taking the edge off. Again. He started his stove, got his coffee going and pondered his next move, because there *was* going to be one.

She was here and he wasn't going to let her get away again.

Kase figured she'd freaked out about how he made her feel and run away from him after a few short months. He'd started off too hot. This time he'd make it a slow burn…

He grabbed his cell phone and called Tyler Bodean, who was in charge of the circuit schedule right now.

"Yell-o?" Tyler said, and Kase heard a bull lowing, the sound deep and familiar as hell.

"Hey, bud. It's Kase." They'd known each other since high school, where Ty had been two years ahead of him. Kase knew he could call in a favor. "Can you tell me if Ainsley Preacher is registered for Giddings?"

"Hrm. That gal back with us? She must be riding for the finals. Hold up."

He heard grunts and a couple "damn phone" and "get off the fucking fence, you ass," then Ty was back. "Looks like, yessir."

"Thanks. Call me if she cancels?" He needed to plan, and he had until tomorrow night if this all worked out.

"I can do that. You hunting, man? She's a bit of a cold fish, from what I hear."

"Yeah, well, I think different." He wasn't gonna snarl, but he wasn't gonna listen to anyone talk against her either.

"Good on you. Holler if you need anything. I got shit to do."

"Thanks, Ty." Kase wondered if his buddy would ever find someone who could put up with how the rodeo came first. Prob'ly not. One way or the other, that was none of his.

Ainsley? Now, that woman was some of his. His business, his girl… She just needed to know it. He headed to the bathrooms, humming some classic George under his breath.

When he came back, Lilith wasn't in her trailer and Kase craned his neck, looking for Ainsley. She was in a clearing, moving fast, her hair back in a ponytail as she rode her mare bareback.

Lord, she was something. She was well past the awkwardness of a girl, but she still had that fluidity, that oneness with her horse that some of the older barrel racers lost. Her breasts moved under her button-down shirt, mesmerizing him.

What he wanted to see, though, was that ink. He wanted to touch it, trace the edges. He wanted to see how far down it went. He wanted to know the story. Who had done the work? Had they been lovers? Fuckbuddies? The Ice Queen bird had flown, dammit.

Why couldn't that frickin' bird have flown for him?

Still, she was here now, horsefeathers and all, so he'd take it as a sign that he was on the right track. He watched her until he couldn't stand the pressure in his belly. Then he hit the latrine and pondered what he could borrow from friends to cook Ainsley some breakfast.

It was time to prove his goddamn intentions. With bacon.

Bacon was one thing he knew they agreed on. Oh, hell yeah. He knocked on Eddie and June's trailer, the old married couple in no hurry to move on.

June came out, wearing her *Buckle Bunnies Suck* T-shirt. "Hey, Kase, honey. What's up?"

"I need to buy breakfast foods. Something I can cook for a lady. Can I raid you?"

"Sure, honey. You always share your good coffee."

"I can pay you or I can go to the store today on the road."

"Just bring us Burger King one afternoon next week. You know how Eddie feels about his Whoppers." June rolled her eyes and pursed her lips, her expression hilarious.

"I do." He could totally do that. He whipped out his phone and made a note on his calendar. "Okay, lady, lead me to your bacon."

June had canned biscuits and eggs, bacon and even a little carton of shelf-stable orange juice. Rock on. Good and good for you. Kase kissed her cheek and gave her a squeeze. "You're my hero."

"You're a man on a mission. Be good, and if that doesn't work for you, son, have fun!"

"I always do that, Miss June." Kase winked and headed off to the next phase of his plan. He had a wee two-burner stove, but he knew Ainsley's trailer had to have a stove with a tiny oven.

He'd be way better off cooking there.

Ainsley was loving on that black bitch of a mare, cooing at her like she was a pampered poodle or something. That meant no one would sound the alarm by kicking the damned trailer wall...

Okay, so maybe it was creepy to sneak into someone's trailer, but he was a desperate man and preferred 'romantic'.

He just wanted to... Shit Marthy, he wanted to know why she'd dropped him like a hot rock when she wanted him as badly as he wanted her. Kase knew she did. He'd heard it in her voice last night.

He'd seen it in the way her eyes had dragged over him as if she was starving.

His body tightened, the desire for her never too far from the surface. The hell of it was he liked her too. Her dark sense of humor, her hard work ethic, even her eye rolling when he was at his most macho cowboy. The way she'd never met an animal that scared her—from bucking bull to fractious horse. Hell, rumor was she'd gotten her jaw broken from a kick when she was nine and only missed two junior events.

Her trailer wasn't locked. Ta-da. No breaking required. Just entering.

That wasn't so bad. Kase left the door open, though. He

was going for surprise, not shock, and God knew he didn't want to get his happy ass shot.

Kase chuckled. Ainsley would probably happily shoot him. Okay, a makeshift pan out of aluminum foil to contain the biscuits... It only took one instance of the breakfast breads melting down through the oven rack for a guy to learn that.

He had to say the tiny trailer was neat as a pin, except for the bed, which was a tangle of sheets and what looked suspiciously like one of his old T-shirts.

It took a lot for him to resist going to look. What if it belonged to some other dude? What if it was just wishful thinking?

What if he was making a goddamn fool out of him...?

"Kase Jakoby, what the fuck are you doing in my trailer?"

"Language! Lord, girl. You got a mouth on you."

A mouth. A gorgeous pair of tits that made him a little dizzy. A tiny waist. And that ass.

Christ, men could write odes to that fine ass.

She stood in the doorway, arms crossed under her breasts, glaring. "What are you doing?"

"Cooking you breakfast. Should be obvious."

"Why?" Sweat darkened the edge of her dark shirt and he knew she had to be hot, so she needed to strip down.

"You don't have to cover up for me, baby girl."

"That's not an answer."

"No? How about I want to trade breakfast for a tattoo viewing?" Kase burned to see that back piece.

"I'm not that cheap." She turned a chair around, straddled it, and he damn near creamed his jeans.

Do not burn the bacon, Jakoby. "I never thought you were. That's just for looking. We'd negotiate anything else."

"You're a nut." And she thought he was charming. The tiny smile playing about her mouth proved it.

"You still like your eggs over medium?"

"Yeah." She frowned at him, leaning on the back of the chair. "What are you really up to?"

"What do you mean?" Kase paused, pan hovering over the burner. "I'm here to seduce you."

"There's not a hot, skinny little blonde around?"

His brows rose near to his hairline. "What?"

"Come on. You didn't get what you really needed from me and you picked that little buckle bunny instead. Fine. Whatever. She decide she wanted someone else?"

"What the hell are you talking about?" Kase pulled the remaining bacon from the pan and turned off the stove. He couldn't make eggs and make sense of this too.

"Sheri Ballard, you asshole."

"What about her?" Kase really didn't get it. Sheri was — well, bless her, she was his best friend Loyal's sister, so he wouldn't say what she was.

"Really? The morning after you tied me... I mean, it was that next day and y'all are stepping out and it's just a thing?"

"Stepping out? Now all he could do was scowl. "What are you talking about, woman?"

"Jesus Christ, do you fuck so many girls that you can't remember? She sure remembered when she told all of us in the arena that afternoon, in loving detail."

Kase blinked. "And you just believed her? Never asked me? Ran off?"

"I saw y'all! I saw y'all behind the trailers! I didn't need to ask." She looked so sure, her eyes snapping with black fire.

There was no way. No way because it didn't happen. How could she have seen something that didn't ever come close to being true? "Tell me what you saw."

"What?"

He sat down, right across from her. "I mean it, baby girl. Tell me what you saw because I ain't never once slept with Sheri. She's my best friend's sister. That was not going to happen, so what did you see?"

"I saw — I remember it was wicked cold that day, heading into fall."

He nodded. They'd been damn near to the finals, damn

77

near to Thanksgiving. The Dallas Stampede.

"I saw you, Kase. You had your back to me, but you pushed her up against the wall of the arena, hands over her head." Her cheeks flamed dark red, and she pushed away from the chair and stood. "I'm going to take a walk. Be gone when I get back."

"No." His hand shot out and Kase grabbed her wrist. "I was never with Sheri, and I mean it. So I want to know what you saw you thought was me."

"It was you. I know your hat, your hatband. That stupid denim coat of yours with the shearling collar."

"This was the day after we had that amazing night? Before or after I rode?"

She blinked at him. "Before. That morning. I was coming to…"

Her cheeks flushed even darker and she waved a hand.

"Oh, man, and I missed it? I wondered where the hell my hat and coat went. In fact I was at the Cavender's in Mesquite, getting a hat and boots. I figured my truck got broken into while I was with you." Hell, he'd bought her a belt buckle that he'd thought she'd like when he was there.

"So, I'm supposed to believe that? Seriously? Someone stole your hat and boots to fuck your best friend's sister up against the wall?"

Kase wanted to growl, but he shrugged easily instead. "I reported it to the rodeo company and the police, baby girl. Wasn't your daddy on the board back then?"

"Yeah. Yeah, he was."

"Then he'll have records. Cost me a thousand bucks to replace my good hat and boots. I was pissed."

He swore he saw a tear balancing on her eyelashes and he had a moment of utter rage. That fucking Sheri, hurting both of them and stealing his shit for what? It wasn't like he'd give her the time of day one way or the other. He knew who he wanted.

"Hey," Kase said, stroking her wrist. "You okay?"

"No. My options are you're a shit or I'm an idiot. I'm not

okay."

He pondered that. "No. No, if someone stole my coat and boots and hat, you were tricked." Kase was going to kill someone. Starting with Sheri.

"She said… She talked about your ink, that scar on your belly." Ainsley's fingers brushed the place where he'd got hooked, down low, right above his cock, and the touch made him curl his toes. She started to pull away and Kase grabbed her hand, pressing it against the scar.

"Oh, Ainsley. I've known Sheri since I was twelve. She's probably seen me naked as much as anyone besides my momma, just because her people have a swimming pool. Her brother is my best friend." Kase frowned. "And he's going to die if he knew about this and didn't tell me."

He'd deal with that shit later. Right now Kase had a woman to woo, to remind that he was one of the good guys, and to cook bacon for.

The bacon was done, actually. "Eggs. Right?"

"Okay. Okay, yeah. You… You want toast?"

"I'd love some." That was the spirit. Fuck, it killed him that he'd lost all this time, all the possibilities. "Oh, wait. Biscuits. I made biscuits. I'm praying I didn't burn the fuck out of the biscuits."

Ainsley's laugh went right to his balls. "I don't smell burned biscuits. I bet you're safe."

"Can you check? I'll do the eggs." Kase grabbed a bite of bacon to feed her, feeling as if a huge weight had fallen off his shoulders. She opened up and nipped it from his fingers.

His breath caught, and Kase stepped toward her, his body on fire for her touch. Ainsley licked her lips and he could smell her, smell strawberries.

Groaning, he bent his head, licking at her lips, wanting her to open up so he could kiss her.

"Don't burn the biscuits," she moaned, but her arms were wrapping around his shoulders, and his hands were on her ass and he didn't give a good goddamn about the biscuits.

Kase lifted her against him, rubbing, and this was Ainsley with him, his girl. God, he'd missed her, missed how her body fit against him. She could say they didn't know each other, but Kase knew every inch and wanted more.

She hooked one leg around him, dragging them together, grinding her hot little pussy against him. Kase hated the clothes that kept them apart.

No one had ever needed like his Ainsley.

He twirled her, turning off the oven with one hand as he propped her butt on the edge of the counter. Ainsley clung to his shoulders, her mouth seeking his again, kisses so hot and fast they scalded like coffee when you drank it too fast.

He pushed at the buttons on her shirt, wanting—no, needing to get some skin. The fact that she had this huge tattoo that he'd never seen or explored made him nuts. Someone had done that. Someone had stripped her down and inked her, touched her.

Now it was his turn. He tugged off her shirt, then started on the undershirt. Her eyes met his, so warm, so dark and hungry that he could fall into them.

"Want you," Kase told her, because he thought the words were just as important as the deed. He should have remembered that before and maybe she would have asked him about Sheri instead of running.

"Still?"

He snorted and rubbed her against his cock. He was so hard for her a cat couldn't scratch it. "Never been a day I didn't want you, girl. Not one day."

"Oh." She touched his cheek before reaching back to unfasten her bra. "Wanna see?"

"More than I want my next breath."

She shivered, her nipples drawing up hard, deep pink and puckered.

Kase saw them, and he had to touch them, had to circle the taut skin with his fingers, had to feel them go even tighter.

A soft moan was Kase's reward, and he bent to kiss Ainsley's throat when she arched her back. He wanted to taste every part of her, love every bit of that hot little body, from her full lower lip to her strong, horse-gripping thighs.

"Do you remember, baby girl? How I made you come just with these sweet, sensitive little nipples? That night just outside Banderas, the one where we had brisket and fed each other fries?"

Her body went tight and he had to smile, because she clearly remembered. Hot, needy wildcat.

Kase went even farther, licking a line down her chest. He nuzzled her breasts, wanting a nipple in his mouth. She moved right into his lips, pushing that taut bud right where she wanted it.

Yum. Kase flicked it with his tongue, pushing that nub back and forth. Her nails dug into his neck, the tiny sting revving him up, and he answered with scraping her with his teeth, careful to let her feel but not hurt.

"Kase." She arched, her legs wrapping around him to hold him between her thighs. "Please."

"Patience." Like that was going to happen. He wanted her—hot and heavy, slamming them together as they rutted like mindless animals.

"No. We wasted too much time." She rubbed up and down his shaft, the seams on their jeans pressing against him until he wanted to shout with the pleasure of friction.

"Jesus!" Kase cupped her cunt with his palm, giving him a chance to breathe, giving him a bare moment to chill the fuck out and to not go off like a virgin.

She smiled, the feminine triumph in the expression as maddening as it was endearing. Then she wiggled against him so hard his ears rang with the rush of his blood. "Let me down so I can turn around."

"I don't know. I like you where you are."

"You don't want to see? You been making such a big deal." She licked her lips, giving him ideas about what to do with her lush mouth.

"I do." He did. And when she wiggled out of her jeans and boots, after sliding to the floor, his heart tried to pound out of his chest.

The sweet, curvy cowgirl tattoo covered the length of Ainsley's back. She was dark-haired and wearing the tiniest pair of cut-offs with her boots, a red button-down tied at the waist, the fabric just barely covering her breasts. Her belly button was pierced, her thigh was inked with a cow skull, and her little bowed lips were parted on a moan. Best of all, her tiny hands were on the saddle horn, wrists bound with rope.

He hit his knees, just drunk on the sight. Kase kissed the small of Ainsley's back. "Stunning."

She glanced over her shoulder at him, hair tumbling over onto her back. "You like?"

He looked up, met her gaze and held it. "I love."

Kase made sure that he watched her, that she heard him, understood him, then he bit her ass, hard enough to sting. "Turn back and spread for me, baby girl. Let me taste your sweet pussy."

When she hesitated, he swatted her some, knowing this was a game she craved. "Now."

He was going to feed that need well enough that she'd never look to sate it anywhere else.

"Now."

God, Ainsley's inner thighs were slick with her need, her ass tingled with the promise of that little swat, and the finest broad-shouldered blond cowboy she'd ever met was kneeling behind her.

She braced herself against the counter and spread her legs. Ainsley decided to trust. She wanted to believe in him.

"Jesus, you smell like heaven." He grabbed her hips, then turned her to face him again nuzzled into her lower belly, chin rubbing her curls below. "Never see strawberries without thinking about you."

"You said." She sank her hand into his hair. Ainsley had started using the strawberry shampoo back when she'd been poor, hell-bent on proving to her daddy that she didn't need him. She'd kept using it after Kase because she couldn't get over him and how much he loved the scent.

"I did." He lapped at her, teasing her. "Open up wider. I need."

She balanced on her toes, bracing her elbows on the counter so she could push up with her hips. Ainsley wanted his mouth at her core.

"That's my girl." Kase hooked one leg over his shoulder and spread her, before zeroing in on her clit, tongue circling her nice and slow. He made turn after turn around her sensitive bud, driving her mad.

"Oh, damn." Now she could ride, swinging her hips, letting him send her soaring like only Kase could. He held her close, thumbs holding her pussy open as her hips rocked. Kase controlled the motion, helping her find her rhythm.

He always was a control freak. "I got it for you," she gasped. "The tattoo."

His moan vibrated against her cunt in the best possible way, and Ainsley tugged his silky, short hair, pulling him into her. She wanted to meld them together, to never let him go again. Her thigh muscles shook with strain, her breasts bouncing as she sawed back and forth. He lashed at her, nudging the sensitive nub over and over, and her thighs began to shake, to shudder violently. A tight spring of need gathered in the pit of her belly, and she pinched her nipple, giving herself a little sting that she was so used to with Kase.

He laughed, a low, sensual sound that buzzed against her skin. Kase knew what he did to her, knew what she craved.

"Quit teasing, you butthead," she told him.

He dug in with his fingers, her soft skin ready for his marks. She wanted everything, and she was going to take it.

Two fingers pressed inside her, filling her pussy in a rush, and he began to suck at her clit in time with the pressure.

She went wild, crying out, her head falling back so her

hair tickled her skin. Ainsley thought about his thick cock filling her in the same way, pushing deep, slamming into her as they came together. No one had ever spread her the way he had, made her strain to take him.

This was her one and only, and Ainsley knew it. Had known it since they met. God, she'd believed the lies... She'd seen them with her own eyes, though. She'd thought—

"Stop it," he growled, his lips shining with her essence. "Pay attention. Right here."

Kase pushed his fingers in to his third knuckle, the heel of his hand grinding into her, making her arch as she gasped.

"That's it, baby girl. You think I can't feel it when you think too much? That's your problem. You need to feel. Need to let me lead." Kase nipped at her hip, her thigh. "Let me give you what you're asking for."

He kept fucking her with his fingers, driving her higher and higher, and all the while, those bright blue eyes watched her like a hawk, memorizing every inch of her body.

Maybe she should have been self-conscious, but he made her feel like a rodeo princess, as if he had eyes only for her. She stretched her arms up over her head, teasing him with the position he loved, counting off seconds to see how long it would take him to stand up and give her what she really needed.

He moaned for her, but his eyes narrowed, his thumb working her clit.

"Kase." Ainsley shook, her belly taut, the spring inside her twisting unbearably tight. "I—God."

"Yes. Come on, baby girl. Let me watch you come apart in my hands, then we'll do it again."

She nodded, her hair flying, because she wanted him with her, wanted him just as crazy for her, no matter what it took.

He circled her clit once more, then pegged her bundle of nerve endings hard, rubbing with a steady determination that she couldn't deny. Electric shocks flowed through her body, beginning at her center and working out. Her whole body drew up, the orgasm right there, ready for her to fall into.

"Beautiful woman." Kase rubbed his chin against her belly. "I got you."

And thank God he did, because she was heading over the edge and there wasn't a thing to be done about it except take the pleasure and soar. Ainsley danced for him, grinding against his hand, against his face. She shouted, the sound ringing out loud enough that Lilith kicked and neighed in the next partition.

"Damn, girl." Kase slithered up her body, leaving wet kisses on her belly, her breasts, her neck, before taking her mouth, sharing her own sweetness with her.

She writhed, her whole self on fire, her hands clenching and unclenching over her head. Kase laughed and grabbed her wrists, keeping her right where she was. Fuck, yes. That was what she needed. Some force.

"Took you long enough to take the hint," she said, and Kase busted out with a laugh.

"Yeah, I'm slow enough you had to tattoo it on your back."

"Shut up." She laughed up at him, gasping when he slid a denim-clad thigh between hers. The rough fabric was almost too much. "Oh, Jesus. Fuck me, Kase. Tell me you have rubbers."

"Uh-huh. I was hoping you'd let me. Bed?"

"Now."

Kase lifted her, but her head bonked against the ceiling, and they both cracked up. So he let her slide to her feet, backing up into the main area of the trailer.

He worked his boots off while she shoved her nightshirt — which had been his, once upon a time — off the bed with the comforter.

Kase chuckled, stripping out of his jeans, his long legs and lean hips almost as fascinating as his incredibly hard cock. Almost. "I missed that shirt," he told her. "Thought it got stolen with everything else."

"I missed you." She reached out to slide one hand down

Kase's belly, tracing each and every ridge. He had that six-pack all the Instagram honeys wished they had.

"I'm selfish enough to be glad." He sucked in his tummy, the coarse hairs there catching on her fingers.

She leaned in for another kiss as her fingers wrapped around Kase's cock, measuring him from balls to tip and not finding him wanting in the least.

"Uhn." Those blue eyes closed, Kase rising up on tiptoe. "Easy now, baby girl. I need a tiny bit of control."

"Do you? That doesn't seem fair." How far could she push him until he stopped her? He hated to lose his tight rein.

"It does if you want me to fuck you." His eyes popped open. "And I want to. I want to slide inside you and feel how wet you are for me, feel how you pull at me." One of his hands wrapped around her hip, drawing them tight together. "Let me in, baby girl. Let me prove that I'm made for you."

"Condom." She hadn't been...active for a while. They shouldn't take chances, right?

"My jeans pocket." Kase jerked his chin toward the bench by the bed.

She nodded and moved to grab it, jumping as his warm hand slid over the curve of her ass.

"I love every curve, Ainsley. I want to do bad things to you."

"I intend to let you try." She gasped as he touched her, fingers sliding through her slick folds again, teasing her. She was almost too sensitive now, but he knew how to rev her up.

"You're wet for me."

"Duh."

He tugged her curls playfully. "I'm going for seductive, woman."

"Oh, right. I know how suave you aren't." She chuckled, remembering the first time, how they'd clunked heads and spilled an ice-cold Sprite all over the bed in the hotel room. He'd gotten way better after that.

"You know a lot about me. Next time you doubt me, remember that I want you, Ainsley Lynn, not anyone else."

She flushed all the way from her cheeks to her nipples. "I wanted to believe you wanted me, but—"

"I want you." He stood her up, turned her around and met her gaze, head on. "I ain't lying."

She reached up and touched his cheek. "Okay."

His eyes darkened to something like cobalt. "Just like that. God, you're amazing."

"I'll just have you killed if you're lying." She tried to play it off, because she wanted this so much.

Kase laughed, then tossed her back on the bed, crawling onto the mattress in front of her. "I bet. Evil woman."

She had to lick her lips, had to. She could smell him now, all musk and heat, and she touched him, gathering up the hot drops leaking from the tip of his cock. He grunted and when she brought her fingers to her lips and licked them clean, he gave her a harsh, needy cry.

"Come and get me, cowboy," Ainsley told him.

"Shit, baby. I'm going to make you forget your own name." He grabbed the condom from her so he could tear it open and slide it on his cock, which Ainsley admired, running one hand down her belly.

She could watch him for hours, watch the way his hips shifted as if he was riding.

"You gonna show me where to go?" he asked, pressing between her legs.

"You don't remember?" She grabbed hold of his shaft and drew him close to her, rubbing his tip against her clit, revving them both up.

"I want you to touch me, though." His heartbeat thundered against her palm, his hardness almost impossible in the laws of nature.

She licked her lips, stroking him from base to tip again, her fingers dragging over the condom. She hated the latex that kept them from being skin on skin, but they had to be careful, smart. Neither one of them needed babies or...

Well, she didn't want to think on 'or'.

Ainsley wanted to believe he cared enough not to pass on anything, including a kid.

"Hey." He reached out and tilted her chin up. "No wandering again. If I have to tie you up, I will."

"Tease. You can have that when you earn it." Listen to her, being all confident and shit.

"I'd better make this good." Kase placed a hand over hers and they both guided him inside her. He flexed his hips, sliding home deep with a single thrust.

Her lips parted as he took her, like she was going to be able to make room that way. God, he stretched her to the limit, made her strain and moan and shiver and ache.

"Jesus, baby girl. I was made for you." His hand was a brand on her hip, solid and so sure, moving her where he wanted her.

When Kase began to thrust, she strained to rise up and meet him, but he controlled the pace. He was giving, taking, not letting her have a bit of the upper hand.

"Trust me. I will get you where you're going. Believe in me."

How could she not? He'd come after her, even though she'd run away. She nodded, staring into his eyes, blue as the Colorado sky of her adopted mountain home. They came together, again and again, a fire lighting between them.

Kase bent to kiss her, lips and tongue taking hers by storm, a sensual onslaught she couldn't resist. She couldn't even think. When he slipped one hand between them to touch her, everything shattered into a thousand pieces.

Ainsley cried out, her body arching until she thought it would break. Kase kept her flying, never letting her down.

His thrusts sped, the heat they were building making her sweat. She grabbed Kase's shoulders, feeling how slick his skin was, how hot he was to the touch.

"I gotta. Baby girl, I gotta."

"Yes, Kase. Please. I want to see your face." She dreamed

of him at night, of his intensity when he came inside her.

He curled over the top of her, his hips slapping her backside as he let himself go. He shot for her, his moan deep and heartfelt, and he gripped her arms so hard she felt each inch where their bodies came together like it would stay with her for days.

He stared down at her, chest working like a lathered horse's. "Lord, woman. You're like a bonfire in July."

"Uh-huh." She patted his arm, clumsy because her brain had shorted out.

Kase pulled out of her, leaving her bereft, got rid of the condom, then pushed close again, gathering her right into his side like she belonged there. "I want to know all about your ink. I want to know about where you've been, baby girl."

"I left Texas." She thought that was the best place to start. "I mean, I got the ink in Vegas. But I'm in Colorado now."

"Yeah? Why'd you come home?"

"Money. I've got a shot for Vegas again and Daddy fronts my way if I follow his rules."

"Ah." He chuckled. "I thought your demon horse paid your way."

"You be good to my baby. She's the love of my life."

Kase clasped his hands against his chest, all dramatic gasps and rolling eyes.

"It's true. She's my good girl."

Kase nuzzled the top of her head. "And are you going to be mine, baby girl?"

"I— Be serious." She pinched his nipple. This was too far too fast. She'd just stopped hating him...

"I am." He pinched back, careful. "I can wait, but I'm serious as a heart attack. I'm not the fuck 'em and forget 'em kind."

"I thought— I'm going to kill something." She really was. Sheri wasn't on tour anymore, so she'd have to start with Kase's buddy Loyal.

"Yeah, you and me both. I'm gonna start with chatting at

Loyal about drowning his sister and then I'm fixin' to have to talk at your daddy."

"My daddy?" Her eyes widened. Nobody talked to Danny Preacher. Nobody.

"Yep. He's my proof, remember? I reported my shit stolen to the rodeo office." He cupped her cheek. "I know you don't believe me, but I didn't fuck around on you. I didn't, and you just up and left like your ass was on fire."

"Shut up. You don't know how it felt, seeing you..." She swatted his chest.

"Hey! Wasn't me!"

"I know." Her chin wobbled, and she hated that she tended to cry when she was pissed as hell. "Someone did this deliberately, and I'm sorry. I should have talked to you, but I loved you so much that I lost it."

"Yeah, sure, but for so long? I called and texted. I went to Preacher's and asked after you."

"Oh, God." Now she was going to kill her daddy too. "No one told me. I dumped a Dr. Pepper on my phone so my brother gave me his and I never got my number back."

And she'd blocked Kase the first few days, sure, but only for a couple and she'd been... Shit. She'd been stupid. Like dumb as a box of hammers. Christ.

"I feel like shit," she told him.

"I do too. Pissed-off as shit and I'm gonna knock a few heads together, but that's all in the tomorrow. Today we got a day for me to look at that tattoo up close and personal."

"That sounds like a good plan." Ainsley gave Kase a watery smile. "I'm glad you're here."

"No tears, woman. I know you didn't cry under the needle, so you just suck it up."

"Butthead cowboy." He made her laugh, though, didn't he, and backed the tears right off.

"Turn over, baby girl." He helped her slide to her belly so he could trace the inked lines on her back. The little touches made her wriggle, and the lighter contact turned to a slow massage. He was so tactile, so deliciously giving.

"I could touch you for the rest of my life, Ainsley Lynn."

"Shut up, cowboy."

"No, ma'am. I did that once and I lost out. From now on you're going to know how I feel." He kissed the small of her back, right where the spurs were on her cowgirl tattoo. "Besides, don't think for a second I didn't notice this girl's wearing my tattoo on her thigh."

"I told you I got it for you." She'd thought it was about closure. That was bullshit, and Ainsley had figured it out the first time someone else had tried to touch her.

It had been about not knowing how to fight for what she wanted.

She was older now.

Ainsley grinned. Now she was going to claw that Sheri's eyes out if the woman even tried to come near her man.

Well, that and she was going to trust Kase enough to ask him what was going on instead of running away.

That seemed like a pretty good plan.

* * * *

The sun beat down on them in the arena, the day too damned hot to be roping and riding, but they were doing it anyway. Kase was trying hard to just sit still and wait for his re-ride, which was coming right in front of the bull riding.

He saw the pickup come out with the barrels, Mr. Franks and Wallace getting them set in the back and to either side. He thought he could hear Lilith in the rear of the arena, whinnying her head off.

Yeah, she'd be ready and rarin' to go, that silly beast. His girl was doing great, winning the last three events. Kase liked to think that was because they were traveling together.

He'd been doing pretty damn fine himself, taking four purses in three events. He was on top of the fucking world.

Kase studied the toes of his boots, waiting for Ainsley to ride. He felt a touch to the small of his back, and he smiled, looking up. "Hey, baby girl."

"Oh, nice." Loyal's sister, Sheri, stood behind him, seeming a little brassy in the late afternoon sun.

Oh, for fuck's sake. "What are you doing here?"

"Came to watch Loyal ride."

"Well, no touching. I am strictly off limits." That was about as nice as he could be for Loyal's sake. He kinda wanted to punch Sheri in the face, which he knew very well he would never do. He couldn't guarantee the same for Ainsley, though.

"Aren't you special? You hook back up with the Ice Queen?"

"No thanks to you." He studied her from her teased hair to her nose, raised up in a haughty sniff. "Why the hell did you do that, Sheri? Set me up that way?"

"I'm sure I don't know what you mean."

"Don't," he snapped. "If you don't want me to go to Loyal and tell him you broke into my truck, don't lie."

"I didn't break into your truck." She couldn't meet his gaze with hers. "Wacey Ford did."

"Son of a bitch. Why? You tell me why."

"She's a cunt. She thinks she's better than us and we were all happier with her gone. It's not like she didn't have her daddy to run to, after all." Sheri wrinkled her nose. "Besides, it was eons ago. It was a prank."

"A prank." He advanced on her, his heart slamming his ribs, he was so fucking mad. "A prank? You got no idea what you did!"

"What, your precious princess had to run away to Colorado? For Christ's sake, Kase, spoiled barrel racers are a dime a dozen."

Speaking of barrel racers, Harry Walkers announced Ainsley's name, and Kase turned to watch her ride. Nothing in the world could make him feel the exhilaration Kase experienced when he saw her on that bitch of a mare. She and Lilith looked like one being, they were so in tune. She cornered like a dream, taking the first two barrels easily before she caught sight of him and Sheri and her body shifted on the saddle, confusing Lilith.

No. No, baby. Don't fuck up because of her.

His girl recovered, turning her head and hands the direction she wanted Lilith to go. Then it was all over but the race to the finish line.

"Go, baby girl! Ride her! Go!"

His girl whipped the end of the rope like a master, Lilith streaking toward the timer lights.

"Fourteen and four, ladies and gentlemen," Harry said over the mic. "We have a new leader!"

"That's my girl!" he hollered, waving his hat wildly. "That's my Ainsley."

"You're such a sap," Sheri told him, and Kase realized he'd forgotten she was there.

"And you're a giant bleeding asshole. You got a point? I got a re-ride in a sec."

"She's a spoiled little rich girl and we're all better off without her stuck-up —"

Sheri was cut off as a hand landed on her shoulder, and Ainsley whipped her around, decking her hard, right in the mouth. His woman had stripped off her sponsor shirt, and she was standing there in all her glory, that white tank top damn near see-through with sweat. The second blow caught Sheri right under the jaw, flattened her ass out.

"Spoiled or not, I sure as fuck can clean your clock, bitch." Ainsley spat on the ground next to Sheri, then turned to Kase, looking about as proud as punch. "Good ride, cowboy. You make the whistle, I'll blow you in the trailer."

Then she walked off, her head held high.

Hoo, yeah. What cowboy could resist a dare like that? Kase grabbed his rigging and headed down toward the chutes, leaving Sheri sitting on her butt.

He had to make the whistle and get in the money. Kase intended to collect on her promise.

"That your girl, man?" one of the little local cowboys asked.

"You know it."

"Hot. You are lucky. That's one helluva tattoo she's got."

"One hell of an uppercut too." Kase winked, then went to settle in at his chute. He had a paint mare named Dust Devil tonight. "Okay, lady. My woman made me a promise. I reckon to collect."

The mare bobbed her head, ears twitching. There, they had an agreement. "It was a slow night, huh? I need a seventy-six."

An eighty would be better.

An eighty-five might earn him a ride of his own. Kase chuckled, and Loyal walked up to the side of the chute to help him load. "You got a heck of a lady there. I got to tell you, I didn't know about Sheri, bud."

"I guess Ainsley dealt with it. Tell her to leave me be."

"You got it. You're buying the beer in Vegas, right?"

Kase laughed. "Ainsley will be. She's gonna take it all."

"I'd like to see that." He helped Kase settle in his rigging, get the flank strap on.

Kase would too. "Thanks, buddy. Okay, I'm fixin' to nod."

Loyal backed away, and Kase jammed his hat down with his free hand before he nodded his head. The chute opened and Kase marked out, his spurs above the mare's shoulders.

Dust Devil bucked for him, strong and steady, rhythm like a train, *chugga-chugga-chugga*. Head down, heels up, she was like a mad kind of rocking chair. Perfect for a good score.

He heard the buzzer, and the safety man hauled his happy ass down. And when they announced an eighty-four five? Shit. He was totally getting laid.

Kase slapped his hat against his leg before clapping it back on his head, then pumping his hands in the air. Hell, yeah.

Money, money, money! He won the round, got himself a tour around the arena, and by the time the crowd went wild for the bull riders, he was heading for a purple trailer.

Lilith was already loaded up, all ready to go, and she

rolled her eyes at him when he walked up, but she wasn't laying back her ears or giving him teeth anymore. In fact, she damn near nuzzled his pockets for sugar. Which he had, of course. He gave her one cube, because Ainsley would yell if he fed Lilith too much. "You spoil her." Ainsley was perched on the tailgate of her truck, drinking a beer and looking at him. "Good ride."

"You too." He stared into her dark eyes, his body reminding him she wanted him. She'd said so. "I was worried you were gonna lose it for a second."

"Yeah, well, I dealt with things." Ainsley smiled for him, her dark eyes twinkling. "Thinking I might head up to the mountains for a while, though, finish out the season there."

"Yeah?" His heart dropped right to his boots, but Kase kept it light. "Cooler up there, and Cheyenne is coming up."

"It is." She chewed on her bottom lip, little white teeth tugging. "You wanna go? We could share expenses."

Up. Down. Way up. Kase lit up like a firecracker. "Hell, yes. Let's find a new kind of dirt for my boots."

"Find a place where I can go back to being something more than Danny Preacher's daughter."

He reached out to touch her cheek, the cool, dark fall of her hair rubbing the back of his hand. "You'll always be more than that, baby girl. You're the best. And you're mine."

"Am I now?"

He loved how she was feeling brave enough to hang out just in her jeans, her tank top, her sparkly little belt.

"You are." Kase said it with absolute certainty. "I love you, Ainsley. Never doubt that for another moment."

He grabbed her, took the kiss he'd been needing since they'd come to work this morning. "Did I tell you I scored over eighty? Took the round?"

"Looks like somebody earned themselves a kiss."

Kase raised his eyebrows. "Now, I just had that. You offered something else."

"Did I?" Oh, little tease. He did adore her.

Kase bent his knees and came up under her belly, lifting her on his shoulder. "Yes, ma'am. I think now is the time."

He patted her ass, heading to the trailer, laughing as she kicked and squealed for him. Kase was a Texan to the bone, but he'd always had a hankering for the mountains. Steamboat, maybe, or Vail.

As long as Ainsley was there, he'd be the king of the goddamned world. And his girl? Well, she could be anyone she wanted—no hiding, no shame, no worries.

She was his, tied and taken.

THREE TO FEUD

NAN COMARGUE

Chapter One

"Get a move on, Grace. The clock's ticking."

Her boyfriend Adam spoke from the doorway. Though they'd worked at the same oil company for over a year, he rarely set foot in her office, clearly considering it a lesser executive's domain. Unlike his office, hers had only a limited view of downtown Calgary and none at all of the famed Saddledome.

With two years' experience over her, Adam was on the verge of a senior executive position while she was still assigned mostly routine accounts. It had been a banner day last week when she'd actually got to go to an offsite meeting, carrying a senior partner's files for her.

Oh, well. It was the way of the world. She was paying her dues.

"I'm ready," she said, lifting out the overnight bag she'd tucked under her desk. The small bag had felt light as air this morning but now it might as well have been filled with accounting tomes.

She'd already shut down her computer and cleared away the files she'd been working on. She liked to leave an empty desk each night, though perhaps that wasn't such a good practice, since other people sometimes commented on her apparent lack of work.

At a big oil and gas concern like theirs, you didn't only need to put in the long hours, you had to be *seen* to be putting in the long hours.

"You look tired," Adam told her when she drew near. He dropped an absent kiss on her forehead. "Long day?"

"Yes," said Grace. "I guess."

He lifted his eyebrows. "You guess? You're not sure?"

She tried to explain. "I am tired, yes, but I'm mostly worried."

"About the trip?"

What else did he think I meant?

"Yes," she said again, "and about my cousins."

"Oh, right, the wealthy Walkers." Adam's tone put a heavy underline beneath the last three words, as if he was quoting a title. The Wealthy Walkers. A prime time drama, perhaps, or a comedy-horror.

Adam put an arm around her shoulders and steered them both out of the doorway. He started pushing her, ever so subtly, down the hall toward the elevators. Time hadn't stopped ticking.

"Tell me about your cousins again."

She'd repeated the story often enough to know that it didn't begin with the current crop of Walkers. No, the story went far *far* back. Generations.

"It all started with the Walker brothers. Three of them. James, Joseph and Jeremiah. They came out together from York — before it was Toronto — to make their fortunes. They came here to the great province of Alberta, worked hard, and bought land. The problem was that they bought the land together, jointly, in all their names."

"Bad mistake," said Adam, shaking his head. "Joint tenancy is fraught with issues."

"Their second problem," Grace continued, "was a woman. Apparently women were scarce in those parts back then and all three brothers wanted her. James married her. Joseph and Jeremiah stopped talking to him, and to each other. And because they never spoke and couldn't agree on basic things like what to grow on the land, the property went downhill.

"The next generation was smarter. One of the sons had the bright idea to divide the land, which they did. They fenced it throughout and did what they wanted with their thirds. One grew crops, one went in for horses and the other raised cattle. But they still never talked, just like their fathers."

"If they never talked, how did they manage to divide up the land?" Adam asked, as he did every time.

Grace glanced up at the elevator numbers. All of them were stuck up on the forty- and fifty-somethingth floors. They were on the tenth.

"How does anyone solve any sticky problem?" she asked. "They arranged the deal through their lawyers. The three cousins went through booms and busts but they all managed to hold onto their lands and pass them down to their sons, along with the feud. By that time, of course, it was a *real* feud. No one cared about the original argument between the brothers, they only cared about not being the first one to give in."

Adam smiled at her. "Delightful people, you Walkers."

Grace straightened up to her full height of five foot three. "I'm a Pratt."

Though her mother had been a Walker before she married.

"Plus you're adopted," said Adam.

"Plus I'm adopted," she repeated. "Who could miss that fact?"

When the elevator doors finally opened to admit them, she had every opportunity to observe exactly how un-Walker-like she was in appearance. Between the crush of bodies, she could glimpse her reflection in the elevator's mirrored panels and it showed not a tall, lithe fair-skinned creature like her mother, but a short, plump brown-skinned woman.

A past boyfriend had compared her to a Cabbage Patch Doll. During the inevitable argument that had followed, he'd insisted that the dolls were cute and so was she. Cute. As if any grown woman wanted to be considered cute.

Years before, she'd been a small, plump baby her parents had adopted from India, back when Indian girl babies were the fad. Grace thought that had come immediately after the Romanian orphan craze, and right at the beginning of the Asian adopted baby boom. Just her parents' luck that Indian babies went out of style soon after she was born.

They never did have any biological children, though if that was a true disappointment to them, they managed to hide it from her. The Walker name continued on the adjoining farms with two more healthy sons, each the last of their line.

Grace snuck a glance at Adam. In repose, his fine features took on a new sharpness. That sharpness bothered her sometimes. She'd had a bit of experience with strong men and they hadn't needed Adam's cutting edge to get their points across. But Adam could certainly be convincing. It was for his sake that she was undertaking this rather unpleasant chore and going back to the rural Alberta landscape where she'd grown up.

She wondered again if he was truly worth it.

Like babies, girlfriends also came and went out of style. Was she Adam Berman's Amal Clooney?

Grace shook the nasty thought aside. She loved Adam. They were moving in together.

She loved him. She really, *really* did. Except she had a sneaking suspicion that her love for Adam was a calculation she'd done in her head and had come out with the expected answer. He was smart and ambitious and… She was doing it again, adding up the numbers.

Who was she trying to fool?

* * * *

For years, Robert Hall had tried to explain to his friends and family that the job of real estate appraiser was not as boring as they might think. Sometimes he got to take long looks inside fabulous homes, a few even belonging to famous clients. And at other times, he was able to visit far flung parts of the country. He'd valued everything from mansions to lighthouses.

Far from being boring, his job was interesting and challenging. Now, he was starting to wonder if it might not also be dangerous.

Standing between two tough-looking cowboys, he definitely felt threatened.

"I-I've got an appointment," Rob repeated, flinching as his childhood stutter reasserted itself after a few decades in hiding. Somehow, he'd known it was merely in hiding and not truly gone. Nothing bad in his life ever truly disappeared.

"So you said," said Cowboy Number One. He was the one with the lighter brown hair and the cool snakeskin boots. A few inches shorter than his companion, he also did most of the talking.

Cowboy Number Two stood with his arms crossed over his chest, glaring down at Rob. His boots matched his hair, plain black, worn to a dusty gray. He was scarier by a long shot.

Behind each cowboy was a pickup — what else? — silver-gray for Snakeskin and shiny black for Black Boots. The trucks were pulled into the wide mouth of the driveway, parked at just the right angle to box in Rob's Toyota. Was that on purpose?

"I'm a real estate appraiser," he said. "The appointment I have is to inspect this property and give an estimate about its worth."

"For who?" Snakeskin squinted at him. "The bank?"

There was more than one bank operating, Rob wanted to tell him, even in Cowboy City, Alberta or whatever this place was called. He saved his breath. For men like this, lean, tan men who towered over him in cowboy boots, men who wore cowboy boots all year round and not just at Stampede time, he was sure there was one Bank and it was run by the man or maybe the guv'ment and they didn't trust either.

Rob wiped his forehead with the back of his hand. He was on an episode of *Hee Haw*. That was it. An episode written by Stephen King.

"The appointment is with a Ms. Pratt," he said, knowing he wasn't supposed to divulge client information, yet unable to stop himself.

He hadn't expected much of a reaction from the two men, yet he got one. Both of their expressions changed, Snakeskin's softening while Black Boot's hardened.

"Grace is coming here?" Snakeskin asked, his tone no longer challenging, but low and musing.

Grace Pratt, yes, that was the name Rob had in his calendar. The name lacked romance, but it clearly held magic if it could alter these two men's attitude.

Rob nodded. "She was supposed to meet me" — he paused to check his smartphone—"twelve minutes ago. Do you know her?"

Snakeskin grinned and Black Boots scowled, yet they spoke the same words at the same time. "I'm her cousin."

Then they both scowled. At each other.

Rob didn't know what to say. Cousins? He remembered being told that the property belonged to an old family, but that had seemed like an innocuous statement. Maybe he'd stepped into the middle of a blood feud. He started to feel afraid for this unseen Grace Pratt woman—and for himself.

A plume of dust signaled a car coming down the road toward them.

All three men squinted at it until the dust cloud resolved itself into a white sedan. By then it was almost upon them. The car slowed, then braked behind one of the pickups. After a moment, a figure stepped out onto the driveway.

The woman was diminutive in height. Her face was round like a cherub's and surrounded by a halo of dark curls. She wore a well-tailored business suit, yet its obvious expense couldn't hide the impact of her generous hips and boobs. Nice, soft boobs, Rob imagined, the kind you wanted to bury your face in.

Damn it, what was he thinking? This was obviously his client, Grace Pratt. And there was no way in hell she was related in any way to the two cowboys.

Rob felt his professional obligations keenly. He stepped up to the woman. "Ms. Pratt? I'm Robert Hall from Perfect

Price Appraisers. I'm ready to perform the appraisal."

And more than ready to get out of the presence of the other two men.

But Grace Pratt wasn't listening to him. She was staring from one cowboy to the other.

"What the fuck are you two doing here?"

Chapter Two

Her entire childhood, she'd been told how nice people didn't have to swear to get their points across. Well, she ought to have known a long time ago that she wasn't too nice.

The last sight Grace had expected to see on her driveway was a pair of Alberta cowboys. Her cousins, Josh and Drake. Since Grace's adoptive mother had changed her name when she'd married, these two were truly the last of the Walkers.

For the past ten years, Grace had told herself that they'd faded from her memory. Now, seeing them in the flesh, she wondered if that was even possible. The two of them were too forceful, too alive to be forgotten, even after a decade.

Josh was the first to react to her rude greeting, stepping near and bending down to brush his lips against her cheek. Just like a real cousin.

"Gracie!" he exclaimed. "It's been too long, girl."

Grace peered up at him with suspicion. What was he doing, putting on a show for the appraiser? For the length of time the two of them would be there, it hardly seemed worth it.

And what was with the guilt trip? She wasn't about to hop aboard *that* particular bus.

"You had my number, both of you, if you'd wanted to reach out and touch me."

Her challenge included both men, though Drake hadn't said anything. He merely stood with his arms folded across his wide chest, tall and implacable. He was always the silent one but now his silence felt like an attack. His muteness was worse than Josh's folksy friendliness and backhanded accusation.

Josh started to say something in response but Drake surprised everyone by breaking into his speech.

"Can't touch what isn't there."

Was that another accusation?

Oh, Lord, she knew she shouldn't have come today. Except she was afraid that sending an appraiser by themselves would have been a recipe for one or both men spotting him and chasing him off the property with the proverbial pitchfork. It was land the Walker men cared about, not people. Not her.

"I'm having the place appraised," Grace said.

Josh pushed his hands into the back pockets of his jeans, but the casual posture failed to hide the keen alertness of his body. "Why? You thinking of selling?"

Sell the property? Now why would she do that? The house might be unoccupied but it was kept clean and well maintained by a local couple, who checked up on it every week or two. The vast farmland surrounding the house was tenanted at a modest rate and planted with canola. The crop made a buttery, golden blur of the landscape. And while all of that was happening, the land kept growing and growing in value. Subdivisions sprouted and sprawled, offspring of the Alberta oil boom, and the developers were always searching for new sites.

She could hold onto the property and grow rich through inertia.

But she knew her adopted cousin wasn't thinking about any of that. He was thinking of that clause that was tucked into every Walker's last will and testament. The Walker Succession Clause, the one that ensured that no part of the three properties could be sold without first right of refusal going to the other two owners.

"Settle down," she said. "I'm not selling the place."

Grace might not believe in the feud, but that didn't mean she wanted to be the one to sell out first. The property made a tidy income and it wasn't bothering anyone. Except for her cousins and neighbors perhaps.

"Then why do you need an appraisal?" Drake wanted to know. His voice, huskier than Josh's, seemed to rumble through her body like a minor earthquake.

No, she certainly hadn't forgotten these two men.

"I need a value figure to put into a cohabitation agreement," Grace explained, "for my partner and me. We're moving in together."

It was more than she wanted to share, but she knew anything less wouldn't suffice. They would want the whole story. Heck, they probably felt it was their right.

"Partner?" Josh repeated the word musingly. "Is that a city term for boyfriend?"

It was Grace's turn to cross her arms over her chest, but she didn't do it because she was tough. She did it as a defense mechanism.

"Yes, I guess so."

"You're moving in with your boyfriend?" Drake's low voice took on an aggressive note. "What's the matter? Can't he afford a ring?"

With a bit of internal coaching, she was able to keep her temper. This was just how they were. Self-appointed dictators. Too bad no one ever told them there was only ever room for one God.

"What he can't afford is me making off with half the value of his condo," Grace answered. "So we're doing it properly, with a contract. Neither of you would want him to make a claim for half of this place, would you?"

"You're going in this relationship already thinking about it breaking up? Doesn't that kind of kill the romance?"

Josh shook his head, the gesture catching sunlight in his hair and reflecting it back in golden gleams. There was sunshine in his smile too. Or there used to be, when he used to have reason to smile at her.

Both Walkers were over six feet, lean-hipped and broad-shouldered, but Drake was taller and thinner. Most people would have concluded that Josh's heavier musculature gave him the physical edge on his cousin, but Grace had reason to know that they were actually quite evenly matched.

Between the two of them, Drake and Josh Walker had taken her virginity in every way possible. Mouth, ass, and the plain old-fashioned way.

Who were they to tell her about the boundaries of a healthy relationship?

"That's a touching sentiment," Grace said, "but considering that I have a potential interest in your property as much as you have in mine—I certainly hope you got a pre-nup before you bought a ring, Josh. You too, Drake."

"I'm not married," said Drake.

"Me neither," Josh echoed.

She'd figured as much. As distant as they'd been the last decade, she would have merited at least an invitation. But, then again, who knew? Men were so inexplicable, these men most of all.

At least with Adam, she had his number and he had hers.

"Well, you should be," she told them impartially. "There should be someone to carry on the feud into the next generation."

Who wouldn't jump at the chance to be the matron of the next Walker generation? From middle school on, Grace had seen what a flutter the cousins caused within female breasts, even though they were years older and out of reach. The state of affairs had continued into high school where Josh, a decade earlier, had been a star football player and whose picture still held pride of place in the hallways.

Drake held a different charm, a darker one. When Grace was a teenager, he'd already been well into adulthood. He was more solitary, no team sports for him, and had once been a good student, though he went on to agricultural college, like anyone else with the limited ambition of running the family farm. He should have been married by now to a sober pillar of the community who was strictly conscientious about volunteering—though what he really needed was someone to lighten him up and make him smile. They both should have been married. Yet, here they were, in their thirties and still single, the Walker blood rusting in their veins.

Oh, the rust didn't show yet. They were still young and vigorous specimens of the male species, but what would happen in twenty years or thirty? Then they would be old, lonely men with the feud denying them even each other's company.

Pricks of moisture gathered behind her eyelids but she blinked them back.

What did she care? They'd chosen their paths long ago, both of them. She'd washed her hands of both men.

"You spending the night?" Josh asked, switching subjects.

"That's up to Robert," Grace said, jerking her chin in the appraiser's direction. He'd shifted a few feet up the driveway and away from the other men. She couldn't blame him. "I packed a bag in case."

Robert shuffled his feet as if they were cold, though the day was mild and dry. "It's a big job," he said, "and we're starting late."

"So we'll work late," Grace told him. "I'll pay you for the overtime."

"It's not that." The appraiser looked at the wide, blue sky. "It'll get dark before long."

"We'll rig up some lights," Grace said. She was slipping on the rural 'can do, make do' attitude like a comfortable old bathrobe — and finding that it fit pretty well. "Come on, don't dawdle. We'll work something out."

Drake stepped forward just as she did, blocking her path.

"You got a hotel room booked?"

It took her a few seconds to realize that the question was directed at the appraiser. Judging from the prolonged silence, it took him a while too.

"Y-yes," Robert stammered. "I booked it when I got the job."

"Good," said Drake, "because you're not staying here after it gets dark."

Grace had to protest. Quitting with the sun was a sure way to turn the valuation into a two-day job.

"Dr-ake."

He ignored her. "You quit working as soon as the sun sets, got it?"

Robert nodded eagerly.

Frustrated, Grace turned to Josh for help but there she saw only a slower, more thoughtful nod.

The Walkers agreed. She looked up. Nope, the sky wasn't falling. Yet.

"That doesn't mean," Josh said, "that you should spend the night all by yourself, Gracie. This is a lonely stretch of road. I don't want anything happening to you."

Was he offering to keep her company? His deceptively lazy, blue stare gave nothing away.

"I can take care of myself."

"You shouldn't have to."

Drake didn't say anything but his silence seemed to be a second vote against her competence.

She waited for few seconds, then said, "Isn't this the part where you call me 'little lady' and imply that I couldn't get the woodstove going without a man to help me?"

Josh grinned. "That depends on the man. How well would your boyfriend do?"

Adam. Flanked by these two men, it was suddenly difficult to recall his face. The memories were stronger. Of her and Josh stuck up in that hayloft, kissing so hard they hadn't heard her mother until she'd called for her, then stifling each other's giggles as they'd struggled not to make a sound.

There were so many firsts. The first time she'd met Drake, a stranger with a face she'd found so familiar. The first time they'd kissed and how he'd pulled away, the muscle of his jaw working, and told her they could never do it again. Josh, gentle, and for once, serious as he'd discovered her virginity and claimed it with care and expertise. Drake, coming back into her life, showing her pleasure in new ways she hadn't believed she could experience.

So many beginnings but so many endings too. They'd both pushed her away, each for his own reason.

Drake had claimed from the start that she was too young. Yet he was twelve years older compared to Josh's eight and Josh had never mentioned the age gap with any concern. When she was twenty-two, back from university, waiting to find out about business school admissions, she'd seen those twelve years as a huge difference, but now that she was twenty-seven and he was thirty-nine, it no longer seemed like a gap at all.

If only he'd waited. If only he'd cared enough to wait.

Then there was Josh, sunny and carefree, yet his big issue had always been the feud. What would his parents think if he got together with her? Now they were both dead, but the feud was obviously still alive in his heart, in that spot where she'd once wanted to take up residence.

What a mess...and what a shame.

"Uh, we should get going, Ms. Pratt."

The appraiser's hesitant voice broke into her thoughts. He was right. Her plans were what mattered. The feud, and the Walkers, could haunt the land after she was gone tomorrow.

Good fucking riddance.

Chapter Three

Grace was having the best dream. That one where the object of her lust was magically delivered into her bed, no questions asked, and it turned out that he wanted her as much as she hungered for him.

Tonight, that dream man was Josh Walker and he wasn't being smart or funny or filled with sunshine. He was concentrating all his energy on fucking her and he was frowning while he concentrated, and that was all she wanted.

"Josh!" She gasped his name, and it was as if that name had the power to transform the fantasy into flesh.

The broad shoulders she was digging her fingernails into were very real. She could feel the crescent marks her nails made, dug into the faintly rough skin.

Yes, this was Josh, knees braced on either side of her hips, pelvis thrusting against hers, his cock balls-deep inside her pussy. Fucking her oh-so-well.

Why had she hesitated to let him in when he'd showed up at her door with a pizza and a bottle of hard liquor? She'd been hungry for her dinner, yes, but she'd been more hungry for this, for the kind of hot, hard, wordless screw that was a specialty of the Walkers. It was the opposite of the collaborative, chatty fucks she and Adam shared.

Adam. For a second she felt an ominous tremor of the guilt she knew would bear down on her in full force in the morning, but then Adam's face dissolved. He became the dream. Josh was the reality.

She moaned his name again as he ground their hips together, entering her with a delicious twisty movement that was uniquely his own.

When she arched up to meet him, her name was wrung from his lips.

"God, Gracie!"

The cry was halfway a prayer, halfway a curse and it was very satisfying. He'd left her once, so she was glad to have the chance to remind him of what he'd abandoned.

"Ride me," she said. "Fuck me!"

"Oh God, yes!"

His face was sweaty, twisted and beautiful above hers. He thrust one hand through the wild tangle of her hair and held her head for his kiss. Lips locked, he swallowed her moans as his cock pounded her cunt.

The mattress joined in the noise, creaking and groaning along with them, the sharp springs giving Josh's efforts an extra bounce. Grace had to grab onto his ass and hang on, her fingers digging deeply into his firm butt cheeks. She felt as if she was riding a bucking bronco the wrong way round. Muscles she hadn't used in years were getting a solid workout. But it was like riding a horse… She hadn't forgotten how.

Josh climaxed with a wild yell, spilling hot sperm inside her. She could feel the heat of his jism through the thin condom and the sag of his body as he surrendered to his release.

But that wasn't the end of it for her. And Josh knew it.

With his dick still stiff enough to fill her pussy, he kept his hips moving in a slow rhythm while he worked his hand between their bodies.

Grace gasped as he captured her clit between sure fingers, rolling it like a toy with his fingertips before pinching it between his thumb and forefinger. It was a good pinch, hard enough for her to feel it all through her body, yet not quite forceful enough to hurt. Pain and pleasure sifted together, like Josh himself.

If she stopped to think about it, she knew he would only hurt her again. So she didn't stop to think.

She was getting close, her pussy throbbing away, clutching greedily at Josh's wilting cock. Time was ticking. She needed this *now*.

Josh rubbed her clit faster. The faster he rubbed, the harder she bucked until it became a balancing act, her strength against his, his patience against her frustration.

Grace closed her eyes, her world shrinking down to his hand, his dick and her cunt.

She pushed against Josh, arching her body and grinding her mound against his hardness, not caring that she was mashing his fingers in the process.

What she wanted was just tantalizingly out of reach, but it was coming closer, circling her like a persistent bee. Reaching for it made it pull farther away. The most difficult thing in the world was staying back and letting it come to her. She was bad at that part. Her hips wanted to move and, like Shakira's, her hips didn't lie.

So close. So...fucking...close.

Her orgasm wasn't a screaming locomotive, it was a jet plane taking off, the propulsion, the pressure, then the ultimate, incredible release hollowing her stomach and make her brain float dizzily within her skull.

She clawed at Josh's back, making him wince, but he didn't move away. In the past, he'd always been willing to sacrifice a few centimeters of skin to her climax.

"Jesus," Josh said when he finally withdrew and rolled off her, ditching the used condom as soon as he could. "I'd forgotten what it was like with you. Or, actually, thought I'd remembered but I hadn't. My memories could never match up with that."

"Thanks," Grace said drily. She thought he described sex with her a bit like an amusement park ride. Wasn't that how he looked at her anyway, as a bit of seasonal fun with no requirement to get a permanent pass?

Well, she wasn't expecting anything permanent either. Not this time around.

He turned his head to stare at her. "That was really

special, Grace."

So was the Mindbender rollercoaster at the annual Provincial Exhibition. Really special for three minutes and a forty-dollar day pass got you unlimited rides. Not on her, though. No frigging way.

"Thanks," she repeated.

The problem was he was right. That was very good sex, the kind a few hundred mediocre sessions in the intervening years had almost made her forgot existed.

But she wasn't about to pour her heart out to Josh Walker, merely because he felt like making maudlin speeches. They were lying in the bed she'd slept in when she was much younger and far more naïve and he was the lover she'd had back then. Not anymore.

Still, she'd cheated on Adam.

He would never find out.

Ugh, was that who she was now?

Grace sat up, pulling the sheet around her as she tried to run her free hand through her messy locks. No luck. Her curly black hair was a mop top on the best of days. Right now it was a rat's nest.

Of course Josh looked perfect beside her. His hair was tousled, but it was a sexy designer tousle, and sex had brought out a healthy flush to warm his tanned skin. He ought to have been smiling, that lazy sunshine smile he had, but his face was serious. Too serious.

"So who's this guy who wants you to move in with him without the benefit of blessing or gold band?"

"Adam," she said. "He's also an executive in the company where I work."

"An office romance?"

Josh, with his arms crossed behind his head, looked as if he'd never set foot in an office in his life. He brought the breath of a wild prairie wind with him wherever he went. Fresh, cool and utterly impossible to catch.

"It's better than online dating," Grace defended. Why was she defensive? Was it because she'd already compared the two men in her head and realized that Adam came a distant second?

Why was she so stuck on something she could never have? She might as well ask for Drake on a platter while she was at it.

"I'm sure it is," Josh surprised her by saying. "I've tried it."

"An office romance?" So much for her assumptions. She hadn't even known Josh had ever held down employment. Running a horse and cattle ranch was a full time job. Heck, it was the equivalent of several full time jobs. If you didn't love it, it could quickly grow into a burden.

It was a good thing the Walker blood ran half-equine. Drake had just as much horse sense as Josh, though he didn't strictly need it for modern day farming, which was all done with heavy equipment.

"No," said Josh, "online dating. It was a bust, as you can probably tell from my single state."

He'd dated online? Hurt overwhelmed her initial surprise. If he was willing to go with a stranger rather than consider building on what they'd once shared…

Damn it, she had to remember that she didn't care. It wasn't her place to judge her adopted cousins.

"Maybe you're too picky," Grace suggested.

"Maybe." He moved his shoulders in an awkward shrug, since his hands were still planted behind his head. "Or maybe my standards are high because I know what's possible. Like what you and me had."

She was sure her heart would have stopped for a beat or two after those words, she'd dreamt about hearing them for so long, but it kept right on ticking away. Stupid heart.

Grace kept her eyes down on the rumpled sheets and tried not to look at his sticky flaccid penis, still a pretty impressive sight.

"You and I…" She paused, then started again. "You said what we had was impossible because of our parents and the feud."

Josh's fingers covered her fidgeting ones. "My father was all about the feud. You would have thought it all went down a year ago rather than over a hundred years ago. But he's gone now. I don't feel the same way about it. I don't even know if he would have felt the same about it since it was you."

"Because I'm adopted?"

He leaned over to look her in the eyes. "Because you're *you*. He would have loved you the same way I do. Because of who you are, not in spite of it."

Loved you the same way I do.

The same way I do.

'Do'. Not did. 'Do'. Present tense.

Coming on the heels of that exhilarating revelation was a load of anger.

"Why didn't you call or contact me in all these years?" Grace demanded. "Why didn't you come to my graduation? I sent you an invitation."

She'd sent both him and Drake invitations. Neither had come. She, along with a few international students, was one of the few people at the ceremony who'd had no loved ones to look on in pride.

"I went to the ceremony," Josh said. "Drake and I both did."

A dozen questions tumbled together in her head, coalescing into a single amazed cry. "What?"

"We wanted to surprise you," he explained. "We bought roses and everything. I booked a suite in one of those fancy downtown hotels—but, of course, I didn't tell my cousin about that part. Then we saw you in the crowd, surrounded by a few hundred new young grads, and I guess it occurred to us at the same moment that we didn't belong in your life anymore. You'd moved on a far distance from Cold Lake, Alberta. You were a city woman and a professional and you probably didn't want to be haunted by ghosts from your country past."

Tears stung her eyes, as if the words he spoke were a

biting wind.

"I wouldn't have sent you invitations if I thought of you as unwanted ghosts. No matter how much time I spend in the city, I'll always be a country girl at heart."

"Really?" He leaned his head against the bed frame and scrutinized her from between narrowed eyelids. "Are you sure it isn't a situation where you would rather visit the ranch and ride a cowboy for a week or two as a vacation from city life? I know you've always had your heart set on being a fancy exec."

"They don't just need professionals down in Calgary," Grace told him. "There are business people here too. Good ones who earn a decent living."

Josh picked up the hand he was holding and brought it to his lips. He was smiling and the result was like a brilliant sunrise over a dark country.

"Tell me that again, Gracie," he urged her. "And use smaller words this time. Not all of us have been to grad school."

"Later," she said, putting her palm against his chest and throwing one leg over his lap. "Right now I want to see if I still remember how to ride a cowboy. I hear it's like riding a horse." She reached down to cup his growing cock. "It's starting to feel like it too."

They were both laughing as she climbed on and showed him that she remembered every hard-won lesson.

Chapter Four

With a wealth of livestock to tend to, Josh was required to keep traditional farming hours, so he was awake by three-thirty and showered and dressed by four. He wore yesterday's outfit, but he managed to make the rumpled jeans and shirt look sexy instead of untidy.

They lingered together in the kitchen, both standing with mugs of coffee in their hands, not touching, not even speaking—just basking in the warm afterglow that came from a night of vigorous fucking. Grace hardly even felt tired.

"I'll see you tonight," Josh said, making the question into a statement of intent. "We can go out. Paint the town barn-red."

Since the town was more or less a series of barnlike structures, that made sense.

"Go out in public?" Grace questioned, glancing at him over the rim of her cup. "I remember you used to be totally against that. 'Being seen together' was the ultimate fear back then."

Josh grimaced. "I was an idiot. Do you have to keep reminding me of how much time I wasted? You could have been frying up my morning pancakes these last five years."

"Five years? Try two. I would have still wanted to go to grad school. And I never fancied being a child-bride."

He put down his mug and stepped closer. "Is that a problem, the age thing? How old was this last boyfriend of yours?"

Funny how he was already speaking of Adam in the past tense, as if it was all done and decided. Grace wasn't so sure. She'd taken an afternoon off work. She was expected back there on Monday. A lot could happen in the next forty-eight hours.

"Adam is twenty-nine."

"Damn, that sounds young," Josh said. "And, before you say it, I know you're even younger. Hell, now I'm glad I didn't try to keep you here all those years ago. You were too damn young."

It warmed her to know that he'd considered trying to convince her to stay.

"You probably could have convinced me."

"I know." His smile was a little grim. "I didn't know it then but I know it now. Only, I reckon the convincing would have been short and the regret might have been long. You were young and you had ambition. My only ambitions are rooted in this place, in this land."

Grace looked up at him, holding nothing back and not caring to try. "I love it too, you know, this land."

Josh curved one hand around the back of her neck, keeping her head tilted up so he could kiss her full on the mouth. When he lifted his head again, his eyes were no longer lazy but bright and sparkling.

"I love you, Gracie."

She had to sigh before she answered, letting out years' worth of pent-up yearning.

"I love you, Josh. I always have."

* * * *

Two hours later, she was back in the kitchen for a second time, following a very satisfying, though rather lonely, sleep. She hummed as she rinsed and filled the coffee maker once more. She nibbled on a slice of cold pizza while she waited for the coffee to brew. She still had another hour before her appointment with the appraiser.

As if by magic, a man appeared in her kitchen with a takeout tray of Tim Horton's coffee and a carry box of donut holes, called Timbits. Her favorite.

"Does everyone in the neighborhood have a key to my house?"

Drake stopped short and stared down at her. "Sorry. I figured you would need breakfast."

"Mrs. Milton stocked the fridge for me," said Grace, already digging into the box. "Ooh, old-fashioned sour cream cake."

Those were really her favorite, followed by chocolate-glazed as a close second. The box contained plenty of both kinds.

"Not much about you I forget," Drake said, pulling the paper cups from their moorings and handing her one.

She folded back the plastic tab on the lid and took a sip. Hot, creamy and delicious. This, she imagined, is how addiction got rekindled. That one tiny sip that led to a long, slippery slope.

She sighed. "I haven't had Timmie's in ages."

Drake ripped the entire lid off his cup and took a lengthy swallow, his Adam's apple bobbing. He didn't sigh but his expression was just as appreciative.

"Now I know they have Tim Horton's in the city," he said.

"One on every block," said Grace, "but everyone in my office drinks Starbucks so that's where all our coffee runners go. I'd forgotten how good a simple double-double could be. At Starbucks, I get non-fat soy lattes because it's easier. Everyone gets non-fat soy lattes."

Drake's eyes raked her up and down. "You're not a non-fat soy kind of woman."

She laughed. "I know you meant that as a compliment so I won't get mad at you but, in case you hadn't noticed, the non-fat soy crowd control the world nowadays."

"Not out here," he said. "Out here, we build how we want, we grow what we want, we set the prices for it and we take the payoff or the hit for it. We take our risks and we earn our rewards, and we do both of them the hard way every time."

Grace gaped at him. Was this the nearly mute Drake Walker she'd known? The man had turned into a frigging poet laureate.

She tried to shake off her strong attraction to Drake. She loved Josh.

"What are you doing here, Drake? Other than getting me hooked on Tim's coffee again."

His eyes were dark and alert, but now they uncharacteristically avoided her gaze.

"I wanted to see you again, Grace. It's been a long time."

Another man might have said 'too long', though Drake didn't need to say the words for her to understand that he meant them. That was a part of the old connection they'd shared, that wordless camaraderie. Where Josh could be a charming talker, Drake used his silences to the same end.

"You're seeing me," she reached for another sour cream donut hole. "Mm, these are good. And fresh. You must have driven to town at sunrise to get them."

"The road's better now," Drake explained. "Progress happens, even out here. It comes slowly but it does come."

He seemed to be trying to make a deeper point with that statement, but Grace was too busy chewing to pay much attention. If he wanted to stand there all hot and remote then it was probably better she didn't look too hard at him. Her mouth was watering for more than fried dough balls... She remembered how salty Drake's balls tasted.

Blood rushed to her cheeks. Damn him. Why did he pick this morning to show up at her doorstep when he'd had five years to do it when she was single in the city? Why did the two cousins have to make a visit to her property the one thing they could agree on?

"What do you want, Drake?"

He looked at her, then down at the long harvest table between them.

"You," he said, "naked and bent over that table."

She sputtered the coffee in her mouth, and only managed to swallow it down after a few dangerous seconds.

"Dr-ake!"

His hands moved to his belt buckle. "But first I want you on your knees."

She could have said no. She *should* have said no. There was Josh. And Adam. Adam! She still needed to call him and break it off. He would be hurt and baffled. He might be angry. He—

Drake had his cock out.

She never could resist his cock.

Josh's penis was a solid seven inches, shapely and probably wonderfully photogenic. It was the kind of penis men were happy to share online in amateur porn pics. It was a penis that was both sociable and came with plenty of social media potential.

Drake's penis was a dark secret she wanted to keep to herself. It was over eight inches long, thick all around and heavy, with a big shiny head that begged to be sucked.

Grace was on her knees in front of him before she realized she'd moved, cupping his dick in her hands, cupping the swaying balls, stroking the velvety head. She snaked her tongue out to lick the slit, teasing it lightly.

Mm, *this* was her favorite.

She had to stretch her lips wide to accommodate the tip of his penis but once it breached her mouth, his cock head filled it perfectly.

For a moment, their eyes met. Hers were dark brown but his were darker, almost black. Like that hole he called a heart.

Then Grace closed her eyes and gave herself up to the pleasure of sucking his cock and wringing the low groans she was soon teasing from his throat. She drew his dick as deeply as she could and twirled her tongue over the sensitive head, then she released it and nuzzled it up and down its glistening length. All the while, she played with his balls, feeling them swell and grow heavy in her palm.

The crotch of her panties was soaked right through to her jeans with her juices. She pressed her thighs together, trying to quell the need before it spiraled out of control. If his cock was all she got, she wanted to enjoy it thoroughly.

Grace lifted his dick higher as she pushed her nose underneath. She licked and lapped his dangling nuts, pulling gently on the sac with her lips, stretching out the tightly packed skin. Then she opened her mouth and took as much of his balls as could fit, sucking it hungrily, tasting the salty-male tang of him. While she teabagged his testes, she frigged his dick with her fingers, getting it good and hard and throbbing.

"Now," Drake ground out. "On the table—before I come in your hand."

He pushed a space clear in the middle of the wood surface while Grace quickly shimmied out of her jeans and panties.

She crossed her forearms on top of the planks and bent her head over them as she felt Drake come up behind her. Her butt was stuck up in the air and angled toward him, making a tempting target she hoped he wouldn't be able to resist.

When his hands gripped her ass cheeks, she knew that this was no neighborly visit, no cousinly pretense of consideration. This was the real deal.

Drake pushed the fingers of one hand into her wet crease. He rubbed it briskly and with a certain detachment that was more of a turn on than anything he'd done so far, as if he was sizing her up for the task of handling his cock, and he wasn't sure yet if she quite fit the bill.

Oh, yes, sir, please pick me!

She closed her eyes as his blunt, male fingers found her clit and rolled it with surprising delicacy.

She was ready. Oh, God, she was ready.

As he stroked her labia, she jerked back against him, trying to ride his fingers. She was hungry for whatever way she could come, in whatever way he was willing to let her.

Her heart froze when he moved back. He steadied her with his hands at her ass. Then he entered her pussy with a strong thrust.

Filling her. Fucking her. *Finally.*

He was motionless for a long minute.

"You all right, baby?"

Some note in his voice, so light and tender, made tears spring to her eyes.

"Yes, Drake."

He moved, not thrusting but angling and twisting instead, managing to gain another fraction of an inch inside her slippery, wet cunt.

"You want more, baby?"

This time the question was more insistent.

"Oh, yes, Drake!"

Part of the tense drama of sex was the way he had to withdraw in order to fill her again, creating a void he soon occupied as master and owner. He did it so well, too, that masterful act. But with Drake, it wasn't an act. He was fully in control of himself—except when they were together like this.

His hips rocked harder against her ass, his balls lightly slapping the underneath of her thighs.

"More," Grace urged him on. "Please, Drake!"

He was braced behind her, holding her in place with hands and locked knees, keeping them both upright as he fucked her with increasing force. Her slick channel grabbed at his cock, trying to hold onto him, but he set the pace and he decided how to take her.

He rode her from behind like a rutting beast, hungry and wild. Grace could only rest her sweaty forehead in her arms and take it. All that existed was his cock in her cunt. Nothing else mattered.

Grace moaned, almost sobbing for release. Drake seemed intent on riding her to the ends of the earth, but she was afraid of the dark place where he was leading her. She wanted to climax here on earth, not on this new plane he was taking her to, but she was afraid to reach between her legs and help her orgasm along. She knew it might anger him.

Drake grabbed her ass, squeezing it until her cheeks were sore, the pain melding with his darkness.

"Please," she tried to cry out, the word a broken whisper on her lips.

Please, let me come.

She didn't even try to speak those words aloud. He was going to give her this experience, even if it meant breaking her in the process. So she would never forget him. So she would never again be satisfied with another man. Not even Josh.

Her pussy was stretched to its limit yet it wanted more. More hard fucking. More delicious cock.

It was too much. Yet it was not close to enough.

She'd never cried during sex before. She was crying now. Crying because she'd never been fucked like this, because she didn't want to know what she had been missing, what she was going to miss from now till the end of her days.

Drake's hips hurtled against her hot buttocks as his rhythm broke, then re-formed, then broke again. He was trying to hold on and hold out against his climax but it was an Olympian task, even for a man with his tight leash on his own needs.

But before he could lose control, he reached beneath her, sliding his fingers between her damp thighs to tug on her clit.

Yes, oh, yes!

She was almost there.

He fucked her harder, ramming his dick into her, almost lifting her completely off the table.

Another tug at her clit. Another delirious riot of sensation streamed through her trembling body.

Then...a feather light stroke of his fingers and she was gone.

Her pussy walls spasmed around his stiff cock as it spurted thick cum into the condom. But that thin layer of latex couldn't diminish the heat pouring off him, filling her vagina with the forceful proof of his orgasm.

Her own body seemed to fight itself, aching as if it had gone through a great battle and glowing as if she had won an important race.

It took a full minute for her heart to stop beating in her ears and return to its usual place in her chest. She uncurled her toes and forced her fingers to unclench.

For a moment she was relaxed, reveling in the afterglow of her climax, but after the pleasurable haze started to dissipate and reality began to reassert itself, she grew tense.

Now was the part where Drake withdrew and ran away with all of the concentrated effort of a criminal escaping from the scene of a robbery. This was when he uttered those familiar words—*We shouldn't have done this* and *God, you're so young*—and forced those terrible cruel excuses into the shape of a goodbye.

Because it was always goodbye with Drake.

Tears pricked her eyes anew but Grace refused to move, refused to wipe them away.

They were both older now. He would have to face her if he wanted to reject her this time.

Drake's hand lingered over the curve of her buttocks as he withdrew from her body. Unlike Josh, he was careful and tidy, wrapping the used condom in a piece of paper towel before he discarded it in the trash, rather than on the floor.

Grace stood slowly, straightening out her cramped limbs. Muscles that had been forced into inactivity from her pose now refused to comply with her brainwaves while other, well-used parts, ached for a nice long soak in the tub. Maybe someone to wash her back…

Of course, it wouldn't be Drake.

He was too busy doing up his black jeans and looking around for the matching shirt. He hadn't even bothered to take off his boots.

She leaned her butt against the edge of the table. She'd found and pulled on her panties but her legs were still bare. Dreading the coldness she knew would be in his eyes, she didn't even feel chilled.

Pride made her speak first.

"Still here?"

Drake looked up, his dark hair tumbled and somehow poignant over his wide brow. "Must be getting slower in my old age."

Grace frowned. Age again.

"You're only four years older than Josh," she pointed out.

He used one hand to rake his hair back. "How do I stack up?"

She stared at him. The sardonic question clearly held a hidden meaning.

"You know about me and Josh?"

He nodded brusquely. "I suspected years ago, but I knew ever since we went down to Calgary together."

For her graduation ceremony. The reminder took some of the chill from her next words.

"You must have had a good time comparing notes."

Drake's mouth moved in a brief grimace. "We nearly beat each other to a pulp over it. Or, should I say, over you."

Grace's hand moved to her chest. "Over me?"

"That's why we couldn't see you after the ceremony," he said. "We had to wear our hats pulled low to cover the black eyes we were sporting. The people seated behind us complained about the Stetsons. But I couldn't have missed seeing you graduate, baby. No effing way."

"Drake!" She flung herself at him.

He staggered but managed to hold onto her. He spoke into the wild tangle of her hair. "Baby girl, this has been a long time coming."

"Too long," she said, her voice muffled against his pecs.

"Too long," he immediately agreed. "Though, I have to think if we'd tried to get together back then, when I first wanted to, Josh and I would have torn each other apart trying to keep you to ourselves."

Noting the past tense, she was able to pull back and ask the question throbbing on her lips without too much trepidation.

"And now?"

"And now we know we might have to make it a package deal if we want to keep you here with us."

The words were plain enough, but Grace was left blinking up at him. Was she hearing him right...?

"Drake—"

"You love us both," he cut in, so quickly that she suspected he might fear what she was about to say—or what he thought she was about to say. "You don't have to choose between us. Not unless you want to."

'You love us both.' Yet, in all the time she and Drake had been together, he'd never told her that he loved her back. At the time, she'd been young enough to be confident that it was the truth, even if he couldn't bring himself to say the actual words. Time had eroded that confidence.

She pushed at the hard wall Drake's chest made.

"You don't love me." Were there any more pitiful words in the dictionary? "You let me go. Both of you."

He didn't try to hold onto her, but allowed her to put a few feet of distance between them. The kitchen was suddenly cold without his arms around her.

"We were young and stupid. Mostly stupid."

"That's not an explanation," she said.

He took a single step, halving the space between them. "It's an apology. Or at least the beginning of one."

"I don't want your apology," she choked out. She wanted all of that time back. All of the heartache. All the lonely years she'd spent in the city, thinking no one cared about her.

On the phone with her parents who'd retired down south years ago, she'd pretended to be busy and happy so she wouldn't worry them, but underneath she'd been lonesome.

All those wasted years...

That, she could not forgive.

Drake's dark gaze was fixed on her face, as if he was trying to read her thoughts through the not insubstantial barrier of her skull.

"Sounds like the two of you have it all fixed up," she said. "What kind of arrangement do you have in mind?"

Maybe they intended to shuttle her back and forth between Josh's ranch and Drake's farm, one week on and one week off. Give them both time to miss her on the off weeks and get hungry again for her during the on time.

Or maybe they would install her in her own property as if it was a brothel and visit her on assigned nights. Josh on Mondays, Wednesdays and Fridays and Drake on Tuesdays, Thursdays and Saturdays. On Sundays, she could rest.

"You come back here," Drake said. "We knock the three properties into one. We put up a house in the middle. Or two houses. Or three. We can work out the details. We just need you to say yes."

Was this really Drake Walker talking? Old-fashioned, quietly stubborn Drake?

Back in the day, she couldn't even have convinced him to be seen in public with her.

He must have spotted the confusion on her face, because his expression changed into a ruefully sympathetic one.

"I can talk so easily about it because I've had years to get used to the idea," he told her. "I know it's new to you. Trust me, I didn't intend on springing it on you like this. It would have been better if Josh could have broke it to you. He can talk. I can't."

"You're doing okay," Grace said huskily.

A tiny smile started to tug at one end of his long mouth. "So you're not vetoing the idea?"

It was nice to know she didn't just get a vote, she got a veto.

Grace shook her head. "I'm not vetoing the idea." A thousand considerations were running through her head. Her job. Her career as a whole. Adam. They all weighed in favor of the city...and a veto. "Not right now, at least."

As if to punctuate her uncertainty, a knock on the front

door signaled the appraiser's arrival.

Drake lowered his head to kiss her hard and quick on the mouth.

"Good," he said, when he drew back. "That means we get the chance to convince you."

The knock sounded again, so Grace didn't have time to ponder what that meant. Whatever it did mean, it promised to be very exciting.

Chapter Five

By noon, Grace was cursing her parents for deciding to gift her the land she was traipsing around, years ago, instead of waiting until they were decorously dead.

Growing up here, she knew the land was vast and varied but now, looking at it through adult eyes, it was also filled with endless possibilities—all of which required endless decisions. Should she sell to developers or hold onto the potentially lucrative mineral and gas rights? Should she worry about the highway pushing out here or suburban sprawl edging up to her property boundaries? If she chose to work it herself, would she earn more ranching like Josh or farming like Drake? If she sold it, should she take into consideration what Josh and Drake were doing on their land?

The funny thing was, she didn't have to sell the property. That wasn't why she was up here at all. The only thing she had to do was value it for the purposes of putting a figure down on the contract she and Adam would sign when they moved in together. Knowing the value would mean they would know how much each was entitled to take of the relationship if they broke up—although the very act of entering into a contract suggested it was more like *when* they broke up. It was actually *if* they moved in together.

Two days ago, there'd been no *if* about it.

There was no hiding it. The 'if' was Josh and Drake. The 'if' was fantastic sex, had severally, to use a legal term.

Could they change that 'several' status into 'joint and several'?

It didn't seem possible that two strong personalities like

Josh and Drake could manage to compromise on anything so life altering.

But Drake's proposal had been clear enough, and when she called Josh later that morning, he'd confirmed it.

The Walker feud was definitely over.

Was it enough of a foundation on which to base the rest of her life?

* * * *

At the end of the day, Grace was dirty, irritable and exhausted. Her shirt and jeans were caked through with mud, since Robert the appraiser had insisted on trekking up every forgotten trail and tramping through every field. Her only consolation was that the job was done—and that Robert had ended up grubbier than she was.

They shook hands gingerly at her front stoop, Robert promising to send the finished report within the week. Though he clearly hadn't wanted to commit himself, the preliminary calculations were higher than Grace's most optimistic guesses. Over the last decade, the province of Alberta had boomed and the Walker properties had boomed along with them. If she ever chose to sell, it would likely result in a bidding war between the developers and the mineral explorers.

Desired by everyone... It wasn't a bad situation to be in.

Except when it came to men...

Grace dumped a load of drugstore bubble bath into the claw-foot tub and dumped herself in after it. The frothy waves enveloped her tired limbs.

She ran her hands down her firm rounded legs, massaging them, frowning when she encountered a hint of stubble. She would have to shave without the benefit of her soothing and fragrant shaving gel. What a bother.

As the bubbles subsided, she ducked her head under the water. There was a tub-like bottle of shampoo to match the bubble bath, the kind that was a dangerous risk to curls, tending to turn a head full of them into a frizzy 'fro. Oh well, she'd have to chance it. Frizz was better than flecks of dirt and dung.

An hour later, she emerged from the bathroom soaped, shaved and steaming hot, wearing a bathrobe that might have belonged to her mother but more likely dated back to her mother's mother.

Two cowboys were sprawled out on her bed, their Stetsons hung at rakish angles on the posts. One black hat, one white. Just like always.

Grace's heart started to pitter patter but she managed to speak evenly enough.

"I'm confiscating both of your spare keys," she said, crawling into the space between them, between their stretched-out legs.

Josh was all long legs and ease but one of Drake's booted feet kept up a frantic beat. It was nice to see she wasn't the only one who was nervous as hell.

"Aw, you don't want to do that," Josh said, with an exaggerated whine. "We'll be good from now on, Gracie. We promise."

Grace's heart was louder in her ears than his voice as she snuggled in between twelve solid feet of hot male. Beneath the worn robe, her nipples were peaked and ready for action. But she'd learned over the years to pay attention to her head as much as her heart and body.

"Promises, promises," she muttered, striving to match Josh's lightheartedness. It was Drake who bothered her, sitting stiff and stern to her left.

"You left the liars back in the city," Josh told her. "Out here, we're true to our word. We promised you peace and pleasure and that's what we'll give you."

Her heart — and her pussy — melted with that impromptu vow.

"Okay, then," she said, all brisk business. "First things first. No boots on the bed. I don't allow it. And, for the two of you, no shirts, jeans or shorts either."

The look the two men shared, a glance of complete understanding, convinced her far better than words that the feud was truly dead. They were more than cousins, she saw — they were friends.

Josh stood, then Drake. Two pairs of cowboy boots hit the floor with thuds. Then came the shirts, revealing broad, well-muscled chests. Then the jeans. Then the boxer shorts.

Two naked Walkers confronted her on either side of the bed, eyes flashing and cocks jutting like restless stallions scenting a mare.

Perspiration sprang out on Grace's freshly washed skin. Two males. Two cocks. For a moment, it was all too much.

She closed her eyes. No, it wasn't too much. This was Josh and Drake, the men she knew best on earth. Two men she trusted and loved. Two men who loved her, even if one of them never said it aloud.

If she let it happen, she could resist the change and they could all go back to living behind fences. Or she could open herself up and push ahead, not knowing how it was going to turn out, just knowing that there was a chance of true happiness beyond the fences and the feuding.

Whether it was one night or it was a lifetime, she had to take the chance and find out.

She opened her eyes again.

Josh was holding his cock, as if giving it a bit of reassurance. Drake, however, stood with his arms crossed over his tanned chest in a classic self-protective pose.

Grace recognized the vulnerabilities in both men.

Cowboys, ranchers, farmers, at the end of the day they were just men. Men she wanted. Men she loved.

All of a sudden, it was simple.

After getting to her knees, she let the robe slip off her shoulders, leaving her naked. Josh was diverted, his eyes swerving to the bounty of her bare breasts, but Drake wasn't distracted. His gaze stayed on her face.

She held out her arms and they came to her, walking then crawling over bedsheets and blankets to reach her. Josh was first, his mouth open and eager. She kissed him briefly but thoroughly before turning to Drake. His kiss was less enthusiastic but no less thorough.

Josh moved down to her breasts, mouthing her swollen curves before he latched on to one nipple, sucking it hungrily.

Grace wanted to watch him as he fed off her tits—that kind of male hunger was a huge turn-on for her—but Drake cupped her chin and kept her occupied with a deep and passionate kiss. His tongue was hot and insistent, probing the depth and breadth of her mouth, making her anticipate a different intrusion.

She let her hands roam their hard bodies, dipping down into the hollows of their spines, then traveling down their lengths to squeeze their tight asses. Both men came by their muscles honestly. These weren't gym-toned physiques but the real tough kind that came from physical labor. Roam as she let them, her two hands didn't seem like enough to savor all of their delights.

Her lips parted moistly from Drake's. Kissing and being felt up were lovely but she wasn't a teenager anymore, to be contented with so little, and she was more than ready to move on.

Cocks, she wanted cocks.

Grace nestled back into the pillows, getting a better view of Josh's flushed face and Drake's taut, dark one.

First, she spread her palms out on each of their chests. Then she slowly slid her hands lower, seeking a different aim.

Their reactions were very different. While Drake's expression grew even more remote, Josh smiled with obvious anticipation, his eyelids lowering to half-mast until his eyes were merely a blue gleam beneath his lashes.

Josh's erect dick looked so good in her hand that she was almost tempted to take a pic—for private consumption only. She traced its smooth length down to the base of crisp, dark-gold hair. Very nice and *very* pretty.

Then she turned to Drake's heavy penis. It filled her hand, as if making a promise of even better filling later. Its thick, swarthy inches weren't pretty but they were very convincing. *That* promise would be kept.

Josh reached down to play with her pussy while she stroked both their cocks. Just like her fingers on them, his rubbing was slow and leisurely.

Drake's hands on her breast brought back the urgency. He pinched and tugged one turgid nipple, sending the blood pulsing through her at a furious pace. Tits, cunt, hands — in all she was well occupied... That was, except for her mouth.

Grace slid farther down the pillows, pouting. "Josh, come up here."

She'd not had a chance to taste his balls yet, and this was the perfect opportunity.

Josh scrambled closer, moving awkwardly on the springy mattress. When he was finally kneeling by her head, she guided him closer to her open mouth but, at the last moment, she switched her focus from his cock head to his taut, golden sac. Lifting his cock higher against his stomach, she had the perfect approach to those tasty testes.

Josh gasped as the heat of her mouth surrounded his ball sac. Coupled with the slow pistoning movement of her hand, her sucking lips held him in sweet captivity.

The sight of her pleasuring his cousin seemed to affect Drake forcefully. He started humping her other hand with increasingly fast thrusts as he kneaded her breasts with both hands, occasionally catching her sharpened nipples between his knuckles and making her squirm. But her abandoned pussy was growing cold as she gave hand jobs to both men and at the same time teabagged Josh. She needed more than her hands filled.

Reluctantly, Grace pulled her lips away from Josh's salty-sweet sac and looked up into his face.

She had a wait a few seconds while he reacted to the loss of her mouth by flickering his eyelids open again.

He cupped her cheek. "What's the matter, Gracie?"

She shifted her hand to a more comfortable angle around his cock while she continued to bear down hard on Drake's big dick, making him groan low in his throat and lean his hips more fully into the action. She kept a watchful eye on him.

Poor Drake, he'd shown the same determined response that morning in the kitchen. It must have been a long time for him. Still, she didn't want him to come before she was ready.

"I want you first," she told Josh once everything, and everyone, was adjusted the way she liked.

His grin flashed out. "Pussy time?"

His eagerness made her laugh out loud. Two handsome cowboys. What more could a woman want?

Josh moved back down to the foot of the bed, taking up position between her sprawled legs. His cock was bright pink, fully hard and raring to go. The sight of it made her pussy walls clench. Yes, it was *definitely* pussy time.

"What about me?" Drake asked, from between gritted teeth. "Don't I get a say?"

"This isn't a voting situation," Grace had to remind him. "Besides, I want your dick in my mouth."

That meant she had to let go of Drake's stiff cock. It emerged from her fist even harder than it had gone in and now it was colored a painful purple shade. Pink and purple penises. She would have to remember these hues when she redecorated the bedroom. She envisioned pink-and-purple striped wallpaper with a gilt trim. It would look like the bedchamber of an opulent harem—except she was the sheikh and Josh and Drake were her consorts.

While her attention was on Drake, Josh had slid his hands under her butt and lifted her for maximum access, with his sheathed penis hovering at her entrance. As soon as she glanced down at him, he thrust inside her wet and ready cunt. With that one push, he was halfway home. He pressed up against her, hips to buttocks, her knees gripping his waist, letting her get used to him all over again.

Mmm, that feeling. That special fullness. Perfect connection. She almost didn't want him to move. But he had to, for both their sakes.

Josh withdrew, only to thrust again deeper, filling her with a single, long plunge. *Oh Lord.*

Grace arched her back, riding the momentum, the echo of his great primal need. It was too much to take in.

She turned her head and Drake's dick was there, offering an outlet to her restless energies. Grace parted her lips and took him inside, drawing down until her mouth fully enveloped the massive head of his cock. Then, with his fingers in her hair, guiding her, she started giving him a hungry, delicious blow job.

She sucked him while his cousin fucked her. Josh was up on his knees, forcing his cock deeply into her with each thrust, penetrating her as he'd never done before, as if their combined desire had been needed for him to achieve such a feat. Her pussy reacted helplessly, clutching at his rapidly pistoning penis, as she writhed her mound against his hips as much as she could before he withdrew again.

As with Josh's cock in her cunt, Drake's dick rode her mouth in the same pounding rhythm. All she could do was try to tease his cock head with her tongue every time he pulled out a little, before he closed up the space once more, giving her as much of his erection as her mouth could hold.

The pleasure was one thing — new, enormous, helpless pleasure — but she hadn't expected the power that came from fucking two men at the same time. Nor did she think any of them had known how much of a turn on it would be to watch and perform for each other.

She sucked Drake's cock, knowing that Josh was watching and loving the show, just as he fucked her just a little bit more forcefully when Drake glanced his way.

Josh was the first to come, flooding the condom in a hot spurt. He didn't linger inside her but withdrew and discarded the condom quickly, before he slid off the bed and onto the floor.

At first she didn't know what he intended. Then he caught her ankles and pushed them up, spreading her well fucked pussy before him.

His head disappeared from her view. A moment later, his warm, wet tongue pushed into her cunt and he started eating her out, lapping up her juices and earning more with every lick and flick of his mouth.

Sheer bliss.

Drake moved to straddle her face, his strong thighs blocking out all else. It didn't matter. She knew Josh was there. She could feel him working his way around her pussy, teasing the outer lips before dipping back into her wet hole, leaving her clit alone, except for incidental brushes that were more maddening that deliberate torture.

Now she could concentrate on pleasuring Drake.

Grace moved to cup his ass, squeezing his muscular buttocks and digging her fingernails in to feel him flinch. A bit of pain spiked the pleasure and made it doubly exciting. He'd taught her that lesson.

Drake threw his head back and groaned as she struggled to relax her throat and take another fraction of an inch. His hips were moving slowly now, so as not to choke her as she devoured his thick cock. She sensed that he was close.

He came in rich gobs, coating the inside of her mouth with his creamy jism. She swallowed and swallowed, and still more came until it escaped her lips and leaked down her chin.

He doubled over, holding himself up with one hand gripping the back of her headboard. Grace kissed his chest and stomach, smearing his own cum onto his skin.

A few seconds later she came into Josh's waiting mouth. It was a climax like no other, seeming to start from the pit of her belly and spread out to her limbs, breasts and pussy. Her hips jerked against Josh's face, anointing him with her juices as she shuddered her way through the relentless spasms of her orgasm.

When she started to subside, Josh licked her clean, tracking down every last drop. A few minutes later he sighed and rested his head in the cradle of her thighs. Then he joined Drake on the bed, who was sprawled out on her other side, and they both curled against her, fitting their hollows to her curves.

They slept.

* * * *

The air smelled of all three of them, a rich musky aroma like an unspoken invitation. Grace woke with that scent in her nostrils and knew she could never tire of it. Sex, on demand, with endless variety. What sane woman would turn that down?

She lay quietly, listening to Drake's deep breathing and Josh's more definite snores. They were in harmony, as they'd been last night, knowing when to move to fill a gap in the lovemaking, and when to hang back to allow the other to take over.

It must be something in the blood, she mused, that gave them that instinctive simpatico rhythm. Two unrelated men probably wouldn't have it. The Walkers of a previous generation certainly hadn't or they wouldn't have ended up at each other's throats, brother against brother.

"Our ancestors were stupid," Drake said.

His voice startled her. Hadn't he been fast asleep just a moment ago? Or had he been shamming?

"What did you say?" Grace stammered. It was difficult to listen closely when she was watching the shape of his mouth. That clever, *clever* mouth.

"Our ancestors were stupid," he repeated, as Josh began to sputter and blink his way to wakefulness on her other side. "Think of how much trouble those first Walker brothers would have saved themselves if they'd thought of sharing that woman."

Grace laughed, tilting her head so it rested against his shoulder. "Three brothers? That would have had to be a very brave woman, especially for back then. Nowadays everybody wants to have threesomes."

"That's not what this is," Josh said, his voice still gruff from sleep.

"No way," Drake added. "It's not a threesome or a ménage, or whatever you would call it, if you ended up in bed with two other drunk people after a party. This is the real deal. You say the word, little girl, and we go out this morning and get you a ring."

"Two rings," Josh corrected.

"Two rings," Drake accepted the amendment easily. "Two rings and no contracts. What we did last night was enough for me."

"Me too," said Josh.

"Me three," Grace said softly.

She'd told herself she hadn't been sure, yet she'd texted Adam in the middle of the night with a rather abrupt break-up message. 'Those two cowboys?' he'd responded, taking it surprisingly well, as if he'd known all along what he'd been sending her back to. Perhaps it had been a test of his and she'd failed — but she'd failed spectacularly.

Those two cowboys had kept waking her up during the night and Grace had always been ready for them. She replayed the past hours in her head, the memories as fresh and vivid as snapshots.

On her knees, sucking both of their big dicks in turn while they'd guided her to whichever one needed her the most and could take the most mouth play without bursting.

On her hands and knees on the bed while Josh had fucked her doggie style and she'd sucked Drake's cock.

On her butt, her legs draped over the edge of the bed, Drake fucking her pussy and Josh behind her, making out with her while he'd kneaded her tits.

All wonderful memories. They might never fill a photo album, but she would carry them forever. Their first night together. The first, she now dared to hope, of many nights like it.

Drake bent his head and kissed her, then whispered the quietest words ever.

"I love you, Grace."

Tears clouded her vision. He hadn't needed to say it—she'd stopped hoping for that—but she realized she'd needed to hear it.

"I love you," she said. "Both of you. Always."

"Both of you?" Josh repeated. "Not 'Josh' or 'Drake'? I guess we're already a package deal, huh, coz?"

Drake's gaze was still locked with hers and she saw the twinkle in their dark depths before he answered.

"She screamed my name enough last night," he said.

Josh grinned. "Oh, right. I must have forgot about that."

Grace snuggled in between them, warm and happy. "Maybe you need a reminder. You always were such a slow learner."

"Hey!" Josh protested, but he shut up quickly when she reached down to grasp his half-awake penis.

The early hour must have helped because his cock was soon fully erect and ready for action, even after the strenuous workout she'd given it during the night.

Grace looked from one man to the other. "I want you both inside me."

Josh's smile widened. "You know I'm always up for that, sweetheart."

But what they'd been doing all night wasn't what she had in mind this morning. This time, after such a declaration from Drake, dicks in mouth and cunt weren't enough to satisfy her.

Drake seemed to sense that as one of his hands moved down to the ample curve of her buttocks. "What do you want, baby girl?"

What did she want? The answer had never been so clear.

She told them what she wanted, and though Josh expressed some good-natured reservations, the fact that she'd already traversed much of the same area with Drake soon eased his mind.

In only a couple of minutes, Grace was lying on her side, sandwiched between the two cousins, their penises sheathed and hard. Josh was in front, readying her pussy with expert fingers, while Drake penetrated her asshole from behind, giving her one finger then two, easing her open for the job ahead.

After she had three fingers in both back and front, it was feeling good. *Really* good.

She was eager for dicks rather than digits.

Drake was first to ease his hand out and his cock into her. The tight ring of her asshole gave some resistance but Josh worked his fingers more firmly into her pussy, making her relax again and giving Drake another inch or two inside her moist anus.

She'd forgotten the stretch and strain sensation of having a big dick up her backside. Adam had been too finicky for anal sex and her previous boyfriends who weren't so uptight hadn't had the inches Drake brought to the job.

"How's it feel, baby?"

It was Josh who asked, lifting his head, his eyes wide and wild as he watched her take his cousin's cock up her backside.

"Good," she said, her voice a little shaky before she steadied it. "Full."

Full was an understatement. It felt as if Drake's cock was choking her from the inside out.

Josh whistled beneath his breath. "I've never seen something like that before. I never thought it could be such a fucking turn on."

Grace wasn't paying too close attention to him anymore. All of her energy was focused on Drake's big dick moving slowly but inexorably deeper into her ass, and his hand looped around her, anchoring her to him. The maple syrupy pace was necessary, at least in the beginning, since it had been a long time since she'd taken it up the ass, but it was also killing her. With a cock like Drake's, it was a damned waste not to be riding it full out.

Drake breathed into her ear. "Still okay?"

She nodded, too caught in the new-old wonder of his penetration to answer aloud.

Josh's fingers had stopped moving. She missed the additional stimulation but it was past time for something bigger and harder in her pussy. She flung her leg over his thigh while she reached down and nudged his cock into the right position.

Josh started to enter her cunt at an even slower pace than the one his cousin had initially set in behind. Sweat dotted his brow. He looked and acted as nervous as a virgin bull rider at his first rodeo.

Somehow she had to put him at ease.

Reaching behind to clutch at the back of his neck, Grace tilted her head and kissed him full on the mouth, passionately and slightly off target. After a frozen second, Josh kissed her back, and in reacting to her opened mouth invitation, forgot to be nervous. He thrust forward at the same moment as she pushed her tongue deep into his mouth, as hungry for the taste of him as her pussy was for his dick.

Josh held her by the shoulder as he moved up into her cunt, sinking into her slick heat.

Grace moaned. The feeling of both of them inside her was better than she could have imagined. Then, when Josh started to really fuck her, she cried out both their names, making it a kind of chant. Josh and Drake. Drake and Josh. *Her* men, fucking her together. Pure heaven.

Drake's hips drove sharply against her buttocks as he thrust rapidly inside her. He reached forward to grab her swollen tit, shaping it into a big cone, squeezing it, milking it the way she wanted to milk his thick cock.

Josh's head dipped down to the breast his cousin held, and he took the rigid nipple sticking out of Drake's fingers into his hot mouth.

The combination drove Grace over the edge, the overwhelming pleasure shooting down to tighten her pussy and anus simultaneously around the cocks that fucked them. She came in a dazzling rush, creaming around Josh's cock while her butt muscles squeezed Drake's dick in an almost painful spasm.

Both men groaned, then shouted out as they reached orgasm. Josh's was fast and furious, his hips pistoning wildly before he thrust one last time and filled his condom with jism. Drake's climax was far more subdued, but no less forceful as he held himself hard against her clenching buttocks and came in a low, slow release.

They continued to move inside her sluggishly. Both her holes were soft and satiated. From now on, she knew, it would take both of them to completely satisfy her.

"I screamed both your names," she said drowsily, after a few minutes, and they eventually withdrew and lay tiredly in the bed next to her.

She rested her head on Drake's shoulder but stretched her hand out to touch Josh's chest. It was important, for some reason, for her to be connected with both of them.

She sensed the two men exchanging glances over her lax body as she snuggled between them.

"Is that a yes to our proposal?" Josh wanted to know.

Grace thought about it—for about two seconds.

"Yes," she told him, before turning to Drake, "and yes. Let's go ring shopping."

She felt the rumble of Drake's laughter beneath her head a moment before Josh's joined his.

"Let's stay in bed for a while longer," Drake said. "There's plenty of morning left."

Josh turned to nuzzle her neck. "I second that."

Grace looked over and saw Drake's lazy smile. Over his naked shoulder was the morning sky, clear and wide and blue. It beat a view of the Saddledome any time.

BETWEEN US

WENDI ZWADUK

Dedication

Once this story got going, it wasn't going to be stopped.
Thank you, NR, for asking me to do this.
SM, thank you. I'm glad I get to work with you again.
JPZ — you know how I feel.

Chapter One

"Where are a couple of farm boys when I need them?" Channon Kennedy brushed her horse, Peaches, and rested her head on the side of the large animal's neck. She liked being around the horses. She could talk to them and not have to worry about someone arguing with her. She'd done enough arguing in the last year for a lifetime.

"I don't know how I'm going to manage," she said. She stopped brushing the horse and looked Peaches in the eye. "I'm one person with three horses and a hundred acres. That's a lot for one person to keep things going."

The horse snorted, then shook her head.

"I get it. We'll figure it out." She sighed and surveyed the stall. According to her father's notes, there were two farm hands living on the property. She hadn't seen anyone, but the state of the stall said otherwise. Someone had cleaned it out recently. She'd need to shovel out the muck and add fresh straw, but it could've been worse.

Not knowing who lived on the farm was her own fault. She'd been at the house for three days, but had only ventured out during the last hour. Between the guilt over not being home when her father died and mourning the loss of him, she hadn't wanted to be out in public. She grieved for the end of her relationship with her former boyfriend, Jack, too. The bastard had cheated on her and dumped her for a younger woman. She shouldn't have been so upset. Getting rid of him should've been a relief, but it wasn't. Seven years was a long time to be with someone, only to be shafted.

Channon climbed the side of the stall and sat on the wooden planks. She leaned against the divider bars between the stables. "I miss the boys the most." She gripped the shelf along the wall. "I could use their help, yeah, but I miss their friendship. Brian and Shaun were here when no one else cared."

Peaches shifted around and bumped her head against Channon's side. Channon hugged the horse. "I miss them. I shouldn't because we're horrible when we're together. I still remember all the times we got into trouble, but it was fun."

She glanced over at Herb, Peaches' brother. "You're eating well. Looks like you're exercising, too. How about you?" She turned her attention to Brutus, her father's horse. "I'm not sure how I'll be able to keep you all exercised, but I'll try."

She paused, listening for anyone else in the barn. She hoped Brian or Shaun would stroll around the corner, but no. Nothing. She blew out a long breath and hopped down from her perch.

"Oh well." She patted Peaches again. "I'll be right back to clean out your stall." She wasn't sure why she'd explained herself to the horse, but whatever. She headed out of the barn. The sunshine blinded her for a moment and heated her skin. She liked the peace of the farm. Loved the privacy and not having to worry about who would show up. In the distance, she heard the hum of a tractor.

Who had a tractor on the property? One of the farm hands? She noticed the red machine moving across the hay field. She shielded her eyes to better see the man on the tractor. Her breath lodged in her throat. Shaun? Couldn't be. He would've told her he was there—wouldn't he?

The man on the tractor steered the machine to the edge of the field and stopped when the mail truck zipped up the driveway.

Channon ran across the lawn. She needed to get a dog to help intercept intruders and so she wouldn't be alone. A dog would alert her to visitors, too.

She stopped in her tracks when the man in the mail truck

left the vehicle. "Brian?" she murmured. *No way.* Someone who either was Brian or looked one hell of a lot like him strode across the short strip of grass. The man on the tractor met the mail man at the fence. She could've sworn Shaun stood on the other side of the barrier. If it wasn't them, then who was intercepting her mail?

"Hey," Channon called. "That's mine." She stopped again when both men turned to her and smiled. "Brian? Shaun?"

Shaun whipped his ball cap off his head and wiped the sweat from his brow. "She remembered us. Only took her three days, but she did."

"Well, we *are* hard to forget." Brian opened his arms. "Give us sugar."

"Sugar? You're holding my mail." She yanked the letters and magazines from Brian's hands. "Since when did you become a mail man?"

"Chill," Shaun said. "We get our mail here, too."

"What?" She leafed through the letters and, sure enough, some had Brian's and Shaun's names on them. "Why? Are you dodging an ex-girlfriend who wouldn't or couldn't handle the both of you?" Brian and Shaun's girl-sharing hadn't been lost on her. She'd dreamed of being the woman in the middle of their man sandwich plenty of times, but they hadn't been interested in her. They probably still weren't and had a girl waiting for them, wherever they were living on the farm. Still, Channon could dream.

Shaun and Brian exchanged glances. "You're done for the day, aren't you?" Shaun asked.

"I'm through with my route, yeah, but I'll have to do my end of the day stuff." Brian folded his arms, then turned his attention to Channon. "I work at the post office during the day and help Shaun the rest of the time. It's worked nicely for five years."

"Oh." In the last seven years, she hadn't really considered what her former friends had done with their lives.

Shaun wiped his hands on his pant legs. "I need to finish the second cutting in the front field, but I'm almost done.

Shouldn't take me more than another hour."

"Sounds good," she said. "Do you have plans tonight?" She probably shouldn't have been asking, but she wanted to know. She wasn't sure she wanted them to be with someone. Truth be told, she wanted to keep them for herself, now that she knew they were still on the property.

"How about we make dinner for you tonight?" Brian grinned and leaned against the fence. "Our cooking skills have improved since high school. I can even boil water."

When he flexed the muscles in his arms, he could've been the poster child for hot mail men. She wondered how many women on his mail route fantasized about him. She did. She wanted those arms wrapped around her.

"Channon?" Shaun tipped his head. He had dirt on his cheeks and smeared across his T-shirt, but he had the rugged style going for him.

Where Brian worked the clean-cut and professional angle, Shaun still had his rough edges. She wanted his arms around her, too. Who was she kidding? She couldn't decide between them. God, she was screwed up.

She met his gaze and shivered, despite the early summer heat. "I'm sorry. I bet once you get *cooking*, you're probably unstoppable." She rolled her eyes to hide her embarrassment. They wanted to make her food, not come on to her. *Jesus.* They probably just wanted to be nice to her, too…and maybe keep her happy so they could keep their home on the farm.

"Well?" Shaun tipped her chin to meet his gaze again. Despite the strength in his body, he had such a light touch. His sweaty shirt was glued to his chest and showcased his taut, muscled frame.

Channon's knees weakened. She widened her stance to keep herself upright and bit back a groan. Either she needed sex or needed him—correction, them—more than she realized. Maybe she'd gone too long without sex and was horny. If they were feeling the electricity too, they weren't showing it.

"Channon?" Brian stood beside Shaun and touched her arm. "Are you in there? Or is Shaun's hot body mesmerizing you?"

"Huh?" She should've been paying attention, not getting caught ogling them. "Sorry. Sure. Dinner sounds good. What time and what would you like me to bring? Where do you want to meet?" *How about my place, my bed tonight and all night long?* Oh man. She couldn't say all that. Not now.

"How about at the guest house?" Shaun asked. "Your dad allowed us to live there if we worked for him."

She stared at them. They lived in the guest house? That explained why she hadn't seen them. She hadn't ventured to that part of the property in years. "I didn't see either of you when I drove in three days ago. Haven't seen you working ground or anything."

"You haven't set foot outside the house in that time," Brian said. "I take the truck out before the ass crack of dawn. Shaun's been working in the barn and on the back forty. It's pretty easy not to see us. We keep out of sight."

"With someone, I'm sure." She wasn't sure why she'd said that. She didn't want them with another woman. She had no claim on them, but still.

"We're alone," Shaun said.

"Really?" she blurted.

Brian sighed. "How about we have a nice dinner tonight and get things sorted out? Yes?"

She shrugged, unsure of what else to do. "I'd like that."

"Good." Brian climbed behind the wheel of the mail truck. "I'll be back in an hour." He drove off, leaving her alone with Shaun.

Channon turned her attention to Shaun. "Okay. Spill. What's going on here?"

"Nothing that I know of." Shaun leaned on the fence. "We want to treat you right tonight."

"Because?" God. Being with Jack had made her quick to question every nice thing in her life. She needed to shake that bad habit and fast.

155

"Just because." Shaun shrugged and tipped his head. "We want to."

"You two never do anything because. Your wanting to always has a proviso." Her lack of trust in almost everyone was showing more than she wanted.

"We're doing it because we want to." Shaun smiled. "You deserve a nice night."

For a split second she could've sworn he said *because we want you*, but she knew better. Still, she didn't trust them. "Oh, well. Thank you."

"We want *you*." Shaun grinned and tugged her into his arms. "Have for a while." He kissed her hard on the lips, then let go of her and strolled to the tractor.

Channon stared at him in stunned silence. She trusted her hearing this time. He'd said they wanted her. Really? She hoped it was real, but her second-guessing came back to haunt her. She hadn't heard him incorrectly, but she doubted they'd want her for long.

Shaun glanced back at her and grinned, then climbed into the tractor.

Channon grabbed the fence post for support. She wasn't about to try to figure Shaun or Brian out. She knew better. She'd tried before and only ended up with a broken heart. She needed to move forward with her life and focus on the future. She had a farm and three horses to take care of, and no time to worry about how her farm hands made her body sizzle.

She forced herself away from the fence and headed back to the barn. She tossed the mail onto the storage box just inside the building. When she'd left Jack in Cleveland, she'd cleaned the shit out of her life. She picked up the shovel and strode to the first stall. Not the glamorous life, but she loved being back on the farm and close to Brian and Shaun.

Chapter Two

Shaun sat on the tractor but didn't turn the machine on. He watched Channon walk back to the barn. He loved the way her ass wiggled with each step and the way her sexy curves had filled out a little. She'd been adorable back in school, but now... She had him thinking of every delicious way to pleasure her. He sent a text to Brian.

She doesn't believe us. Will need to up our game.

He wasn't sure what he'd expected from Channon. She'd been away for seven years, and according to the gossip in town, she'd had her heart broken. He knew firsthand that she was still dealing with the death of her father. She probably wasn't interested in a romantic relationship, but that didn't mean he and Brian wouldn't try.

His phone buzzed with a return message.

Then we pull out all the stops.

Shaun tucked his phone into his front pants pocket and turned on the tractor. He finished mowing the field, but Channon never quite left his mind. She was still beautiful — maybe more than before. He wanted to explore her body until she screamed his name.

From the moment she'd left home to attend college, he and Brian had counted the days till she returned. They couldn't wait to see her again. Things hadn't lined up right away — they'd had girlfriends and she'd had boyfriends, but now... There wasn't much holding them back.

Shaun liked that she'd come home, but wished it could've been on better terms—not because of the death of her father or the breakup of her relationship. Still, he and Brian would be damn sure to be there when she needed them.

He finished mowing the second cutting of straw, then drove the tractor to the barn. He and Brian would have a full weekend of baling ahead of them, but he didn't mind. Working on the farm meant a roof over his head and kept him close to Channon. He could easily handle the manual labor.

As he pulled the tractor into the barn, he noticed Brian standing beside the truck. He waited for Shaun to descend from the tractor seat.

"So, she doesn't believe us, eh?" Brian laughed and a wicked grin curled his lips. "Guess we'll have to turn on the charm."

"We'll have to do more than that. She mucked out the horse stalls. I'd say she deserves the full treatment." Shaun elbowed his friend. "I usually muck those out tomorrow. She helped me. I get the feeling she wants to get her hands dirty and take over. We owe her."

"We do." Brian shoved his hands into his pockets and fell into step beside Shaun. "I was thinking something simple. Grilling some steaks and ear corn. Get cleaned up."

Shaun nodded. "I'll hurry." He didn't want to miss a moment of their time with Channon. He strode to the back of the house and into the bathroom. He turned on the water, then stripped. Getting out of the sweaty clothing helped cool him down a bit, but he wanted to heat things up with her. Once he had a taste of her, then maybe he'd be able to move on—but he doubted it. She was in his soul.

Shaun stepped under the searing spray and closed his eyes. The water sluiced over his body, both stinging and soothing him. He soaped his washcloth and scrubbed his body clean. When he touched his cock, he moaned. He wanted her to be there. Her touching him and pleasing him. Her curled against him as he told her how he felt about her.

He wrapped his fingers around his cock and stroked. With each pull, he groaned. She meant so much to him and Brian. He imagined her with him and getting him off. His skin sizzled and blood rushed to his groin. He leaned against the tile wall and widened his stance. He closed his eyes and pictured her with him.

You like it when I touch you, she whispered.

"Fuck, yeah." He increased the speed of his strokes.

Want me to keep touching you?

"Want you to get me off." He pulled harder on his cock. Heat swirled within him and he gritted his teeth. She should be there with them all along.

The orgasm built low within his belly, then spread through his veins. He panted and tensed from head to toe. "Fuck."

Shaun added a couple of strokes as the orgasm hit. Cum spurted onto the shower curtain, then slid down the drain. His knees wobbled and he sank to the floor of the stall.

Cold water rained down on him. Shit. Shaun remained in the fetal position until the trembling subsided. He needed the change in temperature to get him moving again.

After a few moments, he stood. He rinsed, then toweled off and dressed. When he strode into the kitchen, Brian grinned.

"Thought about her, didn't you?" Brian seasoned the steaks, then washed his hands. "I heard you."

"You would've done the same thing." Shaun shrugged. "I like her. And you've loved her since high school. It's time we do more than hope."

Brian nodded. "She did split from her boyfriend, right?"

"The asshole cheated on her." Shaun pointed to the corn cobs. "What do you want me to do?"

"I'm not grilling anything until she gets here. Stick the corn in the oven when it comes up to temp. I'm going to rinse off and probably fantasize about her while I'm at it."

"Can do." Shaun arranged the corn on the baking tray. "Bri? Why would someone do that? Cheat on someone?"

"Who knows?" Brian stood in the doorway. "Look at how many women thought we'd cheated on them because we had lady friends. They thought we were doing something with Channon, too." He sighed. "If we get our way, there won't be a reason to cheat." He drummed on the door frame, then strolled out of the room.

Shaun placed the tray of corn in the oven, then closed the oven door. He'd said he liked Channon. Who was he kidding? He'd been more than a little in love with her since they were both thirteen. He carried plates and silverware to the table on the brick patio behind the house.

True to his word, Brian took hardly any time at all in the shower. If Brian had called her name, Shaun hadn't heard. But that was Brian. He kept quiet much better than Shaun ever could. Shaun liked everything loud and fun. Brian liked fun, too, but he remained more reserved.

Worry crept into his mind. Channon probably knew the score—he and Brian shared their women—but would she be willing to be shared? What if she only wanted one of them and not the other? Could he step back while she had a relationship with Brian? He hoped so, but couldn't be certain.

Brian strolled out to the patio with the plate of steaks in hand. He'd switched his jeans for cutoffs and a sleeveless T-shirt. "You're deep in thought."

"I guess so." Shaun shoved his hands into his pockets and stared out at the pasture behind their house. "What if this doesn't work?"

"Then we figure things out." Brian switched on the grill.

The clicking grated on Shaun's nerves. "I'm worried."

"For all we know, she doesn't want either of us." Brian closed the grill lid, then draped his arm around Shaun's shoulders. "Or it could be exactly what we need."

"I hope so." He wasn't feeling so positive.

"Speaking of the devil, I heard the doorbell." Brian checked the heat on the grill. "Damn. I'm starving. Wish this thing would heat up already."

"Me, too." Shaun left his best friend on the patio and made his way to the front door. Channon stood on the small porch. She smiled and half-shrugged.

"Look at you." He drank in the vision of her. The shorts hugged her curves and showcased her legs. The tank top barely contained her breasts. He longed to drag her into his arms and kiss her senseless.

"Well?" She lingered on the porch. "I tried to dress casual."

"Casual? I'm in love." He'd used the L-word and didn't care. "Come in." He hadn't been ready to say those words out loud, but he trusted his heart. He loved Channon Kennedy. "You look beautiful."

"Thank you." She sighed and her smile grew. "I haven't worn these boots in forever. Felt good to be myself again."

"It's a good look for you." Shaun escorted her through the small house. "I'll give you the tour later. Bri's got the steaks going. Once I get the corn out of the oven and let it cool a little, we can eat. Want some wine?"

"I'd love a beer if you have any." She hugged him. "I haven't had a good beer in a long time."

"Then let's remedy that." He pulled three beers from the fridge. "If you don't mind me asking, why no beer? Don't they drink that sort of thing in Cleveland?"

She took one of the beers from him, then nodded to the back door. "Let's go outside. I'll explain everything to you and Brian together."

"Sure." He held the door for her, then returned to the oven. If he didn't hurry, the corn would burn.

"Heya." Brian turned the steaks. "How is the corn coming?"

"Done and cooling." Shaun sat beside her. "When those are ready, shout. I'll get the sides and bring them out."

"I can help." Channon placed her hand on his. "I might be your guest, but I'm not above a little work."

"It's fine." Shaun nodded at Brian, then ran into the house long enough to grab the fixings for dinner. He brought the foil-covered baking sheet out to the table, then grabbed the corn. He settled beside Channon again as Brian plated the steaks.

"Right on time," Brian said. He switched off the grill. "Let's eat."

"Thanks." Channon didn't eat. Instead she rested her hands on her lap. "Jack would never have allowed this. He hated anything country or kitschy. Cowboy boots, picnics, cut-offs... I missed my home and you guys."

"We're glad you're here," Shaun said.

"You certainly know how to treat a girl. Steak, flowers on the table and candles...it's like a dream." She shook her head. "I don't deserve this."

"Forget about him," Shaun said. "You're safe and yes, you deserve all of this." Good thing she'd come back, and even better that her ex hadn't joined her. Shaun wasn't sure he'd allow the jerk to stick around. He hadn't even met the guy and still disliked him.

"We only pull out the stops when there's a pretty girl at our table," Brian said. "Funny, you're the first girl to come out here in a long time."

"I'm shocked." She laughed. "Or you're lying."

"Nah." Shaun toyed with the condensation on the beer bottle. "Sulphur Springs is a small town and we've got a reputation."

"You two?" she blurted. "You're angels."

Shaun shrugged. He wasn't about to lie to her. He'd had his share of fun and sowed plenty of wild oats, but he knew where he wanted to land and who he wanted in his bed— her.

Chapter Three

"Honey, some people can't handle us," Brian said. He'd thought long and hard about how to tell her their truths. He might as well just get it all out there. "They don't see why two guys want to share one woman. They think we're wild and won't settle down."

"Oh, I don't know. You'll find the right one."

Brian's heart lodged in his throat. "Maybe we already have." What would she say about that?

Channon raked her gaze over Shaun, then Brian, and pressed her lips together. She picked at the label on the beer bottle with her thumbnail. "Whatever. You're silly and I don't need silly. Safety is what I need—that and quiet." She peeled the husk from one of the ears of corn. "Jack... If he'd caught wind of this place and saw how much he could get per acre if he sold, he'd have had a shit fit. He sees dollar signs, not sentimental value. He couldn't appreciate it here."

"He'd sell?" Brian dropped his fork. He couldn't imagine not being at the farm and not sharing a life with Shaun or Channon.

"He'd sell this place faster than you'd think. It took me forever to see just how awful he was in my life." She buttered the corn. "And now he's in the past."

"Seems like he was a real worm." Shaun took a bite of steak. "Damn, this is good. Brian, you outdid yourself."

"I agree. This is delicious." She smiled and cut a sliver of steak from the larger hunk. "Mind if I talk about my ex? I need to get the words out of my head."

"Go for it," Shaun said between bites.

Channon smiled and tapped her fork on the edge of her plate. "Jack had his moments. Some were good, some were okay and others sucked."

"Are you glad you're back?" Brian asked. The food looked good—hell, he'd grilled the steaks—and his stomach growled, but he only saw her. "We've missed you."

She leaned back in her chair and downed more of her beer. She sighed. "I missed it here. There are rules, but not Jack's rules. He always seemed to be on the edge about something. Like he was never happy or he wanted something he couldn't have."

Brian snorted. "Telling." He'd never liked her ex or the stories he'd heard about the guy from her father. He never understood what she saw in Jack, but then he hadn't thought he or Shaun would be good enough for her either.

"It's still relaxed here." Shaun stabbed the last piece of steak on his plate. "Just me and Bri."

Brian watched Channon and her body language. Since sitting down with them, she'd relaxed more. She smiled and her rosy glow came back. He wanted that look for her all the time. Wanted her between him and Shaun, and safe.

Channon tucked her knees to her chest. She propped the beer on her knee. "I'm glad it's just you two. I need the quiet time to regroup. Jack cut me loose from the ad agency and I've been rudderless."

"Cut you loose?" Brian sat up straighter. What the hell? Now he knew Jack didn't deserve her. "Seriously? That asshole."

"It's for the best. I liked the designs, but not my co-workers. Jack knew how to manipulate people. When I first met him, I thought he was so smart and polished, but in this last year, year and a half, I saw the real man and he's an asshole." She fluttered her hands. "I could use another beer."

Shaun jumped from his seat. "Three beers, coming up." He strolled into the house, leaving her alone with Brian. That was one of the things Brian appreciated about Shaun—he knew when to make a move and when to give Brian space.

Channon left her chair and wandered out to the edge of the field. Brian glanced at the back door, then followed her. He didn't understand what had changed, but felt the tension rising between the three of them again.

She folded her arms and kept her back to him. "I love watching the wind in the field. The swirling is hypnotic."

Brian embraced her from behind and kissed her temple. She didn't pull away, but instead hugged him tighter. She felt so right in his arms and the scent of her lingered in his brain. He wanted more than the kisses or just holding her. He wanted everything.

Shaun strode up beside them and handed Channon a beer. "Have you ever wondered why we didn't leave the farm?"

"Other than it's a free place to live?" Channon tucked against Brian's side and wrapped her arms around him. "Whatever works."

She deserved to know the full truth. They could lose any chances with her, but Brian refused to keep her in the dark and he knew Shaun agreed. Brian dipped his head. "Your dad allowed us to stay here on the farm in return for work, yeah, but he was lonely. You'd moved away and he knew we'd work for cheap. I only got the job at the post office because it had a good health plan and it's a few extra bucks in my pocket. It's a good gig that way — days at the post office and afternoons working ground. I like it." Brian downed half his beer in one draw. "Plus, we got to stay where it feels like home."

"Guess I'll be seeing a lot of you two, then." She kissed Brian's cheek. "I still may get a dog, but knowing you're not far away makes me feel a lot better about being alone."

Brian met Shaun's gaze. He hated to hear her say the word 'alone'. "What are you going to do now that you're back? Just run the farm?" He could think of a few ideas, but none of them would get any work done.

"Actually, I'm starting at the library next week. Already

got that worked out. I'll be at the main desk and reference sometimes. When I'm not doing that, I thought I'd sort through the craft stuff in the attic. Mom gathered it all. I might as well use it and try to make stuff to sell on the craft show circuit. People liked my artsy stuff when I was still in school. Hopefully, I still have the talent."

"They did and they will." Brian had faith in her. He believed she could do whatever she put her mind to and he and Shaun would be right there to assist.

"We'll help if you'd like," Shaun offered. "We're good at lugging tables and keeping company at that sort of thing."

Brian had no idea how to help at a craft show, but he wasn't about to argue. He'd do pretty much whatever she asked.

"That's okay. You've got plenty to do—both of you. Don't you have a girlfriend?" Channon asked.

"Not right now." Brian held her and stood in silence. He refused to deny how *right* she felt in his embrace. He'd always wanted her, even if he'd played down his attraction. He wasn't sure how to tell her exactly how he felt.

Channon pulled away from him and drained her beer. "I should go."

"We're not done." Brian reached for her. "Promise. There's more. I made dessert—kind of."

"I'm stuffed and tired." She smiled and patted his chest. "But thank you."

"Let's work off our dinner together." Shaun scooped her into his arms and carried Channon into the house.

Brian picked up the two empty beer bottles, then downed his own brew in two swallows. He followed them into the guest house. Shaun had set her on her feet and grabbed Brian's guitar. Shaun didn't have to say a word for Brian to know what he wanted.

"How about a dance?" Brian asked. He strummed a few bars of a popular country song. "I haven't had the chance to play for anyone in forever." He continued with the tune. "Come on."

Shaun tugged Channon back into his arms and held her close. "I missed this."

"Our secret dances? Or Brian's concerts?"

"All of it." He rested his forehead against hers. "We never forgot about you."

Brian continued to play the song, but his mind wandered. She'd filled his nights and dreams. He remembered sneaking out of the house to meet up with Shaun so they could drive out to the farm. The memory of countless night swims and the kisses he'd wished would turn into more filled his brain. He wished he was the one swaying with Channon.

"You're silly, but the more we dance, the more I'm thinking I need some silly in my life." She smiled and kissed him on the lips. "I like you." She glanced over her shoulder. "I missed you, too, Brian."

He'd hoped she'd say that all day. Hell, he'd been hoping all his life that she'd fall for him and Shaun.

Shaun palmed her ass and frowned. "Babe? You're buzzing."

"Huh?" Her eyes widened. "What? Oh! My phone. Sorry." She eased away from Shaun and tugged the phone from her back pocket. She swiped her thumb across the screen and frowned. "I need to get this."

Brian stopped playing as she darted past him and out the back door. She wandered onto the lawn. The setting sun bathed her in warm orange light as she paced back and forth through the grass. Shaun nodded to Brian and both men stood in the kitchen.

Brian could hear her end of the conversation. He shouldn't have been eavesdropping, but he needed to be sure she was okay. When she paled and waved her hand, he gripped the edge of the sink. He wanted to rush out to her and make everything better.

"Jack, this is ridiculous." Channon shook her head. "Either you're committed or you're not."

Brian gritted his teeth. He wanted to intervene, but should

he?

"I have no idea what they're talking about, but I don't like the way she's getting upset." Shaun folded his arms. "Call me a territorial asshole, but she's ours. She doesn't deserve to be treated like this."

"You're right." Brian marched out onto the lawn. He took the phone from her and disconnected the call. Jack might have issues with commitment, but he and Shaun didn't.

"You didn't have to go caveman on me." She rested her hands on her hips. "I'm fine."

"You're on the verge of tears." Brian tucked her phone into his back pocket. He gathered her against his chest and led her into the house. He didn't stop until they reached the bedroom. Shaun joined them and eased up behind her.

Brian cradled her jaw in his hands. He knew his heart and it wanted her. "We've never made you deal with commitment issues."

"Because you don't want me." She smoothed her palms over his chest. "Brian."

Shaun moved her hair off her neck. He met Brian's gaze before he pressed kisses on her skin. Channon sagged against Shaun, but kept her hands on Brian.

"I can't," she murmured. She draped her arms around Brian's neck. "You don't want this."

"We don't?" Shaun let go of her long enough to whip his shirt up over his head. "If we didn't want to be here or want you here, this wouldn't be happening."

"Shaun." Channon turned around and allowed Shaun to gather her in his arms. He crushed his mouth down on hers.

Brian groaned and stripped out of his shirt. He couldn't wait. The warm night air kissed his skin, but that was nothing compared to the fever flowing through his body. He eased up behind Channon and slid his hands under her shirt. While Shaun kissed her mouth, Brian nibbled on her neck and shoulder. Each groan and whimper escaping her throat spurred him on. He rubbed the bulge in his jeans along her ass. Despite the layers of denim between them, the heat from her body seeped into his.

Channon glanced back at Brian. "More."

"We'll give you more." Brian helped her onto the bed. With Shaun's assistance, Brian yanked her shirt over her head. He'd tousled her hair, but he liked the look. The blush on her cheeks slid down her neck to her chest. Her breasts strained against the lacy cups of her bra. He'd never seen a sexier woman in his life.

"Beautiful," Shaun murmured. He moved her bra straps down her shoulders and Brian opened the clasp. The lingerie fell away and her blush deepened. She parted her lips and whimpered again.

"Gorgeous." Brian dragged his nose along her neck and nibbled on her earlobe. "I've dreamed of you."

"Me?" she asked. She met his gaze. "Really?"

"Really." Brian feasted on her mouth. When she moaned and opened to him, he swiped his tongue along hers. She wound her arms around his neck and trailed her fingers down the back of his neck. He broke the connection and groaned. "I've wanted this for a long time. We want you."

Chapter Four

Channon hadn't expected him to say such things. Brian and Shaun were forbidden fruit—sexy and commanding, but not hers for the taking.

When Shaun groaned, something in her belly fluttered. She shouldn't have been attracted to them. They'd both done their fair share of getting around. Still, Brian and Shaun blew her mind and when they kissed her, her thoughts turned to mush. The smell of them wrapped around her and their touch sizzled her synapses.

Shaun smoothed his palm across her belly, then popped the button on her shorts. She jerked and broke the kiss with Brian. She knew this was where they were going, but both men continued to shock her. She couldn't wrap her head around them wanting her.

"Don't worry, babe. We won't hurt you." Shaun cupped her jaw and kissed her. "Promise."

She nodded. "I know." She trusted them and believed these two men would treat her with dignity and passion. Channon blew out a long breath. She wasn't afraid any longer. Not of them. She wanted everything with them, even if she had the niggling feeling she'd get her heart broken. But if she didn't give them a chance, she'd never know what could happen. She left the bed long enough to stand and shove her jeans to the floor.

"Babe?" Brian asked.

"Make me yours." She stood nude in front of them. "Please?" She hated to beg, but if that's what she needed to do in order to win them over, she would. She'd fallen for the two ranch hands years ago, and being with them now only solidified her feelings.

Shaun gasped and reached for her. He tugged her across his lap. "We'll do our best to make you happy." He kissed her again and sucked on her tongue. He swallowed her moan.

"Want you," Brian murmured. He covered her breasts with his hands and rolled her nipples in his fingers. "So much."

"Take me." Channon rested her forehead against Shaun's. "I've wanted to belong to you forever. Both of you."

Shaun's eyes widened and he smiled. He turned her around and spread her out on the bed. He unzipped his pants, then shoved the garment to the floor.

Seeing him completely naked stole her breath. The countless hours working in the sun were evident on his tanned skin. When he stretched and grabbed something out of the nightstand, his muscles rippled. He squeezed his ass cheeks together and she bit back a groan. He had the perfect ass for grabbing. When he turned around, her skin heated. He'd shaved the hair from his chest and around his cock. She shivered. She loved smooth men.

"Like the view?" Shaun squirted lube onto his hand. "I do."

She nodded, unable to speak. She'd waited so long for this moment. She spread her legs and palmed her knees. Was he going to fuck her ass? She hoped so. She wanted one man in her ass and the other in her pussy — even if she'd never had two men at one time before.

"Ours." Brian stretched over her and rubbed his face over her breasts. He sucked one of her nipples into his mouth. His teeth raked over her skin and the pain flowed as pleasure through her veins. She reached for him and dug her nails into his shoulder.

"Damn. That's fucking hot." Shaun tore open a condom packet and sheathed his dick. He stroked himself a couple of times before he settled between her thighs. He propped her left leg on his chest. "Babe, you're so beautiful."

Channon sucked in a ragged breath as Shaun entered her. She wanted to thank him for the compliment, but she had no words. Every ripple of his cock massaged her from within. She groaned and tried to relax as he pushed deep inside her. He didn't move for a second, instead he paused within her. She pumped her hips. She needed more from him. Holy shit. She'd take what she wanted if he didn't start moving.

"More," she begged. "Oh my God." She scratched Brian's shoulders as she tried to rock on Shaun's dick. "Please?"

"Slow down, babe." Shaun grasped her hips. He scooted her to the edge of the bed and leaned over her enough to meet her gaze. "Want to make this perfect for you."

With Brian kissing and biting her nipples and Shaun in her pussy, yeah, this was perfect. The only thing that would make it better would be to have both men inside her, but that would have to wait. She winced, then groaned as Brian's teeth raked over her sensitive skin.

Channon released her grasp on Brian and nudged him. She reached between his legs and massaged the bulge in his jeans. Freeing his dick from the denim would be damn near impossible in her current position, but she wanted his cock in her mouth.

Brian groaned. "That feels good." He opened his fly, allowing her to slide her hand beneath the zipper. She wound her fingers around his cock and stroked. "That's right, babe. God, that's fucking hot watching that cock going in and out of your cunt," Brian murmured. "Fuck. I want to join him. Want to take that sweet pussy."

She shivered. Was this how it felt to be consumed by two men? Everything within her focused on them. She bucked her hips, meeting Shaun thrust for thrust. She couldn't breathe.

Brian moved out of her reach and off the bed. He shucked his pants, then settled behind her head. He propped her up on his lap, allowing her to recline on him. The position gave him great access to her breasts and increased her pleasure.

When Shaun pulled out, Brian pinched her nipples. As Shaun filled her to the hilt, Brian eased up. The men worked in perfect harmony.

A moan escaped her throat and she threaded her arms around Shaun's neck.

"Fuck her, Shaun. Make her feel you for the next three days. She's yours. Ours." Brian stopped pinching. "On the edge, sweets?"

"Shaun," she puffed. "Brian." Everything within her tensed. The orgasm built low in her belly, but spread down her limbs. The muscles in her legs trembled. She tugged Shaun closer and kissed him. His hot breath feathered over her cheeks as he slid in and out of her. A bead of sweat slipped down his temple.

"Come for us, sweetheart. Come for us," Brian coaxed. "Do it."

She whimpered and shivered. She couldn't have held back if she'd wanted to — the climax overwhelmed her. She bumped noses with Shaun. Words escaped her and her thoughts muddled.

Shaun grunted and pistoned his hips. The sound of skin on skin echoed through the bedroom. He closed his eyes. "Fucking hell. Fuck." He arched his back and drove into her. "My God." He tensed and curled forward. His cock throbbed within her as he came.

Channon whimpered again. From her head to her toes, she felt wrung out. She sagged against Brian and the bed. Her limbs refused to cooperate.

"Very nice." Brian scooted out from under her, then stretched out on the bed.

Shaun withdrew and left her long enough to remove the condom. He settled on her other side and panted. "Damn. Don't think I'll ever get enough of you."

"Next time, it's my turn." Brian stretched his arm across her belly. "So beautiful. Like you were made for us."

"Then do it." She touched his cheek. "I want more." She gave up worrying. She might as well follow her heart. "I need more."

Brian grinned, then nodded. He didn't say a word as he left the bed. He retrieved a condom, then took his place on the mattress. He tugged her across his lap.

"Ride me," he said, not giving her much of a chance to argue. Not that she'd turn him down.

Where Shaun had moved slowly and with care, Brian didn't hold back. He grasped her hips and pushed deep within her in one stroke. She wobbled on his lap and her nipples tightened. For a split second, the self-consciousness of being naked and on display in front of them overcame her. She covered her breasts with her arms.

"Don't hide from us, babe." Shaun moved her hair off her neck and kissed her shoulder. "You're beautiful."

She leaned into Shaun for another kiss. When Shaun palmed her already tender breast, she moaned into his mouth. She'd come before and didn't think she could climax so fast, but the orgasm welled within her already. She broke the kiss and panted.

"Good girl." Brian held onto her hips and guided her up and down on his dick. He drove into her, filling her to the hilt.

Channon whimpered and rested her forehead against Shaun's. Her lips parted and she stared into his eyes. She could've sworn she saw straight through to his soul.

Shaun grasped her hand. "Ride it out. Feels good, doesn't it?" He kissed her lips. "Better than you ever imagined."

"Yeah," she managed. She wasn't sure how she was able to talk in a coherent manner, since both men blurred her thoughts. She whimpered and wrapped her arm around Shaun's neck. She held onto Brian's arm with her other hand. Her legs trembled and butterflies swarmed in her belly. She tensed and tightened her pussy around Brian's dick. Oh, fuck, did she need to come…

"Won't take him long," Shaun murmured. He kissed her neck and nuzzled behind her ear. "He's been on a hair-trigger since he got home."

She'd been on that same hair-trigger since they'd started kissing her.

"Fuck." Brian swatted her hip. "Up."

"Up?" She sagged against Shaun as Brian eased out from under her. Shaun settled on his back beneath her and held her to his chest. He spread his legs above hers and rubbed his cock on her belly. This position gave Brian better access to her body, but kept Shaun involved — a threesome without the double penetration.

"Relax." Shaun brushed her hair from her face and met her gaze. "We've got you."

"I know." She grasped his shoulders and held on for the ride.

"Hell, yeah. That's better." Brian eased up behind her and guided his cock into her pussy. As before, he didn't use much finesse, but instead filled her to the brim again and increased his speed. When she groaned, he drove deeper into her. He mashed her onto Shaun's chest and swatted her ass.

"Brian." She tilted her head back and arched her body. Her nipples grazed Shaun's chest, adding another dimension of pleasure to the act of lovemaking. She couldn't hold back — not any longer.

"Fuuuuuucck!" Brian slammed into her cunt. His cock throbbed within her. "Oh, wow."

Channon shuddered and sagged onto Shaun's chest. She couldn't move and didn't want to. She'd found her heart with both men. This was where she belonged. She rested her face against Shaun's neck.

Brian's groan filled the silence. He eased out of her and swatted her ass. "Holy fuck, that was good." He collapsed on the bed beside Shaun and closed his eyes.

Channon settled between Brian and Shaun. She needed to shower, but all she wanted to do was snooze between her men. "This is nice."

Brian fell asleep fastest, and within seconds, he'd rolled onto his side. He groaned and threw his arm across her belly.

She chuckled. "Is this normal? Or am I that boring?"

"That's just Bri. He keeps crazy hours." Shaun tucked her tight to his side. "I'm glad you're here."

"Me too." She closed her eyes and ground her ass into his crotch. She drifted to sleep with thoughts of Brian and Shaun on her mind. She wished she'd stayed home instead of leaving for Cleveland. Maybe if she'd have stuck around, she would've had this moment much earlier. But then again, there was a chance things wouldn't have worked out.

The past didn't matter. She was ready to move forward.

Chapter Five

Channon rolled over into something hard. When she opened her eyes, she jerked away. *Shit. What the…?* She stared at the body beside her. Shaun. Oh. The sleepover… How could she forget a night with the men of her dreams? Easy. They'd worn her out. But she had to get up and stretch. She crawled out from between them and grabbed her shorts and shirt.

"Where is my underwear?" she muttered, then dressed and left the bedroom. She'd worry about her lingerie later.

When she strode into the kitchen, the scent of coffee permeated the air. Coffee? She hadn't remembered anyone getting up. She shrugged and poured herself a cup, then crept onto front porch. She sat on the steps and drank in the view. She'd seen the guest house so many times when she'd been a kid and played there when her grandparents came for visits, but she'd never imagined spending the night at the house, let alone having the hottest night of her life there.

Brian and Shaun were like that though — full of surprises. Some of the things they'd said came back to her, along with the memory of their touch on her skin. She warmed to her core. They knew where to touch and how to make her come apart. They'd also known what to say. *They'd wanted her forever. She belonged to them.* She wanted to believe what they'd said, but come on. This was probably just crap they said during sex and nothing more.

Behind her, the door creaked. She glanced over her shoulder and Brian grinned. He held a cup of coffee and a blanket.

"Hi there," she murmured.

"Hi to you." He nodded to the swing. "Sit with me?"

"I was going to sit on the steps, but this is nicer." She snuggled up beside him on the swing. The blanket warmed her legs. She rested her head on his shoulder. "How long have you lived in the guest house?"

"Pretty much the entire time you've been gone. Your dad asked us to stay out here. He needed the help and we were both broke. Shaun lost his job over at K&L Ranch." Brian shrugged. "Kristin only wanted him because she thought she'd piss off her old man. Shaun didn't take the bait and ended up fired."

"That's awful." She held his hand and marveled at how they'd settled together so well — like an old married couple. Even after so many years apart, the three of them were still a team.

"I know why he wouldn't sleep with her. Aside from it being unethical, he has to have an emotional connection to the woman in his life. The only connection she had wasn't to his brain." Brian snorted again. "She just saw a hot ass in tight jeans. Could've been anyone and she'd have been interested."

"*I* want to see his hot ass in jeans...or chaps." She'd fantasized about Shaun in that very outfit plenty of times. "Both of you could dress up that way and I'd be right here watching." Touching, tasting...she stifled a shiver. She'd happily climb in between them.

"I'd dress up for you and I bet Shaun would, too." He let go of her hand and draped his arm around her shoulders. "It'd be fun."

She rested her head on his arm and stared up at the clear blue sky. She should've come home long before she had, but then what? She couldn't be sure they would've made a move back then.

"So you're single?" Brian asked.

She sighed. "Yeah, I'm single and living in my parents' home. I'm a mess." *I'm in love with the farm hands and I want both of them to love me. Definitely a disaster.* "But all this stuff happens for a reason, right? I came back when I did because the cosmos wants me to, right?"

"I believe so." Brian squeezed her shoulder. "Why don't we go for a ride?"

"Shaun won't mind?" She allowed him to walk her back inside. "I'd feel bad if we didn't ask him."

"He did chores already. He's beat." Brian opened the door for her. "That's why there was coffee. He likes to get stuff done just after sunrise when it's not as hot. Plus, it's quiet and it gives him time for a nap. He'll go out around eleven to start the field work."

"Why didn't he tell me?" She ducked under his arm, but stopped in the living room. "My name is on the deed and I haven't done much at all. I owe the both of you for keeping things going."

"Honey, you don't owe us anything." He gathered her into his arms and slid his hands into her back pockets. "Working here has been a labor of love for us. It's fine."

"You're working two jobs," she cried. The guilt washed over her in waves. She wobbled and bile rose in her throat. She needed to step up—big time.

"Slow down." He tugged her toward the front door and kissed her.

Channon closed her eyes but didn't pull away. The guilt lingered, but she gathered her emotions once again.

"I'm working two jobs so I can bring in a little money, yes, but it's also so I could be here at the farm with Shaun and you."

"Brian." She wanted to believe him, but come on. She knew better. She hadn't been enough to keep Jack around. What made her think she could hold onto *two* men?

"We liked having cheap room and board as well as a shed for the vehicles." Shaun shuffled into the room. His low-slung sleep pants showcased his taut body well. His hair stood up in spikes and his nipples were beaded. "I'm not above hard work if it means I've got a stable place to stay." He snorted and scratched his chest. "Give me five minutes to wake up and get dressed."

"We were going for a ride," Channon managed.

"Good. I need to exercise Herb." Shaun wandered back to the bedroom and disappeared. "Don't argue," he called. "We're going."

She met Brian's gaze. "He should be sleeping." He'd worked hard and her arguing had to be what woke him up.

"He's right." Brian kissed her again. "We need to go for a ride." He swatted her ass and left her alone at the door.

"Are you sure?" She hated being so enveloped in doubt, but Jesus. Nothing made sense. "I feel like I'm not in control of anything."

Brian stopped in the doorway to the hall. "Honey, we said a ride, not running off to Vegas to get married. Chill out."

Channon folded her arms. "Can I get changed? I don't even have a bra on." She didn't mind going commando, but not while riding a horse.

"We'll have the horses ready. Meet you in the barn in fifteen?" Brian asked.

"Sure." She turned on her heel and headed out to the porch. She shook her head as she strolled across the lawn. Nothing made sense, but the whole situation felt right. She liked waking up between Shaun and Brian. She loved the way they seemed to care and the passion when they made love to her. But could the good feelings last? She wasn't sure.

As she opened the back door to the main house, she paused. Fuck it. If they wanted to have a good time for now, then she did, too. She'd come home to start over. So she'd fallen in love with Brian and Shaun... She'd accept the fun times for now and deal with the consequences later.

She deserved a little fun for a change.

* * * *

Brian strode back to the bedroom and stopped in the doorway. "She's scared." He trusted his heart and his instincts. Channon was theirs. She just needed a few more nudges to understand her desires.

Shaun had flopped onto the bed. He rubbed his belly and seemed to stare at the ceiling. "We freaked her out, Bri. Christ. We went from *making* her dinner to making *her* dinner. We went too fast."

"Nah." Brian folded his arms. Once he and Shaun had the chance to explain everything to her, he had faith the relationship would work out. They needed to help her overcome her fears.

"Then what do we do?" Shaun asked. He sat up and ran his fingers through his hair. "Give her more time? Fuck her again? Beg?"

"We give her reasons why this is right. Once we show her how perfect we are together, she'll come around." Brian strode across the room. "She's open to the idea of being ours and this ride will help our cause."

"Survey the land and the landscape so she sees what she's got?" Shaun shook out his shirt, then dragged the garment over his head. "We explain we're hers for the taking?"

"Exactly." Brian nodded. "We *are* hers. Always have been."

Fifteen minutes later, Brian strode across the lawn to the barn. Shaun dressed faster and had gone ahead of him to ready the horses for the ride. Most of the time, Brian kept up with his friend, but today he seemed to be moving in slow motion. He rounded the barn and stopped. Channon stood by the pasture with her back to him.

"Channon?" Brian made his way to her. "Ready?"

"Yeah." Her voice broke and she wiped her cheeks with the back of her hand. "Let's ride." She strode past him and into the barn.

He wanted to question her, but didn't. When she was ready to open up, she would and his pushing wouldn't hurry things along.

Channon climbed onto Peaches' back. She didn't wait for Brian or Shaun, but instead headed out of the barn.

Shaun shrugged, then mounted Brutus. "We'll get it sorted out."

Brian gritted his teeth and climbed onto Herb. He loved the freedom of a ride and the times he was able to exercise the horse properly. When he left the building, Peaches broke into a gallop.

Brian clicked his tongue and tugged lightly on the reins. He'd taught Herb to speed up with each click. He needed to catch Channon. Shaun, on Brutus, kept up with her. Channon stopped at the far end of the pasture, by the pond.

Good choice. Brian steered Herb to the edge of the water, then dismounted. "Show off," he said. "You always did like the attention." He admired Channon. She seemed so at ease on the horse, and so beautiful. She'd relaxed once they'd gone out on the ride and she smiled more—except now.

Channon dismounted Peaches and shrugged. Her blush stretched from her hairline to the collar of her shirt. She'd hidden her eyes behind sunglasses, making it hard to read her expression.

Shaun spread out a blanket in the shade under the maple trees. He held up his canteen. "Anyone want a drink?"

"Sure." Channon draped Peaches' reins over the hitching post. "I'm game."

"Good." Shaun grinned. "I brought apples—for us and them."

Brian left Herb beside Peaches, then joined Channon and Shaun on the blanket. He liked the way they fell together. Being with both of them was comfortable and she was the missing piece. The way Shaun looked at her was how he saw her, too.

Channon stretched out with her arms over her head. "This was actually perfect."

"Yeah?" Shaun sidled up to her and draped his arm across her belly. "It could be more."

"Guys." Her gaze vacillated between Shaun and Brian. "You don't have to humor me, I'm okay with what's going on."

"I'm not." Brian's territorial streak reared its head. He'd let Shaun lead the way the first time they'd been with her. Now he wanted his turn. "You're very important to Shaun and me."

"Very." Shaun nuzzled her neck. "Damn."

Brian tucked himself tight to her side and leaned over her. "We want more than one time." He kissed her mouth, loving the taste of her. He'd never get enough of her.

Channon draped her arm around his neck and kept him close. "Make love to me. Both of you."

Chapter Six

Brian met Shaun's gaze. As if either of them could tell her no? He let go of her long enough to yank his shirt up over his head. He wanted to share everything with her. He shoved his pants to the ground and kicked out of his shoes, underwear and jeans. He grabbed the condom from his saddle bag. When he returned to the blanket, Channon already had her jeans and blouse off. Shaun had her stretched out on top of him and he kissed her. Clad in nothing but her bra and panties, she turned him on.

"Suck his cock while I'm inside you," Brian said. "Show us you're ours." He eased up behind her and grasped her hips. "Do it."

Channon glanced over her shoulder and grinned. She allowed Brian to reposition her, to give her better access to Shaun's cock.

"Oh fuck," Shaun bit out. He gripped the blanket. "That's right. Take me in."

Channon popped the button on Shaun's jeans and opened his fly. She eased his dick from his pants and stroked him.

Seeing her pleasuring Shaun added to Brian's desire for her. She wasn't afraid to be with both of them. She glanced back at Brian once more, then took Shaun's erection deep into her mouth.

"Damn," Brian said, drawing the word out. He stroked his cock and grunted. He wouldn't need long and doubted Shaun would either. He shoved her panties aside, exposing her pussy. He lined himself up with her cunt and pushed. Inch by inch, he sank into her wet, hot channel. She blew his mind. Somehow she knew to open to him and when to rock her body.

Shaun propped himself up on his elbows and his head lolled on his shoulders. "Channon, babe."

Brian planted his knees. He increased his speed in seconds as the orgasm built within him. Fuck. Channon was the one person to make him whole—other than Shaun. They needed her more than anything. He couldn't imagine life without her—not again.

With each thrust, he came closer to falling apart. His nerve endings sizzled and the rest of the world melted away, except for her and Shaun. He tipped his head back and groaned. The noise ripped from his chest as he filled Channon to the hilt once more. Channon tensed around him, seeming to hold him inside her. Her muffled cries around Shaun's cock excited him and shredded his restraint.

The climax washed over him from the top of his head to his toes. He shuddered and added a couple of extra thrusts until the shaking slowed. He focused on Channon and Shaun.

"Fuck me." Shaun threaded his fingers into her hair and guided her up and down on his dick. "Fuck. I'm close."

Brian held onto her hips, keeping her upright as she shivered.

Shaun panted and tensed. He gritted his teeth and blew out a whistle. "Holy hell. Fuck, I'm coming."

Instead of pulling away, Channon swallowed him until he let go of her hair. Brian eased out of her pussy and sat back on his heels. He needed a moment for the world to stop spinning, but that was the effect she had on him. She knocked him off kilter in all the right ways.

"Oh hell." Shaun released his grip. "Fuck, I'm sorry." His brow furrowed and the post-orgasm glow evaporated immediately. "I wasn't trying to hurt you."

Channon reclined against Brian and wiped her mouth with the back of her hand. "You didn't hurt me. I loved it."

Shaun sighed and fell back on the blanket. "Thank God. I don't want to hurt you."

"You were fine." She kissed Brian on the lips, then stretched out beside Shaun. "Promise, I loved it."

Giddiness ran through Brian's veins, along with the aftereffects of the orgasm. He settled beside her. He propped himself up on his elbow in order to look at his best friend and their lover. He'd never felt so sure of his feelings in his entire life.

Channon tugged Shaun's arm around her and snuggled up to Brian. "I wanted to be one of your girls since we were in high school. I had such a crush on you both back then. You probably thought I was nuts. I'd dream that one of the nights I snuck off with you two would turn into something hotter than riding the horses in the dark or helping you catch frogs."

He'd wanted their secret meetings to be more than platonic, too, but her father had made sure he and Shaun behaved. Unfortunately, her father wasn't around—or rather fortunately for them. "Do you still want to be our girl?" Brian asked. He didn't dare look her in the eye for fear he'd spook her. "Still dream about us and what we've done?"

"I wouldn't sleep with you—again—if I didn't." She clasped Shaun's hand on Brian's belly. "In my dreams, we had all kinds of sex on my bed and against the wall."

Both places sounded hot as hell to Brian. He kissed the top of her head. "Honey, we've been more than a little in love with you since then. More like *a lot* in love with you."

"And you didn't tell me?" She sat up and covered her chest with her shirt. "Why?"

Brian sighed. "Your dad would've killed us."

"Your father informed us that if we made any sort of move on you, he'd make sure it was our last." Shaun stood and stepped into his pants. He offered up her jeans. "Babe, we wanted to keep you in our lives."

"Exactly." Brian sat up again, but didn't bother to dress. "He respected us as farm hands and with the horses, but not our lifestyle. We were—as he put it—freaks. I never gave up hope that we'd be able to change his mind, but that's why we didn't make a move. We wanted you the whole time."

Channon scrambled to her feet. She clutched her clothes in front of her body. She rubbed the top of her boot-clad left foot along the back of her right leg. "Then let's do it— tonight."

"Think about your choice." Brian stood and yanked his jeans up past his hips. "We're not going anywhere unless you tell us to get bent."

"Once we start, we won't be able to stop." Shaun curled his fingers under her chin. "You're kind of addictive."

Her eyes sparkled. "So are you."

"Then let us get the work done and we'll be around after supper." Brian snagged her in his arms. "If you change your mind, it's okay."

Shaun eased up behind her. "We understand."

Channon whimpered and a smile curled on her lips. "I'm very sure."

Brian held onto hope, but not too tightly. He believed in the passion between them and trusted his heart. She was the one they'd been waiting for all along. But the chance was still there that she'd change her mind. He kissed her temple and ignored his worries. Shaun, Channon and he were meant to be together.

* * * *

Hours later, Channon opened a second moving box. Sorting through her parents' things was turning out to be much harder than she'd imagined. She wasn't about to get rid of everything, but some of the items had to go. She tucked knick-knacks into the box, then paused on her parents' wedding photo. Her mother and father looked so young.

Part of her couldn't believe her father would put such limitations on Shaun and Brian. They were good men and hadn't done anything to make him worry—had they? Sure, they had a reputation and did everything together, but wasn't it better to have two attentive men than to have one man who didn't give a shit about her? The rest of her believed Shaun and Brian—her father wouldn't allow his daughter to be with two men at the same time.

She considered the pros and cons of two lovers. If they wanted lots of sex, she'd be worn out often. The chance was greater that they'd fall out of love with her and want someone else, or they'd want to add another woman to the equation. Being with both of them made getting married someday difficult. She couldn't marry two men—not in the state of Ohio. What if she married one and the other ended up jealous? Could she put herself through that kind of hurt?

Still, she'd have her best friends with her all the time. They'd be even tighter as a trio. Besides, she loved them—always had. Wouldn't the love continue to grow? And she'd have two lovers. Two men consumed with her pleasure. Who was she to complain?

Maybe she should be concerned and keep her heart under wraps, but she knew who she wanted. She'd never been so sure about anything in her life. She could live without them, but didn't want to if at all possible. With Brian and Shaun, she'd be able to heal and have a good life. She'd have so much love.

Channon stood and strode over to the picture window. Shaun, on the red tractor, zipped back and forth across the front field. She didn't have to be up close to him to see the sweat on his skin. Perspiration caused his shirt to cling to his body and showcase his musculature. She bit back a moan. Even dirty and sweaty, she wanted his arms around her. She couldn't see Brian, but the attraction was mutual.

The kitchen door clunked and she heard footsteps on the tile floor. Channon mopped the sweat from her brow and crossed the living room. She expected to see Brian in the kitchen. Instead, Jack stood in the middle of the room. "Jack?"

"Hi, Channy." Jack folded his arms. "This is where you've been hiding?"

Channy... She hated that nickname. "Channon and no, I'm not hiding. What are *you* doing here?" Fear crept into her brain. She didn't trust him, especially not with that wicked gleam in his eye.

"I came to find my girlfriend." Jack eased out from behind the table, but didn't try to hug her. He sniffed the air. "Dirty here, isn't it?"

"It's a farm. We've got dirt everywhere." She gripped the back of the closest chair. "Jack, we split so you could date what's-her-name."

He pushed past her into the living room. "Maybe I realized I was lonely. The apartment isn't the same without you there."

"Because you don't have someone to pick up after you?" she snapped.

"Because I loved you. Still do." He smiled and his tone grated on her nerves. Jack stepped up to her and held out his hands. "If I'd have known how much I'd miss you when you left, I wouldn't have let you go."

She inched away from him. "You *cheated* on me."

"I was wrong."

Part of her had wanted to hear those exact words, but the desire to have him back wasn't there.

"I can see us together—right here." Jack's smile widened. "Our children running in the yard. I can picture it right now. Three kids, all growing up in this house."

Bile rose in her throat and she pressed her lips together to keep from throwing up. The love for Jack was long gone and the more he talked, the more she knew what he meant. He wasn't seeing children—he saw how much he believed he could get per acre if he sold her land. Fat fucking chance.

"Marry me, Channon. You can have everything you've ever wanted." He held up a diamond ring. "Please?"

During their seven years together, she'd wanted to get married and have a family. The temptation to shrink back into her old life was strong…but not strong enough.

"I don't want children," she confessed. Her priorities and desires had changed since coming back to the farm. She wasn't the same girl as she'd been before. Screw Jack and his desire to jump back into her life. He wasn't welcome, because she'd moved on.

Chapter Seven

Shaun stood on the back porch and listened in on the argument. He'd been taught not to eavesdrop, but he didn't trust the guy in the middle of the kitchen. From the moment he'd spotted the silver car zipping up the lane, he'd known something was wrong. He'd parked the tractor and alerted Brian before he'd made his way to the house.

Now the fucker was offering to marry Channon—*their* Channon. He gripped the door handle, ready to barge in at any moment.

"You've always wanted children," the man said. "Ever since we met. I'll give them to you. Just accept my proposal."

Shaun turned the knob. *So this is the ex-boyfriend, Jack. Interesting.* He wasn't anything like Shaun expected. Sure, the guy was tall and had some muscle, but his tone of voice grated on Shaun's nerves.

"No." Channon held her ground. "My priorities have changed."

"Please." Jack snorted. "Don't try to gaslight me."

Gaslight him? Shaun opened the door. He'd had enough. "Fine. If you won't listen to her, you'll listen to me."

Jack whipped around. "Who in the hell are you?"

"A problem for you." Shaun stepped up beside Channon. Out of the corner of his eye, he noticed Brian ease into the living room. Good. He wanted his partner in crime there.

"Channy, you could do so much better." Jack rolled his eyes.

The prick. Shaun stood tall. "I'm sorry. I don't think we were properly introduced. My name is Shaun and behind you is Brian."

Jack's eyes widened for a split-second before he narrowed them. "So you're them? You're the guys who fucked up my relationship with Channon. She never forgot about you two twats, but that doesn't matter now. We're getting married."

Brian folded his arms and flanked Channon.

Shaun notched his chin in the air. "Oh?"

"I never agreed to that," Channon said.

"What's going on then?" Shaun focused on Jack. "Explain."

Channon folded her arms and groaned. "This is all so fucked up. I need some time to think." She shrugged away from Brian and Shaun, then stormed past Jack. She stopped at the back door. "I'll be out with Peaches."

Shaun didn't chase her. If she said she needed time, then he'd give her that time but he hoped like hell she wasn't considering Jack's offer. He turned his attention back to her ex.

"Excuse me." Jack put his hand up. "I need to speak with my fiancée."

"No, you don't." Shaun stepped between Jack and the door. "She wants a few moments. Give it to her."

"Oh I will. I've about had it with her flip-flopping," Jack snarled. "I've had it with you two, too. I'm going to make her see reason."

"Are you kidding?" Brian growled.

"I'm very serious." Jack rested his hands on his hips. "If you two would've fucked her and showed her what assholes you are, then maybe she wouldn't still be hung up on you. You don't get it. I love her. I want her to have my children. Right here." His gaze swept over the room. "On this ranch."

Shaun's temper got the better of him, but he held it somewhat in check. He wasn't about to let her ex-boyfriend take over the land he loved, or to push around the woman in his heart. The asshat just saw land he could sell.

"Right, at the tune of forty-five hundred bucks an acre, I bet." Shaun bit back his anger, despite wanting to forcibly remove Jack from the property.

"She'll do whatever I tell her." Jack sneered at Shaun. "You and your silent partner here can't do shit about it." He paused. "It's over five grand an acre."

"Jesus. The land is worth more than money, asshole," Shaun said. "But maybe I'm wrong."

"You were thinking the same thing." Jack sneered again. "You cozy up to the rancher's daughter and get her all happy, then sell this shitty place out from under her. I've seen it before but I've got the advantage." He grinned, then stormed out of the house. "Where in the hell is my Channon?"

"His Channon," Brian muttered. "The fucker talked about her like she wasn't here."

"If we're not careful, she *won't* be here." Shaun hurried onto the porch, then across the lawn after Jack. He made his way into the barn. He knew exactly where she'd be and didn't bother to look back for her ex. Just as Shaun thought, Channon stood in front of Peaches' stall and petted her horse. His heart ached for Channon. This wasn't how the afternoon was supposed to go.

Jack bent in front of her and gasped for air. "This place is filthy. Don't you clean it? It stinks."

"That's part of being in a barn." Shaun met her gaze and offered a smile. "Say what you need to say, babe. Bri and I are right here."

"What in the hell are you talking about?" Jack wiped his hands on his shirt. "Tell these two you're out."

She sighed. "You never know a person until there's money or property involved." She stared at Jack. "Do you think I'm blind? I know what you're doing. You're back because you think you're going to get in on what I've got. Fuck you."

"Baby." Jack reached for her. "Come on, Channy. We're good together. Think of all the times we shared. We can have them here."

"Leave me alone and don't come back," she growled and

straightened her shoulders. "I'm not giving you any more of my time. You're not worth it."

"Jesus Christ," Jack spat. "Your precious farmhands here want to sell your land, too. They don't give a fuck about you."

She met Shaun's gaze and a tear slipped down her cheek. Did she actually believe Jack? *God damn it.*

"I've got a couple grand in the bank and the money invested in the land," Channon said. More tears streamed down her face. "That's it. I'm not rich and probably never will be, but I grew up here and I'm going to stay here — with someone or alone, I don't care."

"Exactly. You'll be with me," Jack said, and his voice rose an octave.

Shaun grabbed the shotgun from the rack in the front of the barn. He'd have to explain things to Channon later. Right now, he wanted Jack the hell off the property. He clicked the safety and aimed in Jack's general direction. "She doesn't have to explain herself. She said to leave. Get the hell off the property or I'll involve the law."

"You'd shoot me?" Jack shrieked. "You're crazy."

"I doubt you want to find out whether or not that's true." He lined up the sights. "By the way, I've been shooting since I was eight."

"You'd really go to jail because of property?" Jack's hands trembled. "Really?"

"You don't want to know what I'd do," Shaun snapped.

Brian snorted. "You don't want to know what he's already done."

Jack's eyes widened. He backed up a few steps until he reached the front doors of the barn. "Honey, I can't do this. You're on your own. These bastards will kill you."

"You care enough about me to take my money, but not to save my life?" She heaved a bucket in Jack's direction. "Get the hell off my land and don't you ever come back."

"Trust me. I won't." Jack raced out of the barn and out of sight.

"I'll be right back." Brian hopped off the tack box and followed Jack. "I need to take out the trash."

Channon turned to Shaun. She stared at him, wide-eyed. "You'd really shoot him?"

"No. It's not even loaded." He popped the barrel free from the firing mechanism. "See?"

Channon sagged against the side of the stall. "I don't want to be used, Shaun. I'm drawn to you both and I love the way we fit together, but I'm scared. I'm not selling the farm and if you're just getting close to me for that money, you're wrong."

Shaun put the gun back on the rack. Christ. Jack had done so much damage, but so had they, by waiting. "We don't want the land or the money. We've always wanted you. If it hadn't been for your dad forbidding us from dating you, we would've showed you how we felt a long time ago. I love you and so does Brian."

She stared up at him. "You do? Seriously, no jokes, that's how you feel?"

"With all my heart." He cupped her jaw in both hands. "Can't see my life without you and I guarantee Brian feels the same way."

"Then it's a good thing I'm not leaving."

"All I've ever wanted was to take care of the horses, tend to the land and be the man you need. Same for Brian."

"What's the same for me?" Brian strolled into the barn. "I heard my name."

"We both want Channon," Shaun said. "Let's go inside and show her."

"Good plan," Brian said. "The trash is gone and it's time for all of us to move on."

Shaun scooped her into his arms and held her tightly to his chest. He liked the way she wrapped her legs around him. He carried her from the barn, across the lawn and into the house. If they were going to do this, he wanted to make love to her in her bed. He ascended the stairs to the second floor.

Brian followed. "Honey, do you have lube and rubbers?"

"I do." She tightened her grasp on Shaun. "It's not like I've lived under a rock."

"I bet you haven't." Shaun kissed her, then nudged open the door to her old bedroom. "I'm in the right room, yes?"

"Uh-huh." She ground her crotch against his belly. "Like this."

"It's going to get better." Shaun placed her on the bed. He wanted to go slow, but every cell in his body screamed to hurry.

"Shaun?" She sat up long enough to tug her shirt up over her head. Her hair fell around her shoulders in soft waves, and her blush stretched from her hairline to her chest. She reached around to the clasp on her bra. The lingerie fell away, exposing her upper body to them. "I want you inside me."

"I will, sweetheart." He yanked his shirt off, then unbuttoned his pants. "Can't wait."

"I want you in my ass." She palmed her breast. "Brian in my pussy." Her gaze switched between Shaun and Brian. She scooted to the edge of the mattress and shimmied out of her jeans and panties.

Shaun nodded. He'd do whatever she wanted. She flowed in his soul.

Brian stripped and settled on the bed. "Come here, you." He pulled her across his lap and swatted her ass. "You've always had our hearts in your hands." He brushed her hair from her face and kissed her.

She broke the connection long enough to say, "We need a condom."

"Where are they babe?" Shaun asked. He kicked out of his boxers, jeans and boots. "Channon?"

"In the nightstand." She perched on Brian's lap and raked her hands over her breasts. "I can't wait."

"Coming right up." Shaun rummaged through the drawer. He found the box of rubbers and a bottle of lube. Man, she was prepared. He noticed the photograph of

Brian, Channon and him together. He hadn't doubted her desire for them, but seeing the old picture made him more confident. He handed her one of the condoms.

"Thanks." She grinned. "Told you I never forgot." She took the rubber from him and scooted down Brian's legs long enough to sheathe him.

"We didn't doubt you," Brian said. He guided her onto his cock and groaned as he slid inside her.

Shaun placed his hand on her back, letting her know he was still there and to let them build a rhythm. He refused to rush her. He dribbled lube onto his fingers.

"Ready?" Shaun asked. When she nodded, he toyed with the pink pucker of her ass. He eased his middle finger in, one knuckle at a time until she relaxed. "Breathe and bear down on me."

Beneath her, Brian kissed and held her. She whimpered, causing Shaun to slow down. Power radiated through Shaun. He could bring her the utmost pleasure. At the same time, he felt powerless—he couldn't resist her if he'd tried.

He moved his finger, in and out of her ass. He added extra lube to keep from hurting her. With each groan and grunt she made, she nudged him closer to coming apart. He needed her like he needed his next breath. He worked his index finger alongside his middle finger in her ass, opening her.

He massaged her lower back with his free hand. "So beautiful," he murmured. "So ready and so sexy. Want me in here?" He waggled his fingers. "Ready?"

"Uh-huh," she managed.

"Bear down on me." Shaun removed his fingers from her hole, then rolled the condom down his dick. He drenched his cock in lube. "Take me in, babe." He lined his erection up with her ass and pushed. "Breathe."

As she accepted him into her body, she blew his mind. Fuck, the fit was tight. His thoughts melted into nothing. Hell, the rest of the world melted away except for her and Brian and the way they made him feel.

He groaned. As Brian pulled out, Shaun pushed into her body. When Brian thrust into her, Shaun eased back. Between them, they built a steady rhythm. Holy fuck, this wouldn't take long.

Sweat slicked on Shaun's skin and his heart pounded. His dick throbbed. A groan ripped from his throat. "Oh fuck, I'm there."

"God damn it. I am, too," Brian cried. He increased the speed of his thrusts. "Oh Jesus."

Channon shivered and tensed. She buried her face against Brian's neck and moaned. "I need to come."

Shaun trembled and stuffed his cock deep into her ass. His restraint shattered. He curled over her and added a couple of more pushes into her body as the orgasm crashed within him. He groaned from deep in his soul. Beneath him, Channon shivered and came. Her ass tightened around his dick. Brian slapped her ass and moaned.

"Fucking balls, that felt good." Brian sagged on the bed. "Damn."

Shaun had to agree, even if he couldn't vocalize it. He rested his forehead on her back and gasped for breath. He'd been convinced before that she belonged to them, but now the idea was cemented in his mind. He braced his knees against the side of the bed until his world stopped spinning.

After a few moments, he eased his dick from her ass and stood. He ditched the condom in the wastebasket. "Babe, that was… I'm speechless."

"Exactly." She eased off Brian's thighs and collapsed on the bed. "I'm sore in good ways."

"I'm sleepy as fuck." Brian snorted, and sat up long enough to ditch the condom. He fell back against the bed and reached for her. "Come here, you."

"You belong to us now." Shaun cuddled up to her on the other side and kissed her neck. "You own us, babe, and you're between us, right where you belong."

"We're beside you all the way." Brian draped his arm across her belly. "We love you, Channon."

"I always have, really. But Jack's gone, right?" She tensed. "Like gone, gone?"

"He's not coming back. He assumed we'd slept together and he said he couldn't handle a woman who cheated." Brian shrugged. "Can't cheat if you're not together. Besides, he wasn't going to get your property, so that deterred him. If he does come back, we'll call the law."

"What a relief." She sighed and settled.

"I love you both of you and you're who I want." She snuggled up to her men and sighed.

Shaun closed his eyes. He'd found the love of his life with the woman who owned his heart. He had his best friend and his girl between them, where she belonged.

HEALING HER COWBOY

MOLLY ANN WISHLADE

Dedication

For my one true love. XXX

Chapter One

"Well, would you look at that! Jack's back from town and accompanied by a person of interest, if I'm not mistaken."

Barrett Thorne followed the direction of Clayton Quinn's pointing finger. He squinted against the late spring sunshine to better make out the approaching vehicle. It was Jack Quinn's battered red pickup truck all right. He couldn't make out who was inside, but gathered from his best friend's reaction that it must be someone significant. Perhaps it was a new guest, some minor celebrity or other come to spend an exciting two weeks at the Moonglow Dude Ranch, or maybe it was Clayton's latest planned conquest come to visit the ranch for a date. Barrett shrugged. He had neither time nor patience to indulge Clayton if it was the latter, so he turned to walk away but was stopped by a strong hand on his shoulder.

"Hey, Barrett. Don't you want to say hello to the new arrival?"

Barrett froze and took a deep breath. He really had *no* interest at all in who was coming to the ranch, especially if it was a member of the fairer sex. *Especially* if it was another of Clayton's disastrous attempts to try to set Barrett up. He'd told his friend countless times that he wanted nothing to do with women, not now or ever, after what Cara had done to him. Trouble was, it seemed that just as Barrett had no intention of getting into anything again, Clayton had no intention of paying any heed to his protests. He sighed, releasing the air he'd slowly sucked in. "No, Clayton, I don't want to say hello. I've work to do."

"Not even to my little sister?" Clayton asked. "It's

been a while since you last saw her. Hell, it's been a while since I last saw her!" Clayton gave a chuckle, then flung a heavy arm around Barrett's shoulder and led him toward the ranch's reception cabin.

Clayton was, and always had been, a good friend to Barrett, but sometimes he didn't realize how heavy-handed he could be. Had Barrett not been so big himself, he was sure he'd have struggled to accept Clayton's clumsy, tactile ways. He'd wondered at times how Clayton was so successful with women, but then he guessed some women liked their men to act like large, wild bears.

As they approached the wooden cabin that served as the dude ranch's reception, Barrett's stomach gave a flip. He was damned if he knew why. Sure, he hadn't seen Summer Quinn in a long, long time, but she'd never been anything other than his best friend's younger sister. His memories of Summer were fond ones, but not in a romantic way. The last he could remember, she'd been a scrawny tomboy with straw-blonde hair that she'd always braided close to her head, and a splatter of freckles over her nose and cheeks. She'd had the potential to grow into a pretty, perhaps even beautiful woman, but that had seemed a long way off and hadn't been something that Barrett had ever considered too deeply. He knew he'd have done everything in his power to protect Summer from harm—she was as good as family—but that was where his feelings ended. *Honestly.* She was within his friendship circle and he saw her, really, or at least he'd seen her in the past, as one of the guys.

So why did I miss her so much when she went away to college? He shrugged the thought away.

Barrett and Clayton climbed the wooden steps and waited on the porch as the truck stopped. Jack got out, went round and removed a stuffed holdall and a rather scruffy green rucksack from the back. Dangling from the rucksack by their joined laces was a pair of battered brown hiking boots. *Still a bit of a tomboy then...*

Barrett lifted a hand to shade his eyes as the passenger door swung open and a pair of dark red cowboy boots landed firmly on the ground, causing dust particles to drift into the air. He watched with growing interest as the boots gave way to tight denim that clung to curvy thighs and hips. It was not the body he recalled seeing when Summer had returned from college for the Christmas holidays. That must have been during her final semester, and Barrett realized that he hadn't laid eyes on her since, so that would be about seven years ago. Above the jeans was a baggy white T-shirt that hung off one shoulder, exposing a lacy black bra strap and an ample chest. His heartbeat quickened and he swallowed hard, wanting to look away but unable to do so. That wasn't the girl he remembered. Clayton must've been mistaken about her coming home today.

"Close your mouth, Barrett!" Clayton chided. "That's my baby sister you're gawking at."

Barrett forced his teeth together, but he couldn't pull his eyes from the vision of loveliness that now sashayed toward him and Clayton.

Summer Quinn.

All grown up.

And surprisingly, he couldn't deny it, into a beautiful, shapely woman.

As she approached, she swung her hips gently and the wind toyed with the mane of wavy blonde hair that she'd pulled over one shoulder. Barrett watched her smile in recognition as she spotted him and Clayton waiting on the porch, and he noted how her green eyes glowed like emeralds lit from within. Summer was a beauty, no doubt about it, and right now he was struggling to drag his eyes away from her. In fact, he was getting stirrings in his groin that he hadn't felt in some time.

But suddenly he went as cold as if a cloud had passed over the sun.

It didn't matter how beautiful she was. Hell, she could be Miss World for all he cared. There were two reasons

205

why Barrett would never be interested in Summer Quinn — firstly, she was his best friend's little sister and secondly, Barrett had no intention of getting involved in any kind of relationship again.

Summer smiled as she climbed the wooden steps. It was good to be home, despite her concerns that it would be a mistake. Clayton opened his muscular arms and swept her into a bear hug, turning her in a circle and lifting her right off her feet. She laughed and tapped his arm to indicate that he should put her down.

"Clayton! Cut it out!" She was breathless after being squeezed so tightly. As she stepped back, she glanced at her brother's companion. "I thought I recognized you..."

Barrett nodded and offered a small smile, but Summer noted how it didn't reach his eyes. "Summer." His voice was deep and masculine, and it sent tiny shivers through her entire body.

"How are you?" she asked, suddenly wishing she could pop to the ladies' room to freshen up and brush her hair. She'd had a long journey, and she was conscious that she probably didn't look her best, though why she was even worrying about it right now was beyond her. This was just Barrett Thorne, her big brother's best friend and childhood playmate. Their folks had been close, and after they'd died in a car crash when Barrett was a teenager, he'd basically moved in at the ranch. This man was once the boy she'd climbed trees with, raced horses with and competed with in just about every physical activity they could think of, from swimming to running. There'd been a connection between them, but over the years she'd convinced herself that it had just been a youthful exuberance that they'd shared, that the way her heart had flipped when she thought about him was just down to nostalgia for home. Their friendship had been a long time ago, anyway, in a period of innocence, when beating a boy in a race had been all she'd cared about, all she had needed to drop off to sleep with a smile on her face.

That had been before she found out that falling in love with a man could be dangerous, and that heartbreak was about the worst thing she could ever imagine.

"Can't complain." Barrett shrugged, as if accustomed to brushing off unwelcome enquiries about his wellbeing.

Summer watched him carefully for a moment. "Are you here for long or just stopping by?"

Clayton had taken a step backwards and gestured at Summer by pulling a finger across his throat. She gave a small nod. Something had clearly happened to Barrett or he'd be on the rodeo circuit right now. In the past, he'd traveled far and wide to take part in competitions, occasionally returning to Moonglow for a few weeks at a time to help out. He'd been at the top of his game when she'd headed off to college. She'd been eighteen then and he was twenty-two—a young, strong, handsome cowboy with the build and stamina of an athlete. Even so, at thirty-two he still looked pretty fit, so she wondered again why he was here instead of competing in the arena that he loved.

"Come on, little sister, our mom'll be fit to burst by now. She's so excited that you're coming back. She's told all the guests, chewed their ears off, so it's not fair to keep the old girl waiting any longer."

Summer nodded and followed him out of the cabin and back into the sunlight. She gave Barrett a quick backwards glance as they walked across the yard toward the ranch house. Something was wrong with the tall, broad-shouldered cowboy and she was itching to find out exactly what it was, even though she knew it was really none of her business, and that she really shouldn't care one way or another.

After all, what did caring for a man do other than get you a broken heart and an agonizing dose of humiliation?

Chapter Two

Summer entered the big, old ranch house and breathed deeply of the familiar scents of home. Cinnamon. Pine. Cakes. Lemons. A strange combination perhaps, but for the Quinns, it was the smell that told of her mother's hobbies, and of a busy family ranch house where people were fed and watered, where understanding came freely and there was always a warm welcome.

Her throat ached as she eyed the photographs pinned to every spare inch of wall and adorning every surface from shelves to tables. Her mother was a proud matriarch who loved her family fiercely. Summer had been away a long time, leaving for college in New York at eighteen, and even after she graduated, she'd only returned for a few annual visits. Those trips to Moonglow had never left her feeling as satisfied as she'd expected. They'd felt rushed, uncertain and anxious, because she'd always been eager to return to the Big Apple, keen to get back to her boyfriend, Luke, and her burgeoning career in the city. At the time, she hadn't been able to quite put her finger on why she'd needed to be with Luke so badly. Now she knew. Somewhere, deep down, she'd suspected him of cheating whenever she was away, and now she knew for certain that he'd never honored their commitment. Luke had preferred to indulge himself with a variety of women whenever Summer was absent. And sometimes when she was present.

Then there'd been the other matter, lurking at the back of her mind, only banished by keeping busy and trying to forget—her feelings for Barrett that surfaced more vividly than ever when she returned to the sweet air of the Pocono mountains.

But now she was home and in no rush to return to New York. Luke was long gone and so was her belief in love and the possibility of happy ever after.

Summer followed Clayton into the large, open-plan kitchen-diner and was greeted by the delicious smells of pancakes, eggs and bacon. Her mother hurried over to her and hugged her tightly. "Oh, Summer, how I've missed my baby girl!" Summer breathed in her mother's apple-pie fragrance and smiled as Helen leaned back to look at her. "I swear you're more beautiful than ever. A little skinny but we'll soon fatten you up."

Summer laughed. "Skinny is one thing I am not, Mom!" Her cheeks glowed as her mother eyed her from top to toe. One of Luke's complaints had been that she'd grown too curvy and that he preferred her more slimline. It had hurt and battered her confidence, but being in the city and working long hours at her desk job meant that she wasn't as active as she'd once been. She'd tried to pull on her hiking boots and walk around the blocks, but it had been difficult to find time to fit exercise in. So, yes, she had put on a few pounds, but she hadn't minded her new shape. Growing up, she'd been like a beanpole, and her only curves were her knobbly knees, so when she'd begun to develop a more female form, she'd been secretly pleased. However, when Luke had complained about it, she'd become a bit self-conscious. In contrast, outside just moments ago, when Barrett had looked at her… She'd seen what she could only describe as approval in his big, brown eyes, and she was sure he'd even licked his lips. Maybe she was imagining things. Barrett was just a family friend. Last she'd heard he'd married one of those groupies who followed the rodeo, the type who was manicured to perfection and eager to share in his fame. Summer was the complete opposite of such women. She barely even applied a lick of lipstick, preferring to feel the sun and the wind on her skin. Summer loved the exhilaration of thundering along on horseback, and the exhaustion that came from mucking out a stable and emerging covered in hay and dust, smelling like horses and leather. The thought made her chest ache and she rubbed a hand over her heart. She had been too long away from home, too long away from the people and lifestyle she loved, too long pretending to be someone she was not.

Too long acting like I don't care for Barrett?

"Well, I've made your favorite blueberry pancakes, and there's a pot of coffee ready, so let's sit down and you can fill me in on what happened between you and that boyfriend you sacrificed so much for." It was as if her mother could read her mind.

Summer nodded and took a seat, but as her mother placed a large steaming mug and a plate laden with food in front of her, it wasn't Luke she wanted to talk about. She had questions of her own about a tall, dark-eyed cowboy with a solemn air she didn't recall him displaying before.

* * * *

"So you found out Luke was cheating?" Helen asked Summer, as she gazed at her across the large, pine table.

Summer nodded. "With Georgia—my boss at the magazine."

"But how did they even meet?"

"At the magazine's third anniversary party. Georgia insisted that we hold a large party to celebrate and I took Luke along." She could picture him now, so different from the men she'd grown up around, in their jeans, shirts and boots, always tan from being outdoors, smelling of fresh air, horses and leather. Luke had been groomed, meticulously so, from his Armani suits to his expensive haircuts and exclusive aftershaves. He'd been a tall, slim, golden-haired Adonis, and she'd doted on him. For a while. He'd been a distraction, perhaps, from her old feelings for Barrett. But even before she'd found out about the affair, she'd known that something was missing from their relationship. Her doubts had grown in strength just after her father died, when Luke wouldn't make the effort to accompany her to the funeral or to stay at her childhood home for a few days. He didn't like spending time outdoors, preferring to work out in air-conditioned gyms in the basements of tower blocks, rather than taking a brisk walk in the fresh air, or heading out of the city to enjoy some peace and quiet in a more rural setting. Summer loved New York with its vibrant cosmopolitan buzz, but she was a country girl at heart and she missed riding horses, rounding up cattle and feeling the ache in her limbs that came after a day of manual labor.

"If I ever see him again I swear I'll..." Helen ground her teeth.

"Not if I see him first," Clayton added.

"And if I ever catch up with him, he'll be sorry he ever laid eyes on you," Jack growled as he entered the kitchen and helped himself to coffee.

Summer's heart fluttered and she swallowed hard. Here she was, home and safe, surrounded by people who loved her. The remaining Quinn siblings were currently absent from the farm—her brothers Henry and Jordan had gone to purchase some new horses, and her sister Lulu was staying with a friend in Las Vegas—but knowing that Jack, Clayton and her mother were close made Summer feel more secure than she had in years.

Why have I stayed away so long?

She knew the answer to that one.

For love of a man who could never really love me in return.

Am I thinking about Luke or Barrett?

"I guess he thought he was too good for us, never wanting to accompany you when you came home, but seems he just wasn't interested in becoming part of the family," her mother spoke softly. "Your father..." Her eyes filled with tears and Summer reached across the table and took her mother's cool, callused hand. It was the hand of a woman who'd worked hard all her life, but had never shied away from that work, always putting her family and the ranch she'd inherited from her father, and his father before him, first. "Your father never did think Luke was good enough for you. He said there was something not quite right about him, that he never looked him straight in the eye the way an honest man would."

Summer nodded. Her father's death a year ago had been a shock to them all. At fifty-eight, he'd been outwardly fit and healthy, but he'd died from an aortic aneurysm, a 'ticking time bomb' the doctor had called it. Summer had returned for his funeral, but been unable to stay long as work and Luke had needed her in New York. Or she'd kidded herself that Luke had needed her. Being at the ranch after her father's death had been unbearable, and she'd needed to escape as soon as possible. Now she was back, she could feel her father's absence at the ranch. Guilt overwhelmed her, as she thought of how her mother and her siblings had dealt with this sense of loss every day, unable to forget that Cullen Quinn was gone, his vacant chair, empty saddle and unfilled boots a constant painful reminder.

"I'm so sorry I haven't been here. I should have come home sooner."

"You're here now, sweetheart, and that's all that matters. You children all have your own lives to lead. Some of you choose to live them here and some of you live them elsewhere, but that's natural. Your father and I didn't expect you all to stay and help out with the family business."

Summer opened her mouth to say more, to tell her mother that she was back for good, but something stopped her. What if she was wrong in leaving New York and all that it had to offer? Yes, she'd left Luke and the apartment they'd shared for six years and she'd quit her job, after finding out about her boss's affair with Luke and after learning that Georgia hadn't been the first woman he'd cheated with, but still… She *could* carve out a life there. Find a way forward. She just wasn't sure that it was what she wanted anymore. She'd stayed on a friend's sofa for the past two months, and it had been tough, but she could find another place. Make it a home. Couldn't she?

"How long are you staying?" Clayton asked, as if reading Summer's thoughts.

"I'm...not sure yet. But at least a week. Perhaps longer." She chewed her lip. Better to allow herself some time to think, before telling them she'd quit her job and that she was thinking of staying on in Pike County — just in case she changed her mind. She didn't want to cause them any more hurt than they'd already been through this last year.

"Well, while you're here, just as well make yourself useful!" Clayton drained his mug, then stood and grinned at her. Summer returned the smile. It was the Quinn family motto — 'If you're home, you're working,' and she was looking forward to it. If she kept busy, she'd have less time to dwell on what had gone wrong between her and Luke, less time to ponder about how she thought she was in love with a man she really didn't know that well at all. Because, when she'd really evaluated their relationship, she'd realized that she hadn't loved Luke as she'd wanted to. As she'd tried to. His cheating had just confirmed that for her. And now she was home, she could be herself again, think about what she really wanted from her life in the bosom of her family.

"Sure thing, brother!" Summer tucked her chair under the table, then took her plate to the sink. It was good to be back, and she intended to enjoy it, especially if it meant finding out what Barrett Thorne was like after all these years. Would he be like some of the other arrogant rodeo assholes, full of himself and his prowess, or would he be the same old Barrett she'd once known so well? The Barrett she'd once harbored a huge crush on, that she'd never told anyone about — not even her mother. The Barrett she'd loved in her young, innocent way.

She realized that she was looking forward to finding out if Barrett was still the sweet, funny and thoughtful guy she'd once known. Though she knew full well she shouldn't be thinking along those lines at all.

Chapter Three

Barrett guided the afternoon trail ride and enjoyed the warmth of the sun on his skin. Easy pleasures, free pleasures, pleasures without any risk.

He listened to the gentle chatter of the two families who'd signed up for the hour-long trek through the Poconos, picking up on their excitement as they admired the picturesque scenery. He'd ridden the trail hundreds of times before, but the sheer beauty of the land never ceased to lift him. He realized that he could spend his days at Moonglow and never tire of the cowboy lifestyle. Sure, he couldn't take part in the rodeo again, but it didn't mean his life was over right?

Just life as I once knew it.

He missed the excitement, if he was completely honest about it — the adrenaline coursing through his veins and the sheer thrill of facing death, then leaving him empty-handed as he successfully competed time after time. But that last time, just over a year ago, he'd nearly been a goner, and he knew that one more bump to the head could be the end of him. The daredevil in him wanted to tempt fate, especially since Cara'd upped and left him. After all, who would care if he lived or died? But something in him, a soft, low voice that reminded him of his mother's, repeated that all life was valuable and that he'd be a fool to risk even a moment of the time he'd been given. Look at what had happened to the Quinns... Losing Cullen like that had left a gaping hole in their midst. It was a stark reminder to Barrett that life was short and he'd better value what he had. And now... Knowing that Summer was back had him feeling all mixed up. She'd only arrived a few hours ago, but her presence at the ranch had altered something and he wasn't quite sure what it was.

A whinny from the rear of the trail dragged him from his thoughts, and he turned in his saddle to peer backwards. His heart leapt as he saw a familiar figure astride a chestnut-brown mare. The rider trotted past the two families, her red-blonde hair a mane of fire lit by the afternoon sun. As she reached Barrett's side, Summer slowed her horse and fell into stride with him. He tilted his Stetson forward to offer his eyes some privacy as he admired her female form. He couldn't get over how full-figured she was now, how feminine and desirable. Hell, if she'd returned as the flat-chested, narrow-hipped girl he remembered, he'd have been able to respond to her in the platonic way he used to, but this beautiful woman she'd become had a rousing effect on his body and his mind.

"Hey, Barrett!" She leaned over and tapped his leg. Her touch sent blood straight to his cock. He shifted in the saddle.

"Hey yourself, Summer."

"I hope you don't mind me joining you on the trail. It's so long since I've been out here and I really wanted to take in the view."

"It's pretty spectacular."

"You know, it always lifts me." *My thoughts just moments ago.* "I don't know how I've coped for so long without seeing it."

I'm wondering how I've coped for so long without seeing you. He bit his lip to stop the comment popping out of his mouth. *Damn it!* He'd been certain since his wife walked out on him that he could do this, stay celibate and calm, needing nothing more than the active ranch life that wore him out, and a pillow to lay his head on at night, but Summer Quinn stirred him just by being there. He'd have to pull himself together. "So, where's that city boyfriend of yours then? Too busy to make the trip again?" He saw a shadow pass over her face and instantly regretted being so forthright.

"We, uh...broke up."

"Oh, girl, I'm sorry to hear that."

"It's okay." She flashed him a smile. "He was an asshole."

Barrett pushed his hat back a bit so he could see her better. She was still in jeans, but she now wore a checked shirt on top—the Moonglow ranch worker's unofficial uniform—and it was tied in front, above her belt. It was unbuttoned just low enough for him to make out the swell of her breasts. He had a sudden urge to pull her from her horse and bury his face in her soft white flesh.

What's wrong with me?

He cleared his throat. "He *was* an asshole. That time I met him, when he deigned to come out here, I thought he was a total jerk. Couldn't even ride!"

Summer laughed. "Nope. He couldn't ride."

"Ain't a man if he can't ride a horse." Barrett shook his head.

"He liked riding other things, though. Too much." Summer scowled and shook her pretty head. Barrett watched her from the corner of his eye. "He was cheating."

"I gathered that much. The horses didn't seem too keen on him and they're intuitive creatures. Reckon they knew he was bad...or at least that he was bad for you."

They rode in silence for a bit, and Barrett wondered what he should say. He wasn't real good at consoling people. He'd been through it himself but what was the appropriate platitude? *Sorry? Want me to go rip his balls off for you? Bet the other woman's just a whore?* Sometimes, words just didn't seem right for some situations. Barrett was a physical man, a man who knew how to use his body and hands to get a job done, whether that was fixing a fence, holding on to a bucking bull, pleasing a woman or calming a nervous horse. If he had the chance, he felt sure he could soothe Summer's hurts and help her to see what a desirable woman she was. *But I can't! She's Clayton's sister and my old friend. I have to keep my distance.*

Besides, what made him think she'd even want to have his hands all over her, especially now that he was damaged goods? What did he have to offer anymore? That was why Cara had left him.

They rounded a bend and the trail opened out. Barrett turned to the families behind him, and Summer. "You can let loose a little if you'd like, now. Just take care, especially the less experienced riders. We'll be right behind you."

His comment was met with excited squeals from the teenaged girls and boys, and thanks from the adults then they moved on ahead. Barrett was left alone with Summer.

"Barrett?"

He stopped his horse and turned in the saddle to meet her clear green eyes. "Yeah?"

"Why're you here at Moonglow? I asked Clayton but he told me that if you wanted me to know, you'd tell me. You weren't here when I came back for my father's...funeral."

"I know, Summer, and I would've been if I could have. I wouldn't have missed the chance to say goodbye to your father. He was a good man, really good to me. Kind of like a father after my own pa...you know."

Barrett stared deep into her eyes, and searched his mind for the right words to explain why he'd been absent, but they just evaded him. He didn't want to tell her that he was broken, injured by a fall that could've killed him. He didn't want to tell her that his wife had fled after she knew he'd never ride on the circuit again. He didn't want Summer to look at him in any other way than the way she did right now — with desire. He'd seen it in women's eyes before, and he knew what it meant. Summer had been hurt, she'd been sad, but she'd realized that it was time to mend and move on. She needed someone to help her with that. Sometimes, a good time with a man who aimed to please was all it took to get a woman feeling good about herself again. Barrett knew instinctively that he could do that for Summer. He could show her what a fine woman she was, and get her back to her best. But as she gazed at him in the warm afternoon, her hair a golden, her skin like fresh milk and her emerald eyes as clear as a pool, he realized that he didn't want to be just a good time to Summer Quinn. Because being just a good time to her would never be enough for him. This wasn't some stranger he'd met in a bar. This was a woman grown from a girl he'd cared about, and Barrett knew in that moment that if sex and emotions were thrown into the mix together, he'd be in deep, deep trouble.

And if she hurt him, he might never be able to heal.

Chapter Four

Summer took extra care with her appearance that evening, after her shower. She combed through her golden waves until they shone, then even put on some candy-pink lip-gloss, and a coat of mascara that she'd found at the bottom of one of her old drawers. They were holding a barn dance at the ranch as the evening's entertainment, and she was as excited as a girl as she thought of what lay ahead. Silly really, to be so full of anticipation, but her afternoon ride alongside Barrett had filled her with a sense of hope. He was so masculine, so calm, and so in control. He was the exact opposite of Luke and it excited her. Sure, years back, she'd done all the usual teenage things like signing her name as Summer Thorne and daydreaming about kissing Barrett, but now they were both all grown-up and he was, like her, single. That much she'd been able to elicit from Clayton, when she'd returned to the ranch after the trail ride. But Clayton was staying tight-lipped about Barrett's other reasons for being here.

Still, she had the evening to find out more.

She skipped down the stairs and found her mother waiting in the large open hallway.

"Oh, don't you look fine!" Helen Quinn enveloped her in a hug, and kissed her cheek. "You know, I'm so proud of you, Summer. Getting an important city job and writing such clever articles about fashion and celebrities for that online magazine."

Summer took a deep breath and smoothed her hands over her short denim skirt. She didn't want to deceive her mother, but she didn't want to ruin her illusions just yet.

Summer had been proud too, to get the coveted position at the magazine, but it hadn't turned out to be what she'd hoped it would. She'd soon become bored writing the same old articles about the latest shoes and bags, and craved the opportunity to write something grittier, something real. She longed to write about things she cared about, like horses and the rodeo, and the life of real people like her family. Even before Georgia had ruined things, Summer had known that she couldn't carry on writing about topics that held no interest for her. That she would have to make a change. But her mother was so proud, it was written all over her pretty face. How could Summer disappoint her by telling her that she'd walked out on her job to come home? And now, *after* her father had died. She wasn't even coming home to be near him. Her heart throbbed with sadness, and she had to gulp down some air before her grief overwhelmed her.

"What is it, honey?" Helen took Summer's face in her hands and stared deep into her eyes. "There's something you're not telling me."

Summer opened her mouth, suddenly feeling there was nothing to do other than confess, when she was saved by a shout from outside. She slipped from her mother's hold and hurried to the front door. As it swung wide, she grinned to find Clayton and Barrett standing before her in smart shirts and clean jeans. She could have been sixteen again, about to go out riding with her favorite guys.

"You two scrub up well."

"You don't look so bad yourself!" Barrett said, then he winked at her and she lowered her eyes as her cheeks burned. Why was she blushing? This was ridiculous.

"Come on, little sister! There's an empty barn awaiting your presence and some tourists needing entertaining. Let's go round them up and start the evening like we mean to have a good time."

Summer took his proffered hand, then followed him out into the balmy evening. Something brushed against her shoulder, and when she glanced back, she saw Barrett's hand. She took it in hers and walked across the yard between two men she'd grown up loving. Her big brother and his best friend.

Her heart filled with joy.

She could get used to this.

* * * *

"Here, you look like you need this!" Barrett shouted over the music, as he handed Summer a plastic cup of cider.

"Thank you!" She swallowed the drink down, savoring the sweetness of the homemade beverage. She raised her empty cup at Barrett and smiled. "It's good."

"Your family had a fantastic crop of apples last year. Your father would've..." Barrett bit his lip and his cheeks glowed.

Summer placed a hand on his arm. "It's okay. You *can* talk about him. In fact... I want to hear about him. I feel like I missed so much these past years."

Barrett nodded and stared at her hand, where it rested on his arm. What was he thinking?

Suddenly, her free hand was grabbed and she was pulled toward the dancing by one of the holidaymakers. She recognized him from the trail ride, a young man of about seventeen. He was tall and toned, and evidently confident. "You don't mind, do you?" he asked, his blue eyes sparkling.

She shook her head. "No, of course not!"

Summer laughed as they joined in with the dancing. Barrett twirled her, then lifted her and they skipped around the barn until she was breathless. She was partnered by different guests three times, and when a fourth man approached her, she was about to refuse and claim exhaustion, until she looked up and found Barrett staring down at her. She accepted his hand as the music slowed and the fiddler played an old cowboy tune that she recalled hearing in childhood. It was one of her father's favorites, a haunting melody that made images of her family and her life growing up in the Pocono Mountains more vivid than they had been in a long, long time. It was clear to her then that she had done the right thing returning and that this was where she wanted to be. Perhaps forever.

At first, Barrett held her left hand in his right one, his other hand gently resting on her hip, a few inches of air between them, and Summer craned her neck to look up into his brown eyes. But as they danced, round and round, their feet moving instinctively in time, he pulled her closer, until their bodies met from chest to groin. Summer was sure Barrett must be able to feel her heart thundering through her thin shirt. Her breasts were squashed against the wall of muscle that made up his torso, and longing pooled at her core, making her wet and hungry to for him. This was it then, the difference with being around Barrett as an adult. In their youth, they'd been friends, competitive, keen to impress each other. But now, all grown up, their relationship had morphed into something else, something affected by desire. If Summer had stayed at the ranch and seen Barrett regularly, would they have fallen deeply in love, him returning her feelings readily, and been together a long time already? Had Summer's absence and Barrett's rodeo career kept them from surrendering to this electricity that sparked between them now?

It was undeniable.

Magnetic.

Hypnotic in its intensity and Summer was breathless with need and emotion.

When the song ended, Barrett leaned down and whispered in her ear, "I need some air. Care to join me?"

"Sure." She couldn't say more, her throat was tight, her mouth dry. She saw her need reflected in his eyes and knew that their union was inevitable. That it had always been there on the horizon, waiting to happen when the time was right.

She followed Barrett out of the warm barn and into the

cool night air. She was glad that it wasn't as warm as it had been when they'd come out to the barn, because her skin was hot, her body tense and coiled. They walked away from the noise and toward the cabins where the ranch staff lived. Barrett lowered himself onto a bench on the porch of his cabin and patted the seat next to him.

"I'd forgotten how quiet it can be here at night," Summer said, needing to say something to fill the silence, needing to say something that might distract her from the thoughts currently running through her head. "Just the bush crickets and the occasional hoot of an owl."

"The quiet can be healing but it can also be deafening." Barrett ran a hand through his dark hair. Summer watched as it rippled away from his fingers.

"Deafening?"

He turned to her and took her hand between both of his. She gasped as heat flooded through her at this simplest of touches. How could he have such an effect on her when they'd never been intimate, never been more than just friends?

Because this is meant to be.

She shook her head at the thought. Was the cider that strong? Had it influenced her thoughts and awakened a need within her that she'd long since buried? Or was she right to believe that she'd loved Barrett all along? Another thought hit her.

Did I deliberately go so far away to college to get away from my feelings for Barrett Thorne? Did I deliberately fall for a man who was his exact opposite because I knew, deep down, that it would be doomed, that I would never be able to forget this man?

"Sometimes, when I'm out here alone at night, I crave some noise. Something just to pull me from my thoughts. But sometimes, I need the silence. I crave it."

"It's so different to the city. There's so much noise there and you kind of get used to it, but when I come home... I realize how good it is to be away from the hustle and bustle."

"Summer… It's really good to see you." He held her with his dark eyes, and she felt as if she was sinking into their depths. Her heartbeat was so quick, she thought she might faint and she closed her eyes for a moment to steady herself. He pulled her toward him and brushed his lips against hers.

"Sorry. I shouldn't have done that." She opened her eyes. He'd moved away and was staring out into the night. "I don't know why I did it. You're just so beautiful and…"

"It's okay, Barrett. That's been a long time coming."

He frowned.

"I've always wondered what it would be like to kiss you."

"You have?"

She nodded. "And more." She bit her lip. What was wrong with her? She'd sworn off men after Luke's betrayal, vowing that she'd never get involved again and here she was, a few hours after arriving home, throwing herself at her childhood friend, and being more honest with him than she'd ever been with Luke or with herself.

"More?" he croaked, and his eyes darkened.

What harm would it do? No doubt, Barrett would be off on the rodeo circuit again soon, so it wasn't as if Summer would have to see him every day. She'd desired this man for years and it seemed that he was attracted to her. So why couldn't she give herself this, a moment to enjoy, something to lift her, after she'd been left feeling so rejected and undesirable? Why couldn't she surrender to her need for Barrett and make love to him as she'd long dreamt of doing? "Barrett… I'd like to…" Her cheeks flushed and she struggled to say the words.

"Won't they miss us?" He nodded toward the barn, and as if in response, a few loud whoops and hollers came from inside.

"I doubt it. The dance is in full swing."

He paused for a moment. She watched as indecision played across his handsome features. Desire won and he got to his feet and pulled her into his arms. "My place or yours?"

She placed her hands on his broad chest and pushed him toward the cabin, then lowered her hand to his groin and cupped his erection. Summer *had* wanted this for a long time, she could admit it now, there was no point in denying it. And even if it only happened the one time, it would be something she could treasure forever.

Chapter Five

Summer closed the cabin door behind her, and took a deep breath. She was nervous as a virgin, but her body thrummed with need. Barrett switched on a bedside lamp, and she looked around the cabin. It held a bed, a wardrobe and a chest of drawers. One of her mother's homemade patchwork quilts covered the bed, while matching curtains hung at the two small windows. A small door just off the right wall led to an en suite bathroom. The employees of the ranch all ate up at the ranch house, so they didn't need their own kitchens, but there was a small communal kitchen-diner in the end cabin of the L-shaped block for those wanting a late night snack or coffee.

"Summer... Are you sure about this?" Barrett kicked off his boots and socks, then walked toward her and took her hands.

"I'm more certain than I've ever been about anything." And she was. Luke, New York, that life — it all seemed like a hundred years ago, and all she could think about was right here in this room.

"Then come here." His order sent need hurtling through her, and goosebumps rose all over her body.

Barrett tangled a large hand in her hair, then pulled her closer. His act was at once possessive yet controlled, as if he'd thought about doing this before, and Summer felt more wanted than she ever had.

As their lips met, he deftly unbuttoned her shirt and slid a hand inside, caressing her breasts. Her nipples hardened in response. He groaned, then pushed her shirt off her shoulders and kissed her neck and her shoulders then lowered his head and kissed her through the lace of her bra, sucking on her nipples until she cried out his name.

When he pulled at her bra straps, sliding them down her arms, Summer hurriedly undid Barrett's shirt and ran her hands over his smooth chest with its light covering of dark hair. When she moved lower, to his belt, he stopped her. "All in good time," he said. "Let me see you first."

He reached around her and undid her bra, then removed it as he moved backward. He licked his lips, and she glowed with pleasure. Her breasts were one of her best features, she knew it, and Barrett's approval was evident from the large bulge in his jeans. "You're so beautiful. Now take off your skirt."

Summer slid it down her legs, then stood before him in her small lace thong.

"And the rest," he ordered, and she obeyed.

When she stood straight again, Barrett growled, and Summer knew he was pleased with what he saw. That recent waxing had been worth it, leaving just a narrow strip of strawberry blonde curls over her mound. She felt gorgeous, female and desired.

Barrett loosened his belt, then removed his jeans and Summer gazed at his strong masculine form. When he removed his fitted trunks, his impressive cock sprang free, and she ached with longing to feel him inside her.

Barrett pushed her gently toward the bed, then laid her down and ran his big hands all over her body from her collar bones down to her toes. He kissed everywhere his fingers touched and Summer moaned. She opened her legs as he ran his tongue over her needy flesh and lifted her hips, offering herself to him.

When Barrett finally knelt between her thighs, Summer was panting with desire. He ran a fingertip over her clit and a jolt of pleasure shivered through her. She sighed as he pushed her farther onto the bed and spread her legs apart so she was totally exposed. As Barrett stared at her, his eyes dark, his cheeks flushed, he gripped his cock and placed it between her wet folds.

"I wanted to make you wait, Summer. I wanted to tease you some more but I can't… I need you now."

He stroked her wet lips with his erection and she wriggled, trying to encourage him to penetrate her.

"Protection!" He leaned over and rifled through a drawer in the bedside cabinet, then pulled out a condom. He rolled it onto his length, then returned to her.

"Take me, Barrett. I need you," she whispered, afraid that she would climax before he even got inside her. "Take me!"

He held her gaze for a moment, and Summer thought he'd changed his mind, but he pushed into her with one hard thrust. As he filled her and her muscles tightened around his girth, she hurtled over the abyss into the orgasm that had been hovering inside her since he'd first kissed her that evening.

* * * *

Barrett lay on his side watching Summer sleep. They'd made love twice before she'd surrendered to her exhaustion, but he was buzzing with energy. It was as if being with Summer, establishing that connection, had rebooted him and the dull haze that had hung around him since his accident had been burned away.

Was Summer Quinn the cure to his heartache? Was she the woman he'd been waiting for all along?

He shook his head. *Ridiculous thoughts!* He was sure it had more to do with seeing her after so long, and seeing what a beauty she'd grown into. Sure, they had a past, a friendship that went back years, but that didn't make for a fairytale relationship now did it?

He smiled as she sighed in her sleep, and her lashes fluttered gently. The quilt had slipped from her shoulder, exposing the tops of her breasts. Full, round, milky-white with pale, rosy areolae and ruby nipples at their core. Her long red-gold hair was spread out over the pillow and she reminded him of a painting he'd once seen of a fairy maiden—ethereal, too good for this world, this life.

Was Summer Quinn too good for him?

She stirred then, as if sensing that he was staring at her and smiled, her pink lips parting to expose her small, straight white teeth. "Hey, handsome." She stretched out her arms and the quilt fell to her waist. Barrett hardened instantly, his body telling him to take her again, make her his.

He flipped her onto her front, then lifted her hips and knelt behind her as he rolled a condom on. Her rounded bottom was smooth and welcoming. He ran his hands over her flesh then slid one hand between her legs. She was wet and ready, her pussy still swollen from their lovemaking. He slipped two fingers into her warmth, teasing her, and she pushed onto him, clearly wanting him as much as he did her.

"Barrett!" she whispered, as he entered her with his cock. He was so hard it hurt, and his balls ached to empty again. *So much cum!* It was as if he'd saved up a lifetime's worth all for Summer. He thrust into her, filling her time after time with his length, teasing her with the tip before pushing into her so deeply that his balls smacked against her pussy lips.

When she tightened around him as she came, and her juices flowed over his erection, he knew it was his turn, and he pulsed into her with one more thrust, finally spent.

Barrett slid out of Summer carefully and lay on his side, then pulled her into him, spooning her tightly against his body. With his hand over her fast-beating heart, he slipped into a deep and dreamless sleep.

Chapter Six

Summer waited until Barrett's breathing was slow and regular, then she slipped out of his embrace and quickly dressed. She gazed down at him, wanting to climb back into his arms, but knowing that she'd better get back to the house to be there when her family woke. She didn't need further complications right now. She already needed to explain that she intended to stay at the ranch, she didn't want her mother thinking it was because of Barrett.

She leaned over and gently kissed his cheek where the dark shadow of stubble was already beginning to show. He smiled and snuggled deeper beneath the quilt. As she watched him, she noticed a small white scar just above his left ear where the hair didn't seem to grow. How had she missed that before? He was a lot taller than her and he wore a hat most of the time outdoors, so it was no wonder she hadn't seen it. She reached out to touch the scar, then thought better of it. If she woke Barrett now, she'd struggle to leave him, and they'd be caught out.

She picked up her boots, then opened the door and closed it behind her. It was still dark, dawn was about an hour away, so folks at the ranch would soon be stirring. Time to get back to the house, and to pretend she'd been there all night, to pretend she hadn't just experienced the best night of her life.

* * * *

When Barrett woke again, it was light and he was cold. He reached out to find Summer's warmth, but she was gone, only an imprint of her body remaining.

He sat up in bed as loss overwhelmed him.

Gone!

Just like Cara.

But Summer wasn't Cara. She was different. Cara had abandoned him because he was no longer the rodeo star she'd wanted to be married to. He'd heard recently that she was now hanging on the arm of one of his rivals on the circuit, and although he'd experienced a pang of jealousy when he'd first heard the news, it hadn't developed into anything deeper. Cara had been a phase in his life. He'd thought he loved her but the woman he'd fallen for wasn't the woman she really was. Barrett had believed that Cara was caring, funny and sweet. In reality, she was shallow, hard and ambitious for fame.

On the other hand, Summer Quinn had a sweet and kind heart. He'd seen it in her still, the way she laughed at Clayton's stupid jokes and in how she'd graciously danced with the ranch guests and cooed over the younger children in the barn last night. Of course, it could all be a front, but Barrett felt in his gut that he wasn't wrong about her. There was an air of vulnerability about her that made him want to wrap her up in his arms and protect her. Add to that how fucking desirable she was and he could see that she was the whole package.

But how would the Quinns feel about him and Summer being an item? What did he have to offer her, now that he couldn't compete any longer? He wasn't even a partner at the ranch, just a casual employee. He had to have something to give, something to prove that he was a man she could rely on.

If she even wanted him—that was. He'd thought just yesterday that he'd try to show her how beautiful she was, to help her to move on from that cheating creep in New York, but he'd ended up feeling emotions he'd never expected. Emotions that he had no right experiencing at all, unless he could prove himself to be a worthy provider, someone who Summer could rely on. It might have seemed old-fashioned, but Barrett was the kind of man that had to have something to offer a woman.

His woman.

Summer Quinn.

* * * *

Summer pushed her eggs around her plate. She was so buzzed about the night's events that her stomach was a tight ball, and she could barely force down a mouthful of food. Instead, she swallowed the remainder of her coffee in one gulp, then refilled her mug.

Helen, Jack and Clayton had long since finished their breakfast. As Helen and Jack took care of the dishes and chatted to the ranch workers who'd come up to the house for their morning meal, Clayton sat next to Summer and took her hand.

"How you doing, Summer?"

She willed herself not to give anything away.

"I'm good. It's great being home."

"You had any thoughts about staying on this time?"

She met his questioning gaze, afraid that he'd see right through her, but she found only love and compassion.

"I...haven't said anything to Mom yet but I..." She chewed her lower lip.

"You quit your job, right?"

She nodded. "How'd you know?"

"Well, I know you, little sister. Perhaps better'n you think."

"I don't know what I'm going to do now, though, Clayton."

"There's always a place here for you. Mom would be thrilled to have you home."

"Are you sure?"

"We've got a family meeting scheduled for later today, so we can all discuss it then."

"Don't you think she'll be disappointed that I'm no longer the successful magazine journalist?" Summer's stomach flipped at the thought of letting her mother down.

"I think you'd be surprised at how much she's already guessed and... Well, I don't want to say too much but she has some ideas about where things could go from here. She might just actually need your help more than you realize." Clayton winked at her, then stood and held out a hand. "You coming to help out with the junior jumps?"

Summer smiled as she took his hand. "Of course!"

As she followed her brother from the house, she wondered what Barrett would think about her considering staying home. Would he be glad, or would he regret making love to her if he knew that she wasn't heading straight back to New York? After all, perhaps she was just a good time to him, a one-off.

But remembering his tenderness in the night and the way he'd held her so tightly as he drifted off to sleep, she found it hard to believe that he didn't see her as a whole lot more than a one-night stand.

* * * *

Barrett didn't go up to the house for breakfast or lunch, and he was famished by two in the afternoon. He'd made some toast in the employee kitchen-diner, but he was a working man and he needed more than that to fuel his body. Clayton had invited him up to the house for a meeting at two-thirty, so he hoped Helen would be serving up a snack then, or he might just have to wait until their evening meal.

He washed his hands and face in his bathroom, then changed his shirt. As he flung the used one in the wash basket, the image of Summer lying on his bed, legs akimbo, sprang into his mind and his cock hardened. He'd been with his share of women over the years but when he'd met Cara, he'd thought that was it, that she was the one. He'd been wrong about her, and he wondered now at how his feelings for Summer had burgeoned so quickly. Since seeing her just yesterday, he'd been filled with need and… hope. For the first time in a long time.

He frowned at his reflection. If there was a chance that he could make a go of things with Summer, then what could he give her? *Other than your love.*

Yet if Summer came home for good, he knew things at the ranch could improve again. She was like a breath of warm flower-scented air, lightening hearts and minds, stirring loved ones to smile and laugh again. It wasn't that the Quinns had wallowed in misery the last year, but something had been missing and Barrett was convinced since he'd seen the Quinns' reaction to Summer's return, that she could be the key to their healing.

Hell, to his own healing too.

But would she want to stay? She had a good job in the city, a life there to live. Did Moonglow have enough to offer her? Did Barrett have enough to offer her?

He tucked his shirt into his jeans, then left his cabin and walked up to the house. As he climbed the steps he could hear Summer's laughter, tinkling like a brook over stones, and he smiled.

Summer had come.

Chapter Seven

The Quinns sat on the sofas in the lounge, Helen in Cullen's old armchair before the fireplace. They were smiling and talking, and only Summer looked up as Barrett walked in.

He nodded at her and she grinned, her nose scrunching up and her cheeks coloring slightly.

Damn, she's beautiful!

"Hey, Barrett!" Jack said, as Barrett sat on the sofa next to Clayton.

"So I guess we're all here." Helen folded her hands in her lap. "I've spoken to the others—Henry, Lulu and Jordan—and informed them about my ideas and they're in agreement as long as you guys are."

Barrett watched Helen's face carefully, suddenly terrified that she was going to sell the ranch, or even send him packing. He scanned his actions over the past few weeks, had he done something wrong? Had he upset a guest or missed a job?

"Mom…" Summer broke into his thoughts. "I have something to tell you."

Helen gazed at her daughter, and Barrett's stomach lurched. Was she going to tell them about last night?

"Go on, honey."

"I'm not going back to New York. I mean…I am but only to get the rest of my things."

Helen paused for a moment, then smiled broadly. "I had a feeling this was coming."

"You don't mind. You're not disappointed?"

Helen shook her head. "Of course not! You think I'm not thrilled at the thought of having all my brood back here under my roof?"

"But...you were so proud of me getting the job at the magazine."

Barrett watched Summer carefully. He wanted to grab her and hug her and kiss her.

She's staying!

"Summer, I'd be proud of you if you swept the streets. Honey, I love you all so much—you too, Barrett—and yes I thought it was wonderful that you were making a go of things in the city, but I did wonder how you managed without horses and fresh air and...and space." Helen laughed then, and Summer visibly relaxed.

"In fact, Summer," Clayton broke in, "that's one of the things we wanted to talk about." He nodded at his mother.

"Yes. We need to move forward, you know, with the business and we've got a website, but it really needs updating. We also need new ways to appeal to tourists and a blog might be the way to go."

"And a newsletter," Jack added.

"You have a talent, Summer. So as long as staying is what you want, we'd like you to run the website, the blog and to send out a monthly newsletter. If you'd be happy doing that?" Helen raised her eyebrows at her daughter.

Barrett held his breath as Summer looked around the room. Her face was blank as she contemplated her family's suggestions, then she clapped her hands together. "I'd love to! This is perfect! I can write about the things I love and live back here...where I belong."

Barrett's heart slowly sank to his boots. Summer had a role here, a purpose. That was wonderful news, but what did he have? He'd been a casual worker since his accident but he needed some security himself. Perhaps he should think of moving on. He knew he wouldn't be able to bear being around Summer and not having her in his arms. What if he'd been a one night thing to her? After all, he was damaged goods. He couldn't even go out on the rodeo and prove himself to her again.

"And, Barrett?" Helen made him jump with her somber tone.

"Helen."

"We have a proposition for you too."

"You do?"

"I'm signing the business over to the kids."

Barrett swallowed hard. He'd suspected that something like this would happen sooner or later. It was a way of giving them security, and he knew that since Cullen's passing, Helen had been more aware of her own mortality.

"Obviously, though," Helen continued, "I'm sticking around for as long as there's breath in my body!" She grinned then, and Barrett nodded. "But you're like a son to me, Barrett. You know, Cullen loved you as if you were one of his own. You've always been around, ever since you and Clayton were knee high. I see you as one of my own and I know that Cullen would've wanted you provided for too. Since your...accident, I know things have been tough for you."

Barrett hung his head. He hadn't spoken much about it to anyone, but losing the ability to act as he had before that final fall had left him scarred physically and emotionally.

"However, I want you to become a more permanent member of the ranch. Give you something to keep you around. You need security as much as the rest of us do, even though you're too macho at times to admit it." She winked at him.

Barrett scanned the Quinns and found them all smiling.

"Barrett, we want you to accept a partnership in Moonglow. You'll be equal with my other children. You're as valuable a worker — as valued a family member — as they are, so we want this to be your home too." Helen perched on the edge of the chair and stared at Barrett. He opened his mouth, needing to say something, anything, but he couldn't find any words.

Seconds passed, feeling like hours. The clock on the mantle ticked loudly, reminding him that he needed to reply. *Say something. Anything.* But his chest hurt and his head ached. He was overwhelmed and he needed air. He leaped to his feet and coughed out, "Excuse me!"

Then he left the house and ran down the steps toward the stables. He couldn't believe what he'd just been offered and he needed some space to let it sink in.

* * * *

Summer stared at the open door that Barrett had just disappeared through. She wanted to chase him, but she didn't know if she should. Surely, her mother's offer was a good thing?

"Mom? What..." Summer's throat closed over and she swallowed hard, on the edge of tears.

"I thought it might be a bit much for him," Helen said, as she stared at her children.

"He'll come round," Clayton said. "It just surprised him is all."

"Are you sure?" Helen asked.

Clayton nodded.

"Is he okay?" Summer asked, directing her question at Clayton, as Barrett's closest friend.

Clayton held her gaze and Summer's heart thundered at his serious expression. "He's had a rough time of it, Summer. A really hard year."

"I know... I mean, I know some of it. But what hasn't he told me?"

"His accident in the rodeo back last year was almost fatal. He was thrown from a bull and he took a blow to the head. It mightn't have been so serious for any other rider, but as he's suffered so many bumps and breaks in his time, the doctors told him that one more could be the end of him. And if it didn't kill him, he could end up with brain damage and unable to walk, talk or take care of himself."

Summer gasped and tears sprang into her eyes. "So his career ended."

"He couldn't even make it to Pa's funeral. He was in the hospital and we wondered for a while if we'd be going to his funeral too."

"You didn't tell me about this!"

"How could we?" Helen asked. "You were dealing with your father's loss. How could we add to that by worrying you about Barrett? You were so close growing up."

Summer nodded, understanding their reasons yet angry that she hadn't known, somehow, instinctively that Barrett had been so close to death.

"Then Cara left him when he was still healing," Clayton added.

"How did he take it?" Summer asked, afraid to hear the answer.

"He was quiet, for a long time," Clayton said. "Couldn't get much out of him. He healed physically, just a scar on his scalp to show for it, but I'm not sure how he feels about Cara now. I've tried to set him up a few times, but he won't have anything to do with women. First time I've seen his face light up was when you arrived yesterday." Clayton flashed Summer a knowing smile and she blushed. Had their attraction been that obvious?

And now… Summer had a chance to rebuild her own life in the heart of her family and on the land she loved. Barrett had an opportunity here too. He could be a partner, stay on at the ranch. He didn't need to leave and neither did she.

"I'll go talk to him," Clayton said as he stood.

"Let me go." Summer pushed herself off the sofa. "Please."

"Summer? Is there something else going on here?"

Summer met her mother's curious eyes, and tried to shake her head but she couldn't. She couldn't lie to the people she loved. "It's complicated."

"Well, as long as you take care, sweetheart, you have my blessing. I love you all and just want you to be happy. Life's too short not to grab what you want with both hands."

Summer nodded.

"Well go on, then!" Helen waved at Summer and Clayton

followed her onto the porch.

"I always knew you two would be good for each other."

Summer glanced at him, wanting to feel relief that her family were letting her know that they would approve of her and Barrett—if that *was* what they both wanted. But right now, she didn't know if she was what Barrett wanted. He'd been hurt and she needed to find him. She'd love him no matter what, she knew that, and her heart ached for what he'd suffered. But her mother had always said that life wasn't easy, it was a series of jumps all lined up to test even the most experienced rider.

Barrett couldn't risk another fall.

Summer wanted to reassure him that she wouldn't let him fall, ever again.

Chapter Eight

Summer squeezed the horse's flanks with her feet, encouraging the chestnut mare to hurry. She thought she might know where Barrett had gone. She hoped she was right.

She slowed the horse as she neared the clearing, and listened carefully. She could hear the waterfall, flowing crisp and cool down the mountainside into the pool where she'd spent hours swimming and diving and messing around as a child. Always accompanied by her siblings. And by Barrett. A whinny nearby told her that there was someone else here.

She slid her leg over the mare, then jumped down and tethered the reins to a tree. After checking the horse was secured, she followed the small rocky path into the clearing and saw Barrett's horse grazing near the pool.

Then she stopped and stared.

On a ledge of the waterfall, standing right in the flow, was Barrett. His head was bowed as if he was deep in thought, allowing the water to wash him clean, to clear his mind.

He was naked.

Muscular.

Perfection.

A sigh escaped her lips, and her whole body flooded with heat.

She pulled off her clothes and approached the pool, staring at Barrett. As if sensing her arrival, he looked up.

They gazed at each other, and Summer's heart threatened to leap from her chest. She walked into the pool, shivering as the icy water caressed her skin. When she was immersed to her waist, Barrett leaped from the ledge and dived in, causing ripples to rush toward Summer. They lapped at her body, the water splashing her breasts and turning her nipples into hard, rosy peaks.

She gasped as Barrett grabbed her hips, then emerged in front of her. As he stood, his sleek, wet body pressed against hers, and his erection pressed against her stomach.

"Barrett..."

"Shhh!" He covered her mouth with his and silenced her, kissing her hard, plundering her mouth with his own. Then he lifted her and wrapped her legs around his waist so that his cock pressed between her folds then slid inside her, filling her and making her whole.

They stood like that, barely moving, just holding on.

And Summer *knew* that she was in love. That she had always been in love. That Barrett was everything she had ever wanted and needed.

As if reading her thoughts, Barrett hugged her tighter, then waded toward the bank. He lowered them both to the ground so that he was under Summer then he lay down on the grass.

"Barrett. I know what happened to you. I know what you've been through."

"I want to be enough for you Summer. I need to be a man for you."

"You are all the man I need."

Summer placed her fingers over his lips before he could say more, then she rocked her hips, taking him deeper into her body with each movement. Barrett reached up and cradled her breasts, squeezing her nipples between his thumbs and forefingers until she came hard.

"I can't come inside you, Summer," he said, as she increased her movements, circling him and sliding up and down his length.

"Don't you trust me?" she asked, still moving, still taking him as she had always longed to do.

He stared deep into her eyes.

She reached a hand around and cupped his balls, cradling them in her palm and feeling their weight.

"Summer!" he cried out as he climaxed and she sighed as his seed filled her core. He had claimed her as she needed him to.

Epilogue

Summer leaned against Barrett on the sofa at the ranch house, his arms wrapped around her. The logs on the fire crackled comfortingly. Outside, the wind howled, and fat, white snowflakes drifted lazily from the sky, only to be whipped up by the gale and sent flying in all directions.

Barrett kissed the top of her head and peered over her shoulder at the laptop balanced on her thighs.

"Looks good, angel."

"Thanks! I'm hoping it will encourage a new range of guests to come visit in the spring, as well as keeping our regulars interested."

"You do realize we'll be busier than ever by then, don't you?" He blew gently on her neck and she giggled.

"Nonsense."

"He's right, Summer!" her mother said, as she entered the room and placed a tray of cocoa on the table in front of them. "This spring will be your busiest yet. Now let me have a look at that latest newsletter before you send it out."

Summer handed the laptop to Helen, then relaxed against her husband as he ran his hands over her swollen belly.

"You two decided on any names yet?" Helen asked with feigned nonchalance.

"There's only one name for him," Barrett replied. "Cullen."

"Cullen *Barrett* Thorne," Summer announced, and smiled as her mother's eyes shone.

"Really?" Barrett whispered in her ear.

"Absolutely."

"I love you, Summer Thorne."

"I've always loved you, Barrett."

And she had. But now life was better than ever as Barrett had accepted the partnership in Moonglow and they'd moved into the ranch house as a couple. They'd married in a quiet family ceremony in the autumn as the leaves turned red, gold and brown. Finding out that Summer was pregnant had been the icing on their wedding cake.

"You've healed me, Summer. I owe everything to you."

"Well, after a lifetime of loving you, healing my cowboy was the least I could do." Summer giggled as Barrett turned her gently toward him and kissed her.

And Summer knew for sure, as she gazed into her husband's eyes, that Barrett had healed her too.

CADENCE FALLS

BETH D. CARTER

Dedication

Big thanks to Totally Bound and Sue Meadows for all your
help. I'm honored to work with you!
Dedicated to one of my best friends, CR Moss, whose
opinion, time and notes are invaluable.
And for anyone who thinks they can't have a do-over.

Author's Note

Shadow Wolves are a law enforcement unit of Native
American trackers that fall under Homeland Security.
Their primary goal is to track smugglers along the
Texas-Mexico border in Arizona. This group is small,
consisting of anywhere from fifteen to twenty-one officers,
comprised of nine different Native American tribes who
have an esteemed history of tracking passed down from
generation to generation. Their main method of tracking
is called cutting for sign, in which they search and analyze
even the most minute detail in an effort to locate their
target. They have been utilized worldwide in teaching
other law enforcement, as well as hunting terrorists along
the border of Afghanistan and Pakistan.
Most people know very little about the Shadow Wolves.

Chapter One

The town hall was filled to capacity and then some. Amanda waved the leaflet she'd been handed earlier in her face, trying to generate some air flow. The building hadn't been designed for people to be packed in like sardines. Then again, no one had expected to be faced with the threat of an escaped convict in their midst either. Now, here was the entire population of Pine Bluff, Montana, waiting for the federal law enforcement officer to come out and give them details about what the hell they were going to do.

As she waited, melting little by little, she looked around and her gaze met and locked with Cooper Haith, her once best friend. One of the men she'd thought she'd spend her life with and now the one man she could never be with. Her heart stuttered with remembered love. Remembered pain. She really was masochistic to continue living in the same town with him and not have him.

Did he remember how good it used to be between them? Because she did. His touch, his kiss. Their clumsy fumbling in the tall grass, after riding all afternoon. The bubbling water of Cadence Falls providing the soundtrack to their lovemaking. Of course, back then, they'd also had Everett with them, and it had been absolutely perfect. She'd had their future mapped out, filled with love and laughter, as they worked their own ranch.

But that was a long time ago.

Amanda tore her gaze away from Cooper, acutely aware of him now, and where he stood. Her body flushed with longing and an overwhelming need rushed through her. It was an ache that never went away. Even after all these years, she still wanted him.

Luckily, she was saved from continuing down memory lane with the appearance of the town sheriff at the front of the room. Coyote Leigh McCoy was a tall man, more portly than slim, although she'd seen him move pretty fast once when a horse went on a bucking rampage at the annual Strawberry Festival. Sheriff McCoy had managed to capture the reins and soothe the beast before it trampled the gawking spectators.

"Thank you all for coming," he said, nodding in a general way to the people crammed inside the too-small room. "As you know, I received word a few days ago that an escaped convict, who goes by the name of Harold Godfrey Mock, was spotted only a few miles from Pine Bluff."

A fearful murmur swept through the crowd. Amanda couldn't help the small shiver of fright that snaked its way through her, because like everyone else, as soon as they'd gotten the news, she'd Googled the man. Drug smuggling, murder and kidnapping were just a few things on his long list of crimes. She'd been jumping at any and all small noises lately. Of their own accord, her eyes darted over to Cooper, and he stared grimly back at her. If she didn't know him so well, she'd have said he seemed immune to the fear sweeping through the assembled crowd. But she could see the shifting emotions in his clear blue eyes and knew his calmness was just a façade.

"Earlier today Federal Marshalls, working with Homeland Security, arrived in order to help apprehend the fugitive," the sheriff continued, capturing her attention. "They've gotten permission from the Tribal Council in Browning to coordinate the immediate capture of Mock."

"Homeland Security?" a man asked from the crowd. "Are we looking at a terrorist threat?"

The low murmur suddenly rose to an excited fervor. People stood and started yelling questions. The barely contained panic threatened to blaze out of control.

"No," the sheriff shouted into his mike, but it was no use.

Terror was more formidable than a microphone. "Please, everyone quiet!"

At that moment, a man walked out from a side door and gestured for the sheriff to step back. He was dressed in khakis, a navy button-up and a windbreaker with the words *US Marshall* printed in gold over his heart. There was something about him that screamed authority, because with just a piercing sweep of his eyes, the crowd fell silent.

"Sit down," he said in the microphone, his voice deep and cold. Everyone standing plopped back into their seats. Amanda was quite impressed.

"Now," he continued in a tone that brooked no argument. "I am Federal US Marshall Thomas Fletcher. Thank you, Sheriff McCoy, and to all the residents of Pine Bluff for your cooperation in this matter."

No one made a sound as they stared at Fletcher. By the way he held himself and looked down upon everyone, Amanda could tell he was used to being in charge and having people listen to every word he uttered.

"Two days ago, we received data that the escaped fugitive Mock had last been located in the Glacial National Park, and as of this morning I am taking control of the situation to apprehend Mock with the help of a Shadow Wolf from Homeland Security. And, before you ask what the hell is a Shadow Wolf, he's a highly trained tracker who was brought in because he knows this area well. Being so close to the Canadian border, it is imperative we recapture the fugitive before he disappears from our reach."

Someone who knows the area? Amanda cocked her head and waited, hoping Marshall Fletcher would elaborate on this development.

Then Fletcher gestured to the door he'd walked out and it opened again. Amanda blinked, wondering if her eyes were playing tricks on her. All the blood drained from her head, leaving her slightly woozy as Everett Apisi walked across the stage to join the agent behind the podium. Unlike Fletcher, Everett wore a dark suit, although he looked extremely out of place in the clothes. He was more suited to blue jeans and a flannel shirt, riding hell bent for leather over the Montana plains, rather than official business attire.

It had been almost twelve years since she'd last seen him. Since the day he'd walked out of Pine Bluff without a word of goodbye and had broken her heart. Yet there he was, larger than life, facing the assembled crowd and staring blankly at the far wall. He was still handsome, classically beautiful. His Native American features dominated his face, hard angles that stood out in prominent relief. His black hair was cropped short and shone almost blue under the fluorescent lights, but any softness of youth was gone. His gaze was impersonal, not acknowledging at all that this was his home. She didn't blame the people gawking at him. She was sure she was one of them. Gone was the boy she'd known. This Everett was a stranger.

"This is Officer Everett Apisi. Many of you might remember him, since he grew up in Pine Bluff. When we learned Mock was using this mountain passage to make a break for the Canadian border, ICE graciously sent Apisi to help us track and recapture the fugitive."

After Fletcher's introduction, Everett glanced around the room. He paused for a second on Cooper before continuing. Then his gaze landed on Amanda and time seemed to stand still. For a brief moment, the cool detachment left his dark eyes, and she saw *her* Everett once more. Her friend. Her confidant. And once upon a time, for one magical night, her lover.

His features softened for an instant and it hit her heart like a softball. The frozen shell that had formed around it after his desertion cracked and she couldn't stop the wobbly smile she sent him. Then his gaze darted back to Cooper, before his face returned to stone. He resumed his mindless stare toward the back of the room, leaving her shaken from the raw encounter.

"We ask everyone in the community to exercise caution," Marshall Fletcher continued. "No going out alone, no hiking and obey the curfew time we've implemented."

He went on and on about how to be cautious and smart, and Amanda tried to listen, but she only heard muffled instructions that didn't really register. All she could focus on was the pain of seeing Everett again and remembering that once she'd held happiness in the palm of her hand before it'd been snatched away. Whatever the hell was said, people were clapping and the meeting ended. Everett turned away and walked to the door, once again leaving her life without so much as a goodbye. Or one more glance in her direction, as if she meant nothing at all. Panic blossomed inside her and the abandonment rushed back in full force. Amanda jumped to her feet, intent on reaching him before he disappeared again.

"Excuse me," she muttered as she trampled toes and banged into knees. "Sorry."

Finally, she reached the aisle and hurried to the door. Just as she turned the knob, a hand on her arm halted her. She looked around and her gaze clashed with Cooper's angry countenance.

"Don't," he said harshly. "He made his choice long ago."

"I have to," she whispered. "I saw regret, Cooper. Come with me."

As she reached for his hand, he pulled back.

"I can't forget this is all his fault," he said.

Cooper turned and walked away, leaving her at a crossroads, but this time she had a chance to know. Taking a deep breath, she opened the door.

Chapter Two

Fuck!

As soon as the door closed behind him, Everett loosened the tie that threatened to strangle him. The entire time he'd been on display, it had tightened a fraction every second until he could barely breathe. Knowing both Cooper and Amanda had been scrutinizing him had been almost more than he could handle, although it did puzzle him as to why they weren't sitting together. Not enough seats?

Does it really fucking matter?

The little voice in his brain was in a right foul mood today. Not that Everett blamed it. Being back in Pine Bluff dredged up a lot of unwanted memories. Brought up a lot of questions as well. Was Cooper was now running the ranch? Was Amanda able to breed her horses like she'd always dreamed of?

Were they married?

Did they have children?

That one hit him hard in the heart. Best not to think about that question too long because it could drive him mad. Cooper may have been the man to take her virginity, but it hadn't diminished the pleasure Everett had found in her arms.

As soon as he entered her wet depths, something meaningful singed through his blood, as if their souls had joined, becoming one.

"Oh my God!" he groaned when he bottomed out inside her. His balls rested snugly against her. "Baby, you feel amazing."

"I need you so badly, Everett," she whispered in his ear.

Her plea drove him wild and as he pumped into her, his heart filled with love. Harder, deeper. Her tight little pussy sucked him in. He was fast losing control and he so wanted this moment to never end. She felt so damn good wrapped around him, skin to skin.

"Christ, baby," he ground out. "I can't hold on."

"Yes!" she cried. "Yes! Come in me, Everett."

He reached down between their bodies and touched her clit, and that was all she needed to fly apart. Her pussy spasmed around his cock and her incoherent cries of pleasure pushed him over the top, and he came with a loud shout.

And he knew. This was it. This was his girl. Just as sudden as that.

"Excuse me, you're not supposed to be back here."

Marshall Fletcher's annoyed baritone cut through the memories, and he turned to see the object of all his fantasies standing in the open doorway, staring at him with turbulent blue eyes.

Her beauty took his breath away. It always had.

"It's okay, Fletcher," he said. "I know her."

Although he didn't see Fletcher leave, since he was too busy staring at Amanda, he sensed the other man had left them in private. He'd often wondered what he'd do if he found her alone one day, and if he'd be able to keep his hands and feelings in check. It wasn't much surprise that he found himself waging a war between his conscious and his heart.

"Hello, Amanda," he murmured.

"Hello." She shifted from foot to foot. The nervousness looked unnatural on her. Amanda had always been fearless, but now she seemed a little lost. "It's been a long time."

"Yes." He didn't know what else to say. All coherent thought seemed to have fled. Standing this close to her turned his brain to mush.

She nodded thoughtfully. "So you work for Homeland Security?"

"Yes." Great. Now he was starting to sound like a broken record.

"And how long have you been working for the government?" She appraised him up and down, and from the look in her eyes, it wasn't a very flattering appraisal.

Just how much information did she want? Then again, how much he was willing to share with her?

"About ten years," he replied. "When I left Pine Bluff, I went to join the military but came across the desk of Immigration and Customs Enforcement instead. After several interviews, I was sent to the Tohono O'odham Nation in Arizona where I've been training and working ever since as a tracker."

"Because all Native Americans can track?" she asked sarcastically. "Isn't that a little racist?"

"I've had worse stereotypes heaped upon me," he said, shrugging. "That one happens to be true. My grandfather taught me how to track animals. I've since learned how to follow humans. And I'm damn good at what I do. My team and I have seized thousands of pounds of illegal drugs trying to make their way across the border."

She seemed to wilt a little before his eyes. Her shoulders drooped, just a fraction, and had he been anyone else, it wouldn't have registered. But he knew this woman, inside and out...or at least, once upon a time he had.

"Then I guess I can't bitch too much, can I? Not if you're making a difference." She gave him a wobbly smile. "I'm proud of you, Everett. Come by the bar. First drink is on me."

He cocked his head. "What bar?"

"I work at the Dew Drop Inn," she said. "Every night but Sunday and Monday."

Now he was the one confused. "How does Cooper feel about that?"

"Why would Cooper feel anything about where I work?"

"Aren't you and he..."

He tapered off the question when a shuttered look came down over her face.

"No, Everett," she said. "Lots of things changed when

you left. I'm not with Cooper. I'm not with anyone. I'm a bartender at the Dew Drop and I rent an apartment above it. May not be the best, but at least I'm never late for work."

For once in his life, he was speechless. Every idea he had, every vision of what Cooper and Amanda's life was like without him, had just been blown to smithereens.

"We have to go, Officer Apisi," Marshall Fletcher said from behind him.

Everett balled his hands into fists. For the first time since he'd joined law enforcement he didn't want to do his duty. He wanted to stay right here and hash this out with Amanda, find out what the hell had gone wrong between her and Cooper.

But the rational part of his brain reminded him of why he was back in Pine Bluff in the first place.

Fuck!

"All right," he muttered. "Give me one more moment, please."

Fletcher nodded. "I'll be waiting with the task force in the SUV."

He waited until the man was gone before giving his full attention back to Amanda. Holy hell, she was still beautiful after all these years. Her hair was still the color of the sun, worn shorter now, but still just as wild as when they were teenagers. Not a wrinkle marred her flawless skin.

She crossed her arms in front of her chest. "You'll never cross the mountains in trucks."

"I know," he said. "We'll need horses."

"Cooper has horses."

"He took over the ranch?"

"Yes," she replied. "It's still a cattle ranch but he's got good, sturdy horse stock."

"Then I'll go talk to him."

"Why do I have the feeling horses won't be the only thing you'll be discussing?"

Everett ran a hand over his face. Hadn't even started his job and already he was weary. "Why aren't you married?"

"Why did you leave?"

He wanted to grin at her grit. Amanda always did have one helluva backbone.

His phone buzzed in his pocket.

"Damn it," he said. "I have to go. Can we…talk again?"

She shrugged. "You know where to find me."

Suddenly, the tension was back between them, and it was painful to feel. All Everett wanted to do was pull her into his arms and kiss her until they both passed out from lack of oxygen. Even after all these years, she still moved him in ways no other woman ever could. She hadn't even touched him, yet all he felt was her presence wrapping itself around him.

"All right," he said. "I'll see you later, Amanda."

She let out a rueful little sigh. "There was a time when you called me baby. Guess we really are different people now."

She turned and left the way she had come in, shutting the door behind her with a soft click. Her departure had him feeling empty and frustrated. This wasn't the result he'd had in mind. His phone buzzed again, and with a low curse, he went to work.

Chapter Three

Cooper drove back to his ranch as if the hounds of hell chased him, pissed beyond anything. If truth be known, he'd been angry for quite a while now, ever since Everett had left. Ever since Amanda had broken it off. Ever since his father had up and died, leaving a nineteen-year-old boy in charge of a ranch with a debt hanging over his head. The bank had come calling three months after he'd buried his dad, and fuck if he remembered what he'd said, but somehow he'd convinced them to give him more time.

The only way he'd been able to save the main part of his home had been to sell off most of the land. He was still bitter over that part as well, but it was easier to compartmentalize everything, and since Everett had shown his face back in town, might as well go with the obvious compartment. It had been so fucking easy for Everett to just walk away, leave all his problems behind. Forget all about him and Amanda. A tiny voice of reason chattered away in the back of his mind, telling him he was being an unfair prick, but he didn't care. Not right then. Not when the love of his life, and his *ex*-best friend, had been in the same room with him for the first time in a decade. Sure, he'd seen Amanda around town, as well as down at the bar a time or two. But with Everett there, it had brought back the sharp pain of lost love and a summer that he'd give his right arm to relive.

The three of them had once been inseparable.

Nothing could've torn them apart.

Funny how the one thing that Cooper would've sworn was solid as a rock had become their weakness.

He screeched to a halt in front of the generations-old

farmhouse and hopped out of the cab, taking much-needed gratification in slamming the pickup door shut. He eyed the front door of his house. The last fucking thing he wanted to do right then was be cooped up inside, so he diverted his course to head around back to the stable where his horse greeted him with a friendly neigh.

"Hey, Coop," his stable hand, Pete Red Feather, greeted. "How was the meeting?"

Cooper grabbed a saddle blanket. "Great. Super. We have a maniac convict running loose somewhere in the wilderness. Which reminds me, I want you and the others to wear guns. Grab the ones from the tack room."

"We all carry shotguns," Pete said. "Mandatory when riding the fences."

"No, I want pistols on them." Cooper ran a hand down the horse's flank before setting the blanket on his back. "At all times, until this convict is caught."

He heaved the saddle off a stand and settled it onto his horse before buckling and tightening the cinch.

"No problem." Pete scratched the scraggly hair growing on his chin. "I'll let them know when they come in for the night. Looks like a storm coming so they'll probably be in soon. So, who's tracking down this convict? Do we need to set up patrols?"

"Nope. Federal Marshalls are here. And they brought in their own expert tracker."

"Expert tracker, eh?"

"Yep," Cooper replied grimly. "A former resident of Pine Bluff. Go figure."

"You don't say?" Pete sniffed. "Wouldn't be Everett Apisi by chance, would it?"

Cooper glared at him. "How the hell do you know Everett?"

"Because I'm older than dirt and know everything," Pete said smugly. "I knew Everett's grandfather, Walking Bear, who was an amazing tracker. And I remember when he was your best friend. Only one other person was able to put that frown upon your face, and that was that little *áápi* girl you two ran around with."

Cooper stomped over to grab a bridle. "Maybe you *should* retire, Pete. After all, the dinosaurs died out eons ago."

Pete flipped him off. "Yep, must have seen both of 'em."

Cooper ignored him and led his horse from the stall. He mounted and headed off toward the northwestern border of his ranch, the one that that backed up to the mountain. The one that the Federal Marshall had said the fugitive Mock had to be running through to make his escape into Canada. Although it sounded like a plot from a bad movie or something, the one thing that stood between the border and a jail cell was exposure and starvation, and his ranch was close enough that it might tempt a desperate man to do something stupid.

The wind was kicking up mighty fierce as he rode across the wide open plain. Clouds moved rapidly through the big, blue sky, casting shadows upon the ground. If he squinted he could see some of his cattle grazing the distance. Wasn't as much as what his father and grandfather had raised, but it was enough to keep his family land in the black.

Inevitably, his thoughts strayed back to Amanda. And Everett. And the last time they'd been together. They'd ridden across the land, much like he was doing now, until they'd hit the falls. They'd gone swimming in the pond, had food, drank a little. And when the sun had slipped over the horizon to bathe the range in twilight, the magic that existed between them flared into uncontrollable lust. He remembered that Amanda had initiated it, kissing Everett first and then him. He hadn't known exactly what was going to happen, that it would lead to them all losing their virginities, but all he'd known was that somehow it was meant to be.

Everett slid his hands around Amanda, cupping her breasts and filling his palms with the heaviness of their weight. He massaged the plump mounds until she thrust out her chest, moaning with rising passion.

Cooper leaned over her, kissing his way down her body as he unbuttoned her shirt and peeled it from her body. He nipped and licked all the way down, until he fell to his knees in front of her, unsnapping her pants and pushing them down, exposing her inch by inch to his gaze.

"Her pussy is so pretty, Everett," he murmured as his fingers slid through the blonde curls that protected her femininity. "I've never seen anything as lovely."

Amanda bucked her hips as he touched her slit, sliding with ease at the wetness he encountered. His heart pounded with excitement because he couldn't believe she was naked, in front of both him and Everett, letting them look at her. Touch her. He'd never had sex before, but he knew the mechanics of it. Having Everett watch, however, was almost too exciting.

"How does she taste?" Everett asked in between the kisses he laved against her neck.

Cooper pulled away and stuck his finger in his mouth. "She tastes like honey."

"I want you both," Amanda gasped, arching against the hands playing with her body. "Please."

Cooper lifted her away from Everett and laid her on the thick grass near the creek. He spread her legs wide and kissed her inner thighs, working his way up until he latched on to her pussy. She let out a strangled moan as he swept his tongue into her channel, licking up and down, easing his middle finger into her. She came, crying as she convulsed in pleasure, and he knew now was the time. They were both about to lose their virginity. He glanced up at Everett and saw his best friend watching through aroused black eyes, his gaze locked on Amanda's beautiful body.

Cooper rose onto his knees between her thighs to drape her knees over his arms. The position thrust her hips up, and all he could do was stare as he slid his cock tip up and down her fold. He was holding on to his sanity by a lick and prayer.

Then he pushed forward.

She cried out and when he glanced into her eyes, saw pain shift over the pleasure. His body tightened up.

Holy fuck!

She was squeezing his dick hard, but she was wet and warm, and all he wanted to do was pound into her until he came. However, he knew he had to make this good for her. So he looked once more at Everett for help.

"Take a deep breath, Amanda," Everett murmured.

"It hurts," she gasped.

"I know, but relax your muscles. Just breathe."

Amanda did as he said, and Cooper felt her body relax, little by little. Thank fuck!

Slowly, Cooper pulled out, only to push back in again.

"Oh," she moaned. Her eyes flew open and he saw her desire reawakening.

"You feel so good, Amanda," he said. "I love you. I love you so much."

"I love you too!" she gasped.

They came together, his world exploding into such fierce love it left him winded. He vaguely remembered Amanda reaching for Everett. He lay on his back, gasping for breath, as Everett took his place. He and Amanda moaned together, declared their love for each other, and all he knew was everything was right in his world. Nothing could tear them apart.

Cooper shook his head to clear himself of the memory and grimaced as he shifted in the saddle, trying in vain to alleviate some of the pressure his hard-on was giving him in the unyielding seat. His cell rang, thankfully diverting his attention. Cooper brought his roan to a halt before digging the phone out of his pocket.

"Yes?"

"Boss, we got company," Pete said.

"Company?" Cooper asked. What kind of company could make Pete recall him to the homestead?

"The badge kind," he answered. "And the kind that pisses you off."

Everett.

"Keep them busy," he replied. "I'm on my way back."

"I'd suggest not taking the scenic route."

"God damn it," he snarled and hung up. He turned his

horse around and rode back the way he'd just come.

Chapter Four

The first thing Cooper saw as he crested the homestead hill were three black SUVs and men wearing dark vests with the words *Federal Marshall* splayed in bright white across the back. They swarmed around a pop-up tent, which had been placed smack dab in front of his house, like hungry ants seeking any scrap of food. Anger burned through Cooper and he nudged his horse forward, intent on getting the fucking assholes off his property.

"Boss!" Pete shouted at him, and Cooper came to a stop as the old man hobbled out of the barn.

"Pete, what's going on?"

"Showed me a paper." Pete thumbed toward the cops. "Something fancy and legal looking saying they were going to be using the ranch for their base camp."

"Son of a bitch!" Cooper glared at the assembled law enforcement angrily. "We'll see about that."

He dismounted and handed the reins to Pete before stomping toward the so-called base camp. He saw Marshall Fletcher staring at a map. Beside him stood a man dressed in army fatigue pants and a black T-shirt with the word *Police* to the left. A patch beneath the lettering showed a wolf in profile, a feather hanging from its fur...

Everett.

"What are you doing here?" he demanded.

Both Fletcher and Everett looked at him.

"I'm glad you showed up, Mr. Haith," Fletcher said, with a generic insincere smile plastered on his face.

"Cut the bullshit," Cooper snapped. "Get off my land."

Fletcher shook his head apologetically. "Afraid I can't do

that, Mr. Haith. We've need of some horses."

"There are other ranches," Cooper replied.

"Yes," Fletcher agreed. "I'm actually surprised to see a white man running a ranch on tribal land."

"My great-grandmother was Piegan Blackfoot," Cooper replied, with a shrug. "Why don't you use dogs to track this fugitive?"

"Because dogs can't do what I can," Everett said.

Copper ignored him. "Like I said, you can bother other ranchers for horses."

"Not at this particular location."

Cooper frowned. "What's that supposed to mean?"

"Mock's last GPS ping was at Cadence Falls," Everett said. Cooper glanced at him and their eyes met. Held. Everett was a blank slate, not revealing anything he might be feeling or thinking. Once upon a time, they'd been able to share anything. As close as brothers.

It was just one more thing that pissed him off.

He crossed his arms over his chest. "So what, you provide all your inmates with cell phones?"

"Trackers," Fletcher corrected. "Under the skin. The last location was at Cadence Falls, which Officer Apisi tells me isn't too far away."

"Not far at all," Cooper replied grimly.

"Excellent." A satisfied gleam settled on Fletcher's face. "We'll need several horses, Mr. Haith—"

"No," Cooper said immediately. "I've got four wheelers you can use. Not my horses."

Everett shook his head. "Too noisy for this job. Mock would hear me coming and hide. We can't use helicopters because of all the natural canopies. I'm afraid this job is all by hoof."

"Can I talk to you in private?" he asked Everett.

Everett hadn't even finished nodding before Cooper turned and marched away, not caring in the least if he followed. Actually, he did care. He needed to know *why*.

When they were far enough away from Fletcher so as not

to be overheard, Cooper turned and put his hands on his hips, tensing for a showdown.

"What are you doing here, Everett?"

Everett glanced at the mountains behind him. "My job."

"Bullshit!" he yelled, focusing Everett's attention on him. "Not one God damn word in all these years and now you act like nothing matters?"

"Finding Mock is all that matters right now," Everett muttered. "But...once, you and Amanda were all that mattered to me."

"Again, I say you're full of it. You walked away without looking back. Without once calling, or writing, or even leaving a fucking note. It destroyed her, Everett. It destroyed *us.*"

His anger boiled over and without even realizing what he was doing, he struck out at Everett, pushing him in the chest with a mighty shove that caused him to stumble. That definitely knocked Everett off his emotional flat line. Before Cooper knew it, Everett was pushing him as well, causing him to flounder a few steps.

"I did what I had to do, Coop!" He advanced, his face contorted with anger. "I saw the way she looked at you and you at her. You loved her."

"You loved her too," he snarled. "Don't even try to deny it."

"I'm not. I can't!"

"You asshole." Cooper charged, taking a swing that Everett easily ducked. "She refused to have me without you, and that's the reason why she's not here now. That's the reason I lost her!"

Everett blinked. "But...I made it easy for you to have a normal relationship. I left—"

Cooper took advantage of his distraction and swung his fist again. It landed on Everett's chin and the man went down to one knee. The punch made him feel a hell of a lot better, even though his hand now ached like a motherfucker.

Everett cupped his jaw. "I thought I was doing the right

thing for both of you."

Cooper sighed and glanced at the endless big blue sky. The sun warmed his skin and the smell of the earth seeped into his bones. This was the only life he knew, living on the land, and all he'd ever want. He looked down at Everett, who still knelt on the ground, rubbing his face.

"My father died not too long after you left," he said quietly. "The ranch was in the red. I had to sell off most of the land to save this part. The homestead."

Everett stood slowly. "I'm sorry. I didn't know."

Cooper sighed. "It would've been nice to have my best friend there to talk to. To help me figure things out. I was so angry, Everett. I've been angry for a long time and it never gets any better because every time I see her, I'm right back there at Cadence Falls. It's where everything was perfect for one single moment of time."

"I've never forgotten either," Everett admitted. "I'm good at my job. I like what I do, and how I make a difference. But...I'd give it up in a heartbeat if I could relive that day."

"You still love her," Cooper said.

Everett met his gaze. "I never stopped. I love you both. My best friend and my girl."

Suddenly, the apathy was gone, replaced with sorrow. Regret stared back at him in the mirror of Everett's eyes, begging for understanding. For forgiveness. It made Cooper pause, and in that instant, he recognized the fact that he stood on a cliff. Did he go back to the way things used to be, with anger and everything eating him up on a daily basis? Or should he take the leap and jump into the unknown of letting go? It was a strange concept, because only a moment ago he had wanted to pound the shit out of Everett and pour out all his frustration on his ex-best friend. But truth was, he was tired of hurting. Of being alone. As much as he missed Amanda, perhaps he missed Everett a little more. After all, they had been closer than brothers. Had shared everything growing up, including the love of one woman. Cooper knew which way his heart had to go.

Cooper gave a wry smile. "Then I guess we better catch this asshole fugitive so we can sit down with Amanda and talk things out. Life's too short not to be happy, and I'm about twelve years overdue for some."

"We?"

"Hell, it's been years since you've been to Cadence Falls. These mountains can be a bitch. You might have known the terrain back then, but I know it now."

"Fletcher will never agree."

"Fletcher doesn't have a choice," Cooper said. "You may be a tracker, but I'm going to be your guide."

Chapter Five

The last thing Amanda wanted to do was serve coffee and beer to the lunch crowd when the town meeting broke up, but it was her shift and she never shirked her responsibilities. Her heart hurt like hell and all she wished was to lie in bed and pull the covers over her head, but being an ostrich had never been appealing. Even when Everett had first left, and Cooper had expected her to carry on without him as if he'd never existed. She couldn't hide then and she wouldn't hide now.

Her feelings should've changed over the years. Gone away or grown old. The odd times she'd seen Cooper through the years hadn't been as excruciating as today. Then again, it'd been a long time since both of her men had been in the same room.

She caught herself on that mental note. Her men. When she'd been eighteen, the thought of loving two men hadn't been nearly so taboo. It had been as natural as breathing. Cooper and Everett were her men. Why couldn't she have both? Why couldn't she *love* both? She did, and that was the reason why she couldn't betray her feelings for Everett by staying with Cooper. If the roles had been switched, with Cooper leaving, she'd have done the same to Everett. There simply was no way to have one without having the other.

But it sure was lonely.

"Table six needs more coffee, Amanda," her boss, Ted, cut through her musing.

"On it," she replied.

She grabbed the carafe and headed out from behind the bar.

"You okay?" Ted asked.

She flashed him a small smile. "Just a shock seeing Everett."

"Yeah," he replied. "Be careful. Once they catch that fugitive, he'll be gone again."

She nodded. "I know."

As she refilled coffee cups and took orders, her mind kept straying back to that one perfect day next to the falls. Over the years, she'd tried sleeping with different men. Dating. It never worked out. Perhaps it was time to confront the past and lay it all out there. The more she thought about it, the more she realized it was the only way she'd ever get her answers and heal. She was tired of having a broken heart.

At the end of the lunch shift, around four o'clock, the sheriff came in and sat in her section. He'd be her last customer for the day.

As she approached him, coffee cup in hand, he reached for his phone and barked out his name.

"McCoy here." Pause. "What? Is Cooper dead? Okay. I'm on my way."

He stood up and their eyes met. Locked. His shoulders stiffened, bracing like he always did when he had bad news to report. She didn't even realize she'd stumbled until he caught her shoulders to steady her, but was too late for the mug in her hand. She dropped it and it shattered at her feet, splashing coffee everywhere. She absolutely didn't care. Her entire world was falling apart around her with thoughts of Cooper hurt, and she suddenly wished she *was* an ostrich. That had to be less painful than waiting to hear if one of the men she loved was dead. Or dying.

"What happened?" she whispered, pushing the words out of lips that seemed stiff and cold.

"Ah, Mandy," he muttered. "Damn it. That was Pete Red Feather. I guess the fugitive was hiding out in the ranch's main barn. He's got Coop."

"Is he…"

She couldn't finish the sentence.

"As far as I know, he's alive. I'm heading to the ranch now."

"I'm going with you."

"I don't think—"

"I wasn't suggesting. Come on, Sheriff."

She stormed out of the place, not even bothering to tell Ted where she was going. Fuck it all. She'd just gotten both of her men back in one town, she'd be damned if she let a fucking fugitive take one away from her now.

* * * *

It had been a long time since he'd ridden, and Everett had to take a moment to enjoy the feel of the powerful animal he rode, the wind hitting his face, and the sense of freedom that the open range instilled. As they approached the base of the mountain, the trees thickened. The increased foliage provided a denser path through the forest.

"I don't remember this tree line," he said.

"A few years ago, conservationists came to me, asking to plant trees," Cooper replied. "I didn't see the harm in it. Didn't affect my cows this close to the mountain. But this is why you needed me along. The path to Cadence Falls has been obliterated."

As predicted, Fletcher had flatly refused until Everett had pointed out they were losing daylight by arguing. Reluctantly, he'd agreed, but the other Marshalls now patrolled the base of the mountain, and Everett had to report in regularly. It was something he was used to, being part of the Shadow Wolves. The unit was small, as was their branch in Homeland Security, which was why they had to stick together. He and his fellow officers made a good team, they made a helluva difference in their fight against illegal narcotics, and yet, he'd walk away from it in a heartbeat if it meant having a second chance with Amanda.

The thick foliage made riding slow, but he took comfort from that, because if it was difficult for a horse, it would be difficult for a man. Mock would be forced to slow down, giving Everett time to find him. And find him, he would. He was a damn good tracker.

It was mid-afternoon by the time they made it to the falls. The water fell from a hidden spring deep in the mountains, bubbling melodically as it crashed to the rocks below. It brought back so many memories it almost stole his breath away. The land around might have changed, but the falls hadn't. A small river fed the northern part of the tribal land, winding through the Blackfeet Reservation, dumping into the Cadence break before continuing its serpentine course. The falls had always been a favorite of teenagers in the past, but looking it over now, Everett knew it had been a long time since people had last visited. Grass was overgrown. Froth lined the banks of the pond, where the sand stood undisturbed. He brought his horse to a halt and dismounted.

"A lot of people have left the lands," Cooper said from behind him, as if able to read his mind.

"Why?"

"Most people are living below poverty level. Kids hit sixteen and they're practically running to bigger cities for jobs. Food. A life. The land is hard work."

"The land is pure," Everett murmured. A patch of flattened grass caught his attention and he cautiously made his way over to it. "I've got blood."

Cooper moved beside him. "Where?"

Everett pointed to a small rock. A small drop of dark crimson stained the flat, gray surface.

"Shit," Cooper said. "I would never have seen that."

Everett stood and looked around. "More than likely he dug out the tracker here and tossed it in the water."

He saw a snapped branch about two yards away and headed over to it.

"He's moving north. Come on."

As he retrieved his horse, he placed a call to Fletcher, telling them of their position and what he'd seen. The bramble thinned as they moved away from the water source, but a high-pitched neigh and Cooper's cursing stopped him.

"Shit!" Cooper swore.

"What?"

"My horse cut his leg." Cooper dismounted and bent to inspect the leg. A gash split the horse's flesh open, deep enough to let the blood flow freely. The poor beast stood trembling, wide-eyed as he breathed heavily through his nostrils. "This needs to be attended to."

"Then go back," Everett encouraged. "I can take it from here."

Cooper frowned. "You need someone to watch your back."

"It's all good, Coop. I'll stay in touch with Fletcher. I can't let Mock go and you can't make your horse lame."

Cooper took a deep breath and stared at him. "You'll be careful?"

"I'm always careful."

"Still a cocky bastard, I see."

Everett grinned. For the first time in a long time, his soul felt light. It was good to smile. "Go on. I'll see you soon. I've got daylight wasting."

Cooper nodded, grabbed his horse's reins and turned the animal around. He couldn't ride him so he'd walk him home.

It didn't take long for Everett to reach a clearing, so he dismounted and studied the ground. Tracking could be tedious work, but most of the time criminals didn't know how to hide their tracks well enough to completely disappear. They tried, but he was trained to spot even the most minute of clues.

The clearing was large, and by the time Everett had found what he was looking for, almost two hours had passed. Mock, however, hadn't continued north like he'd expected. The evidence pointed south, back the way he'd come. Had Mock gotten lost?

His phone vibrated, and he answered it immediately.

"Apisi here."

"Storm is coming in," Fletcher told him. "You're going to lose any hope in following after the son of a bitch."

Everett looked up. Gunmetal-gray clouds had rolled in with the sudden whipping of the wind. And now that he'd been made aware of it, he felt the electric charge in the air.

"Come on down," Fletcher ordered. "I was told flash floods are possible. We're going to have to find Mock another way."

Everett hung up and studied the ground again. Details never lied, and the tracks were as clear as day to him. Mock must have felt the change in the atmosphere as well and had decided to head someplace for shelter. He wracked his brain, trying to think of the closest place Mock would head. The years could've brought hunting blinds, or deer stands. Or even a cabin or two. But something in his gut was telling him that Mock had a bigger target. If he couldn't make it to Canada on foot, then he'd need a plan B.

Everett looked south, down the mountain, and he followed the panic underlining his instinct. He turned his horse around before he mounted the roan. He made his way back toward the homestead, all the while trying to convince himself he was wrong. Marshalls were patrolling. There was no way he could avoid them all. Could he?

It was a question he couldn't simply say no to and move on.

Chapter Six

When Cooper reached the foot of the mountain, he found Pete waiting with the trailer. He'd called him to bring it, not wanting to subject his horse to unnecessary pain, and by the time they'd loaded the horse inside, the eastern sky was growing dark.

"Are the men back?" he asked.

"Yep," Pete replied. "Did you catch the bad guy?"

"What do you think?"

The old man shrugged and stepped a little more on the gas. The truck rattled over the ground, although the trailer prevented them from going too fast.

"You talk with Walking Bear's grandson?"

Cooper sighed and leaned his head back. "It's none of your business."

"I'm only guessing here," Pete continued, as if Cooper hadn't said anything. "But based on your attitude today, I assume that your bad mood for the past twelve years has to do with the *áápi* girl and the long-lost tracker."

"Stop calling her the white girl," Cooper ordered.

"She *is* the white girl."

"I'm white."

"You are part Blackfoot. Not the same."

"Her stepdad was Blackfoot."

"She is still the *áápi* girl," Pete replied. "But, if she will make this bad mood go away, I will open my arms to her."

Cooper couldn't stop a small smile from touching his lips. "I'll hold you to that."

When they reached the main barn, he brought the horse out and let Pete bandage the leg while he went to grab a gun. The sky continued to darken, and Cooper knew Everett would need help. He might have all the Federal Marshalls out there helping, but Cooper didn't feel right simply sitting at home twiddling his thumbs.

As he entered, all the horses were in their stalls, having been properly tended to. The men were, no doubt, in the bunk house eating dinner. There wasn't much to do on a ranch when a storm hit. He pulled the keys from his pocket to open the tack room, but he noticed the lock hung lopsided on a badly dented bracket, which made it look as if it had been hit by something big and heavy. Cooper slowly opened the door and looked inside, but a scuffling behind him had him spinning around. He spun around to find a tall, thin man standing in the shadows. The torn, dirty jumpsuit was all Cooper needed to see to know that this was Harold Godfrey Mock.

"Thought you were on the mountain, making a run for the border," Cooper said. The sudden rush of adrenaline had his heart pounding heavily. It was an effort to remain calm, like staring down a rattler slithering through grass. Mock held one of the ranch pistols down at his side. "How'd you make it here before I did?"

"You and I both know I'd never have made it to Canada," Mock replied. He pointed to his left foot. "Not with this."

Dried blood covered his plain slip-on shoe. One handcuff still engulfed his left wrist, while the empty side dangled down. A bloody scrape wrapped around his right wrist.

"I had to remove that damn tracker with a fucking shank I made in prison," Mock explained. "I knew they'd be bringing in dogs or something to find me. So I decided to come up with a better plan."

"Hiding in my barn?"

Mock shrugged. "It seemed to be a lucky break. I heard you talk about the guns. And now I have a hostage."

Cooper shook his head. He didn't know why he felt so calm. Perhaps it was because Mock himself wasn't showing one ounce of fear or anxiety. That in itself was slightly worrisome. "Marshalls will never negotiate."

"Then you'll drive the truck," Mock said.

"Pardon?"

Mock pressed the gun to Cooper's chest. "Canada is only a few hours away, so you're going to drive me there."

"And then what? Canada has an extradition treaty with the USA. You'll be right back where you started."

"Maybe," Mock said. "But I bet no one will be looking too hard for me there, at least long enough for me to get out of North America. So come on. The storm will help us get away."

"Hey, boss, the horse is—"

At Pete's surprise entrance, Mock spun with the gun still pointed. It went off, but Cooper couldn't tell if Pete was hit or not. He didn't waste the distraction and attacked, jumping on Mock and pushing the barrel upward, while trying to get the gun away. Mock was surprisingly strong as he fought back. Both grappled for the weapon. Mock elbowed Cooper, who let out a painful *oomph*, and managed to wrangle the gun away from Cooper. Thinking quickly, Cooper kicked Mock, and the man doubled over with pain etched on his face. Cooper dove for the tack room and shut the door as a bullet slammed into the door frame.

Cooper grabbed one of the other pistols from the rack. Making sure the chambers were loaded, Cooper waited, straining to hear any noise outside the tack room. The thunderous hammering of his heart made hearing difficult.

Minutes passed, long moments that had Cooper wondering if perhaps Mock had moved on. He couldn't leave Pete, who may have been hurt, out there alone. Taking a deep breath, Cooper stood to the side and used his foot to nudge the door open. When no bullets came flying at him, he peeked around the corner and didn't see anyone. Gathering his courage, he ran to the barn door and again, glanced out to see if the coast was clear. A big something smashed into his back and Cooper flew forward. He dropped the gun, which skidded out of reach. Cooper rolled in time to see

Mock point the barrel directly at his forehead. At such a close distance, there was no way he could possibly miss.

Mock's eyes were black and dead. "You can either live and be my hostage, or you can die and I'll take the old man as my hostage. You choose."

"You'll never make it to Canada," Cooper said, trying to stall. He didn't know how much that tactic could help, but it was worth a shot.

"I guess that's your answer."

Cooper's eyes widened and he held up a hand. "Wait!"

In that split second, only two things ran through his head. The first was Amanda. The second was Everett. He wished he'd had a chance to say goodbye to them.

A gunshot rent the air. Cooper flinched, expecting pain to sear through his body, only it didn't. It took a moment to realize he was still alive, and relief slammed through him hard. Mock fell back with a stream of blood trickling from the bullet hole between his eyes. Shaking, Cooper sat up, looked over his shoulder. Everett stood in the doorway, his gun still aimed at where Mock once stood. Tears of relief gathered in Cooper's eyes. He hated to cry but the powerful emotion couldn't be released any other way. His best friend had saved him from dying.

"Holy shit, I'm glad you're a good shot," he managed to choke out.

"What are you talking about? I was aiming for his heart," Everett replied deadpan.

Cooper gave a gruff chuckle. "Asshole."

Everett smiled.

At that moment, a black SUV arrived. Marshall Fletcher got out from the driver's side and stalked over to Everett.

"I see you got the fugitive," Fletcher muttered. "We were supposed to bring him in alive, Apisi."

Everett shrugged and put his gun back in his holster. "What was I supposed to do? Let him kill a civilian, who happens to be my best friend?"

Cooper gingerly got to his feet. He didn't want to stare at

Mock's body, with the knowledge that a mere second later, it could have been *his* dead body everyone was looking at.

"I can assure you," he directed to Fletcher. "I am relieved to be the one not dead."

The work hands stumbled from the bunk house, all looking confused. As the other Federal Marshalls swarmed around, collecting evidence and taking pictures of the scene, Pete staggered from the other side of the barn.

"That's okay," he yelled out, waving a hand. "No need to worry. I'm perfectly fine."

Cooper smiled.

* * * *

"Hurry," Amanda urged, bouncing in the passenger seat of the cop car as it sped toward Cooper's ranch. Her stomach churned as her mind kept flashing from Cooper to Everett, and the fact that one of them might be hurt. Or dead.

Suddenly denying herself either of them the past twelve years seemed stupid. She should have tracked Everett down. Forced him to talk about why he up and left. She should never have walked away from Cooper. Life was too short without her rancher and shadow wolf.

"Calm the hell down," Sheriff McCoy grumbled. "Haith is going to be okay. Everyone is going to be just fine."

"You don't know that," she snapped.

"I know Cooper is a smart boy," he countered. "He wouldn't risk his men or himself."

"Not unless he was forced to." She shook her head and took a deep breath, forcing the anxious tears to stay away. "I could lose him. I could lose both."

"Both?"

"I love two men, Sheriff," she admitted softly. "I always have."

The sheriff didn't comment, and for that she was glad. She didn't feel like having to explain anything, from the past or where the future was headed. Not knowing was, perhaps, the worst thing in life.

As the car flew over the last ridge to Cooper's house, its siren disturbing nature's peace, she saw a swarm of Federal Marshalls crawling over the barn area. The sheriff's vehicle zoomed up the gravel driveway, and in the middle stood Everett and Cooper. Alive. A tidal wave of relief rolled over her, and even before the car had come to a halt, she jumped out to run to them.

First she hugged Cooper, giving a silent prayer of thanks he was unhurt. Then she let go of him to embrace Everett. As she snuggled into his chest, she watched the Marshalls cover Mock's body in a black tarp, thankful it was over. In that moment, everything seemed right in her world.

Chapter Seven

The approaching storm made the Federal Marshalls hurry to wrap up the case. Mock's body was put into a black zip-up bag and driven out, seconds before the rain hit. Fletcher made Everett promise to come in for a formal statement before releasing him. Amanda waited on the porch with Cooper, unable to get over how she finally had her two men with her again. Nothing else mattered except that she understood what had happened all those years ago, and to make sure she held on to both of them for the rest of their lives. She wasn't going to let Everett or Cooper go without putting up one helluva fight.

Cooper held the door open for her, and Everett followed. Once inside, the three of them stood in the living room staring at one another as if they were complete strangers thrown into a weird situation together.

"Why?" Cooper's single word broke the awkward silence as he stared at Everett. "Tell her."

Amanda couldn't take her eyes off Everett, and he stared back at her like a dying man glimpsing heaven. The binding that had wrapped around her heart all those years ago, when he'd left, loosened just a little.

Everett cleared his throat.

"Amanda," he said. Emotions clouded the clear tone in his voice. "Back then...I saw the love between you and Cooper."

"I did love him but I loved you too—"

"And I'd believed your love for him exceeded what you'd had for me."

Shock tore through her. "What?"

He took hold of her shoulders. "I couldn't get in the way of that. So I left. So you two could be together."

Amanda didn't know whether she should've been angry or surprised that he'd thought he'd been making a sacrifice for her and his best friend.

"You stupid, stupid man," she whispered.

He gave a twisted, self-deprecating type of smile. "I'm sorry. God, am I ever fucking sorry."

Perhaps the one thing she *did* know was that life was too short to hold grudges. She stroked his cheek. "I wish you had come and talked to me, to us, before you made such a decision. I loved the both of you equally. Still do." She wrapped her arms around him. She needed to hold her men, feel them, make sure they were really all right and let them know all was forgiven.

"Me too," he murmured into the crook of her neck. "I wish I could go back in time and change everything."

Cooper laid a hand on each of their backs. "We can't go back in time, but we can move forward."

Everett pulled back and looked at Cooper. "I would like that."

"Amanda?" Cooper asked.

She looked between each of them. "I want that too, but I can't, not if either of you walk away again. I wouldn't be able to handle that."

"I'm not going anywhere," Everett said. "I let you go once. I can't walk away again."

Everett placed his hand behind her neck and pulled her close. Amanda rested her hands on his chest, and she could feel his heat burning through his shirt, his muscles rippling with every breath he took. Cooper moved in behind her, effectively sandwiching her between the two rock-hard bodies. Feeling them against her rendered her senseless and before she could gather her wits to process what was happening, Everett's mouth swooped down and covered hers.

As he probed the secret places of her mouth with his

tongue, an electrical current charged through her body. His lips were voracious, taking everything she had to give and demanding even more. Need pumped hot and heavy through her blood.

"Amanda," he moaned as he broke the kiss to lick his way down her neck. "Lean against Cooper. Let him hold you up while I make you come."

The words sent her up on flames. She wiggled until Cooper clamped his hands around her hips to hold her still. Everett claimed her lips again, sliding his tongue into her mouth to dance with hers, the rhythm of the kiss mimicking his hips. His hard cock rooted against the very spot where she craved him to be. They both seemed to sense what she needed, because while his hands cupped then rubbed her breasts them through her shirt, Cooper unzipped her pants so he could slide inside and under her panties.

As soon as he touched her clit, she just about jumped out of her skin, moaning.

"You are so fucking sexy," Cooper murmured in her ear, his voice heavy with need. "You've always been so sexy."

"And ours," Everett said. "Right, sweetheart? You're ours."

"Let's take this into the bedroom, shall we?" Cooper suggested.

With a smile, she took their hands and led them upstairs, into the master bedroom. Clothes melted away, discarded in haste along the steps and onto the floor. Amanda could barely believe what was about to happen. A dream come true, one she'd never thought to experience again.

A faint whiff of horse lingered on Cooper's skin. Everett smelled of sweat and sun. The scents swirled around in a dizzying burst that heated her blood and had her senses swimming. As Cooper slid a finger into her, Everett pinched her nipples. She bucked her hips, seeking something and going crazy when the men continued their ruthless assault on her senses. They teased her, revving her up little by little until she could no longer contain her climax. She exploded, riding Cooper's fingers as Everett swallowed up her passionate cry of release.

"That's it," he breathed against her mouth. "Come for us, baby. Give us your cream."

She humped Cooper's hand, milking her orgasm until she slumped, exhausted. As she slowly filtered back to reality, Cooper removed his hand from between her thighs but kept his hard body pressed against her back. Everett gave one last swipe with his fingers against her nipples before cupping her face to give her one last light kiss.

"Holy crap," she said, panting.

"Just wait," Cooper told her as he brought his fingers up and licked them. That was when she realized he was licking *her*.

"We're going to take you together," Everett added.

Her eyes widened. She knew what he meant and a sliver of fear shot through her. Would it hurt? She'd read about anal sex but had never had the thought that she wanted to actually do it. Now, it seemed, the decision had been taken out of her hands.

Everett rubbed feathery strokes along her slit. Pressing inward, he bent one finger to rub along the back wall of her pussy while his thumb found her clit and played with it. In and out he used his fingers to heighten her pleasure. Suddenly, he withdrew and ran one hand over the curve of her bottom, down the back of her thighs then up between them, to touch her intimately. His thumb circled around her hole, then pressed in, just a little. His finger, slick with her own juices, easily slid past her tight rosette. Not enough to hurt, but the pressure he applied made her squirm. The invasion burned, yet as her body adjusted, desire blossomed. It surprised her and she moaned for more. Using the wetness from her pussy, he pressed a finger into her anus. She vaguely realized that he was preparing her, opening her up for his penetration.

"You're so fucking hot," Everett groaned. "So wet. Feel how wet she is, Cooper."

Cooper teased down her stomach and slid through her curls. When he found her slit he let his middle finger dive into her warmth. Both men teased her, playing her body like a musical instrument. Slowly, they rotated until Cooper was in front of her. He dropped to his knees to kiss her belly button and licked his way south until he reached the apex of her thighs. He nudged them apart and a second later he was licking her and sucking on her clit. He pushed one finger into her then began thrusting, back and forth, hitting her G-spot and driving her out of her mind.

"So wet," Cooper replied. "I want to fuck this pussy. Would you like that, Amanda? Would you like my cock buried in your tight little cunt while Everett discovers the delights of your ass?"

She panted, the images turning her on so much. "Will it hurt?" she asked.

"It'll burn, but in such a good way, baby," Everett told her. "Relax and trust us."

"I do," she said. "I love you both so much."

Everett kissed the back of her neck and eased away so they could reposition her. Cooper settled on the bed, his legs spread, and Everett helped her sit on his lap, straddling him.

She opened her eyes and locked gazes with Cooper as he lifted her hips and brought her down onto his cock.

He began to slowly move her, letting her find her center and ride him.

Behind her, Everett slid a finger back into her ass. Amanda halted and stiffened, not sure if she liked the feeling of having both holes filled. As she adjusted to the odd sensation, he edged in another finger, widening her, and the burning thrust took her breath away.

"Oh!" she groaned. "It burns!"

"Relax, baby," Everett murmured in her ear. "I have to stretch you. I don't want to hurt you."

He manipulated her body and she found herself pulled upward, sandwiched between both men. Everett angled his cock against her ass and pushed in. She gasped at how both men filled her.

"Holy hell," Cooper moaned. "You're so damn tight, baby!"

The burning returned and Amanda held her breath, not sure if she enjoyed the new sensation. But just as she thought she wanted to stop, Cooper pulled out of her a little to give Everett more room, and he pushed in all the way. Amanda gasped, unable to believe the feeling of being totally consumed. It was amazing, beyond words. Beyond anything she had imagined.

Everett's breath tickled the back of her neck as he held her hips still.

"That's it, baby," he said. "You're so fucking beautiful, sandwiched between us."

"She's so tight," Cooper said. "She's gripping my cock like a vise."

Amanda moaned. "Please, do something. Move! Fuck me! Please!"

Everett's hips bucked and Cooper followed the rhythm. They moved as one, so in tune with each other. She bounced between them, her hands resting on Cooper's shoulders. Sweat rolled off their bodies, breaths mingled together. No words were spoken and they didn't need them.

They moved in tandem, as one went in the other pulled out. Moans echoed through the room as they spiraled together. The spring recoiled and she was launched into a kaleidoscope of sensation.

"Not gonna last," Cooper muttered from behind her. "Oh shit, oh shit! Fuck!"

Everett shouted as he followed them both, feeling his cock jerk deep inside as his hot essence filled her.

She collapsed next to Cooper and his arms folded around her panting body. Everett wrapped his arms around her front and they rested together, sated, as their heartbeats returned to normal.

"I love you," she murmured. "Both of you. I want this for

the rest of my life."

"Me too," Cooper said.

Epilogue

Amanda sat on the verandah, watching the sun rise on the eastern horizon. For the first time in a long time, she felt whole. Content. The pieces of her fractured world put back together in such an unexpected way. A day ago she'd been merely existing, and now she was blissfully happy.

The screen door opened and Everett stepped out, a cup of steaming coffee in both hands. He handed her one.

"Still take it black?"

She nodded and took the mug. "Thank you."

He sat down next to her. For several moments, they simply watched the day dawn.

"I was wrong to leave all those years ago without talking to both of you," Everett said in a low tone.

"Yes, you were," she replied.

He sighed. "I'm sorry."

"Did you apologize to Cooper?"

"Yeah." He rubbed his jaw. "His right hook told me he forgave me."

She chuckled.

He held out his hand to her. "I'm not going anywhere, Amanda. Never again. My soul is here. With you and Cooper, and with this land."

She took his hand. "You're willing to walk away from your career?"

"Fletcher had mentioned that we need a shadow wolf patrolling this area. Maybe I'll look into that. If not..." He shrugged. "The only regret I have in life is leaving you two behind. This may not be a conventional path to life, but damned if I'm going to ignore what my heart is telling me to do. Not anymore."

Cooper came outside, smiling. It had been a long time since she'd seen him so happy.

"You could start working with horses, Amanda," Cooper said. "Just like you always wanted to do. We could build this ranch into something great."

"The three of us," she replied, smiling, happy to feel like her life was getting back on track again now that she was with her loves.

She held out her other hand to Cooper and he took hold, uniting them.

Bound to the Billionaire

Excerpt

Chapter One

'Bared to Him' by Sierra Cartwright

"Which floor?"

"Twelve, thanks," Myka said slightly breathlessly. He'd patiently held the elevator door open while she hurried across the lobby of the downtown Denver office building. She'd been at lunch too long—the quarterly gathering with her college girlfriends had been too scandalously delicious to leave. As the waiter had brought a second glass of wine for each of them, they'd shared stories of their sex lives—the thrills and droughts—and now she was running late for a meeting with a client.

The man pushed the button for the twelfth floor and then fifteen, presumably for his. The elevator doors slid shut.

"How's the book?"

Self-consciously she moved the bestselling paperback

behind her. "I just borrowed it from a friend." Borrowed it? Prised it from Kathleen's unwilling fingers was more like it. Everywhere Myka went, it seemed people were talking about the book, and, after some of her friends' confessions over lunch, Myka had been desperate to read it. She knew little about BDSM, yet what she knew intrigued her. But where would she find a man into that kind of kink? Her last boyfriend had freaked out and left when she'd brought out scarves and asked him to tie her up.

"Do you know anything about the book?" he asked.

She took a second look at him. He was taller than her, by at least six inches, and that said something since she was unusually tall. In heels, she wasn't used to looking up at many people.

He appeared to be in his late thirties. His dark hair had a smattering of appealing grey at the temples. It added to his distinguished good looks.

His eyes were a startling green. She had the odd sense that he saw through her tough exterior into her innermost secrets.

She knew she was staring, but she couldn't look away. His scent seemed to brand the air — something crisp and outdoorsy, a stamp of primal male power and intrigue. Even his clothing captured attention.

Myka made a decent living as a financial adviser, and she recognised quality. The suit that had been exquisitely tailored to fit his toned body cost at least a month of her salary.

"So, do you?"

She was lost. "Do I what?"

"Do you know anything about the book?"

He captured her gaze. Instinct told her to look away, but she couldn't. Unnerved, she stepped forward so she could exit quickly. "It's hard not to," she said. "It's being talked about everywhere." Realising she was in danger of babbling, something she did not do, she countered, "Have you read it?"

"I haven't read it, no. There's no need."

A bell dinged, signalling that she'd reached her floor. "No need?" she asked.

"I live the lifestyle," he said.

The doors slid open.

He moved forward, crowding her space. She'd have to brush past him to exit. He pressed the button to keep the doors open. "Look me up if you're curious."

This man, tall and broad, had an air of easy command, as if he was accustomed to issuing orders and having others obey. She had an insane urge to treat him with respect he'd yet to earn. She felt her body grow warmer.

He stepped aside, and she exited the elevator. The doors slid closed.

'Made for Him' by Desiree Holt

I'm not making a mistake. This is the chance of a lifetime. Everything will be fine.

Teri Choate locked her fingers together in her lap, watching through the helicopter window as the Friday afternoon sun lit the waters of the Atlantic Ocean below her. A representative of Micah Sheridan's had arrived at her condo in San Antonio at noon to take her to the private airstrip where the Sheridan Worldwide helo awaited her. Now, as they got closer and closer to his private island off the coast of Maine, as the weekend loomed before her, she forced back the case of nerves that kept trying to take over her body. This weekend was a test, for both her and Micah Sheridan. He wanted to push her, to see if she could fully match his needs as a Dom. What would he ask her to do that would show him she trusted him completely?

She wanted desperately to unlock his heart, because she'd had the misfortune to fall in love with the man and that was a disaster in the making. Could she submit to him as completely as he demanded, no matter what level he took her to? And could he finally unlock the shackles he kept around his emotions to make their relationship emotional as well as physical? Commit to something long term?

She had struggled for so long with the clash between her submissive nature and her strong personality. It had been a big step for her, even before she'd met Micah, to blend those two parts of her. Two sides of the same coin. The result had been some less than satisfactory relationships, leaving her to constrain her sexual activities to impersonal sessions at The Castle, the private bondage club she belonged to. It never ceased to amaze her that while she ran an executive employment agency that served clients everywhere, making decisions that involved power and money, once she took off her clothes she turned into someone else. She was sure that was the reason she'd never been able to build a lasting relationship.

Until Micah Sheridan. The man she knew could take control without controlling her.

At thirty-eight he had amassed a global fortune and was both respected and feared in business communities all over the world. The world saw him as a man in elegantly tailored clothing with a sharp business mind and a ruthless attitude, yet still playing with all the toys a man of his wealth accumulated.

She'd done her homework on him. She was aware that this home she was on her way to was only one of many. He had a villa in Cannes, one in Acapulco, a condo in Hong Kong and a chalet in Switzerland. He raced cars for fun, skied both the Alps and the Andes, kept fully outfitted yachts at each of his villas, and never carried a suitcase because every one of his homes was outfitted with his needs.

'Waiting for Him' by Natalie Dae

Shara twirled a lock of her dark hair and stared across the spacious penthouse living room at her Dom. Naked and spreading her legs, she leant back on their black leather sofa and waited for him to notice her. To say hello and smile. To give her that look, the one that told her she was his world and he'd left work behind.

He'd swept in minutes ago, long black hair streaming behind him, and dumped his briefcase on the walnut sideboard that housed alcohol and crystal glasses, napkins and their best silver cutlery. He'd seemed preoccupied, acting as though she wasn't even there. That stung a little. Hadn't she been eagerly anticipating his arrival? Hadn't she been glancing at the clock, seeing only a minute or two had passed since she'd last checked? Hadn't her heart been hammering, her pulse racing, her mind conjuring images of how their evening would go? Yes, she'd experienced a pang of hurt, of regret that, despite their talking to one another via computer for the best part of the day, his mood had changed rapidly since they'd last had contact.

Something had happened in between. Someone or something had upset him.

She could only hope he still wanted to play. Still wanted her.

He appeared lost, leaning his folded forearms on the top of the armchair like that, gazing into space somewhere in the vicinity of the large mirror hanging above the roaring fireplace. She wondered what he was seeing, what he was thinking, and whether she could erase it, make it all vanish so he never had to go through a moment's hurt for the rest of his life. People thought because they had money they had no worries, but they didn't know a damn thing. Life still went on for them much as it did for those who earned less, except their cash could solve the minor issues or remove boredom by allowing them to disappear on their boat for the day or dine out. He'd had a hard morning at the office, she knew that much, preparing for a meeting later in the afternoon, and all the money in the world wouldn't take that tired, strained look from his face. Only she could do that by preoccupying him, or listening to what was on his mind and suggesting ways to solve issues.

I want to hold you, John.

She couldn't, though. She'd have to wait as she'd been instructed, until he pulled himself back to the present.

His hair fell forward off his shoulders, partially obscuring his features, the rise of his cheek and the tip of his nose the only things she could see. The light from the chandelier caught his hair, giving that dark sheet a silver glimmer. She longed to touch it, to sift her fingers through the softness then fist it tight, forcing him to look at her, to acknowledge that she'd been waiting for him like this for an hour. To let him know if they needed to abandon their plans that was all right. It would be a letdown, considering she'd worked herself up into a state of frenzied excitement as he'd told her to do, but she was prepared to forgo play tonight if that was what he needed.

Look at me, John. Speak to me. Tell me what's on your mind.

But that wasn't the way it worked — the way he worked. He would only tell her what was wrong once he'd mulled it over, once he had to admit that he couldn't find the solution alone. He hated to burden her.

'Come to Him' by Justine Elyot

She should have expected a lot of paperwork, but somehow the number of times she was required to sign on dotted lines still came as a shock to Erin.

"And the non-disclosure agreement," said the lawyer smoothly, passing another sheaf of printed material across the desk.

She read it through, trying to take her time and be level-headed, but her vision skittered across the page, picking up legalese phrases here and there. The gist was that she was never to discuss what passed between her and the lawyer's client with any third party — most specifically she was never to publish any account of her experiences with him, nor ever mention his name in connection with hers.

Picking up the pen and signing, yet again, she let her eye fall on the printed-out copy of her original advertisement on MasterMe.com. That nervous moment of pressing the button and making her plea live to hundreds of thousands of fellow fetishists seemed a million years from today. She could barely read it without cringing now.

"You've all heard of the girl who auctioned off her virginity. Well, I'm no virgin, but I do need funding for my MA in Women's Studies, and I can offer something that might well appeal to those dominant men among you.

I'm offering my submission.

Subject to agreement of limits etc. for a period of one calendar month — will probably have to be August owing to academic commitments — I can obey your every command and satisfy your every whim.

Tempted? Please apply to downcasteyes@submail.com.

I look forward to hearing your orders."

A blizzard of interest had buffeted her inbox, most of it spurious, but in the end she had narrowed down the field of bidders to three.

The winning bid had taken her breath away.

One million pounds.

Enough to fund a lifetime's research, let alone the tract she intended to write on the contrast between Victorian and medieval attitudes to female sexuality. She had almost vomited when she had seen the email with the offer.

Of course, it had to be a hoax. Nobody would offer that. Nobody in their right mind, surely.

But communication over the telephone with 'Mr Nobody's' legal team had convinced her that it was serious, and now she was meeting his solicitor in his London office to finalise the arrangement.

It didn't help that a couple of journalists had seen her advertisement and posed as bidders themselves, hoping to get a story about what kind of woman might do such a thing. Erin had sniffed out their misogynistic agenda straight away and blocked them, but she was wary all the same.

'Play to Him' by Wendi Zwaduk

"You're going on another date with him?" Kayla wrapped a lock of Rhiannon's hair around the barrel of the curling iron. "I didn't think he dated anyone twice."

"This is our third date, but who's counting? And, really, what's a date? We're not going anywhere special. I'm just playing music for his customers. Nothing exciting." Rhiannon stared at her reflection in the mirror. Talk about scoring the best stylist in the business. She trusted Kayla to make her look beautiful before each show. Rhiannon pursed her lips and pinched her cheeks. The fat curls accentuated the sunken qualities of her face. She frowned. At twenty-seven, she already looked old. The black liner made the blue in her eyes pop and contrasted with her ivory skin well and paired with the inky colour of her hair nicely, but she worried everything looked too dark and moody. She shrugged. She played moody music, why not look the part? "Do you think I should ramp up the liner?" She squinted. "It's too light, isn't it?"

"You're nervous for a not-really date, that's a very-much-so date."

"I'm not nervous." What a liar. Rhiannon rubbed her sweaty palms on her thighs. Hell yes, she was nervous. Sebastian Chastain, billionaire playboy and owner of Rock Hard Toys and Gear, didn't give second engagements. Unless the woman really tickled his fancy, he rarely offered a first chance for a play date. He'd signed a contract with her to play whenever he wanted and she'd agreed.

She shivered. Tingles radiated over her back from the memories of his whip spread over her skin. Her pussy creamed and she clenched her knees together. Besides, there was a chance the concert wouldn't lead to more.

"Whatever." Kayla rolled her eyes. "Your hair is done. Thoughts?"

Not bad. Rhiannon twisted the cascade of curls on the top of her head. "I like it." The updo would keep her hair out of the way during the session with Sebastian. "Thank you."

"Cool." The stylist gathered her brushes and the bottles of hairspray. "Good luck. Maybe this guy will be the one who gets you to settle down."

"Settle down? Kayla, I don't want to be tied down to a family and responsibilities. I want to be free and figure out who I am."

"And not be lonely." Kayla winked and strolled out of the room.

That word. Lonely. Rhiannon frowned at her reflection and sighed. She'd been without the affection from a man for so long. But she had a reason for keeping things separate. She stood and turned away from her image. Sebastian, though detached in the emotions category, gave her the kink she needed. And he was stable. He understood her boundaries.

'Die for Him' by Amy Valenti

What kind of billionaire holds a business meeting in a nightclub?

I put the finishing touches to my lipstick and clicked the cap back into place, then put it back on the dresser, not without reluctance. I'd have loved to take a purse with me, but it would just get in the way if I needed to move quickly.

"You ready?" Rick called from the living room.

"Think so." I picked up my only essential item for the evening, my trusty Glock pistol, and tucked it into its holster at my hip. After taking a last look around me, I headed out to meet Rick, who was staring, perplexed, at the collection of extreme sports gear piled in the corner.

"I thought you were on jury duty this week, not snowboarding and skydiving."

"Oh." I eyed the corner distractedly. "I keep meaning to pick that up, but I use it all so often that there doesn't seem like much point."

He shuddered. "Man, I don't know how you keep throwing yourself out of planes and down mountainsides and stuff. That would freak me the fuck out. Aren't you scared of dying or something?"

I should be so lucky. I bit back the words before they emerged. I didn't want the guys I worked with to know I couldn't find much to live for these days and needed a good jolt of adrenaline to get my kicks. That'd get me suspended on psych leave, or worse, fired. I could hardly handle two days of jury duty, never mind a life of leisure with no wages to fund my need for extreme sports.

Rick turned and looked me up and down. "Nice. I love the way the Kevlar brings out your eyes."

"Thanks." I rolled my eyes and adjusted the vest below my black shirt. Said shirt was the loosest piece of what could pass as clubwear I owned, but to a trained eye like Rick's, the body armour was easy to spot. Luckily, I wasn't trying too hard to pass myself off as a civilian—I was only covering up the vest to avoid freaking out the rest of the club's patrons. It wasn't a sexy look, but it was functional. "Remind me where this club is, again?"

"Just off Miller Street." Rick switched to businesslike, heading for the door, and I followed, locking up behind us. "I'll drive."

"And you're sure it's an invitation-only night?"

"Positive. While you were sitting around taking it easy on jury duty, we were vetting the guest list and checking out the venue. You're gonna love it."

Judging by the grin on his face, I wasn't too sure about that.

I slid into the passenger seat and buckled up, waiting for Rick to do the same on the driver's side before continuing the conversation. "So why is he having a business meeting in a nightclub anyway? He's only got one more night until the big meeting that's put his life in danger to start with. Wouldn't he be safer waiting until this is all over?"

More books from
Totally Bound Publishing

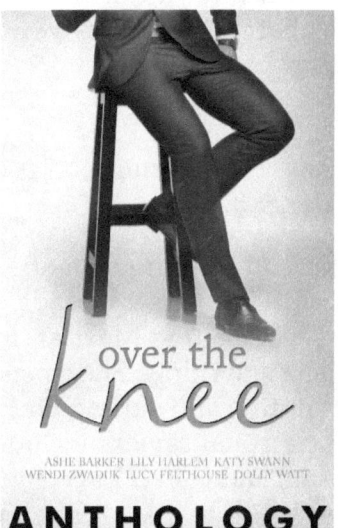

over the
knee

ASHE BARKER LILY HARLEM KATY SWANN
WENDI ZWADUK LUCY FELTHOUSE DOLLY WATT

ANTHOLOGY

About the Author

Alysha Ellis

Alysha Ellis lives in Australia and when she isn't busy drinking champagne, eating chocolate and letting her inner tart run free, she writes erotic comedy. Her favourite quote comes from Mae West… A hard man is good to find. Who could argue with that? Alysha tries very hard to be bad, because bad girls have all the fun.

BA Tortuga

Texan to the bone and an unrepentant Daddy's Girl, BA spends her days with her basset hounds, getting tattooed, texting her sisters, and eating Mexican food. When she's not doing that, she's writing. She spends her days off watching rodeo, knitting and surfing Pinterest in the name of research. BA's personal saviors include her wife, Julia, her best friend, Sean, and coffee. Lots of good coffee.

Nan Comargue

Nan Comargue is a thirtysomething romance and erotic romance writer who has been reading romance novels all her life. She prefers sexy confident heroes who win over slightly introverted heroines (read: nerdish types) but she writes about everything from angel-warriors to cowboy ménage.

Nan is Canadian, eh? So naturally she's written a contemporary romance with a professional hockey player

Wendi Zwaduk

I always dreamed of writing the stories in my head. Tall, dark, and handsome heroes are my favourites, as long as he has an independent woman keeping him in line.

I earned a BA in education at Kent State University and currently hold a Masters in Education with Nova Southeastern University.

I love NASCAR, romance, books in general, Ohio farmland, dirt racing, and my menagerie of animals. You can also find me at my blog

Molly Ann Wishlade

Molly Ann Wishlade has always been an avid reader and writer of stories. Her lifetime of reading has taken her from the magical worlds of The Faraway Tree and The Borrowers, to the Greek myths and legends, to Sweet Valley High and Judy Blume's Forever, to Asimov's science fiction, Jane Eyre's torment and Stephen King's masterpieces. More recently she has wandered through the vivid historicals of Philippa Gregory; the bubbly, gritty delights of Adele Parks and the fast paced thrillers of James Patterson. She loves getting lost in a novel and often regrets finishing one as the characters are usually missed like old friends. She regularly indulges her insatiable hunger for romance and passion in the delicious worlds created by romantic novelists and is working on several of her own!

What precious spare time she has is spent with her family (one gorgeous husband and two bright and beautiful children), taking long walks around the beautiful Welsh countryside (although she's still waiting for the rescue greyhound she wants to accompany her), cooking her own secret recipe curries, drinking Earl Grey (in copious amounts) and discovering delicious wines. Oh, and she also loves to ski and can't wait to go again! And buying shoes!

She wants to take readers on the rollercoaster that is life through the creation of her own characters, relationships and worlds.

Beth D. Carter

I like writing about the very ordinary girl thrust into extraordinary circumstances, so my heroines will probably never be lawyers, doctors or corporate high rollers. I try to write characters who aren't cookie cutters and push myself to write complicated situations that I have no idea how to resolve, forcing me to think outside the box. I love writing characters who are real, complex and full of flaws, heroes and heroines who find redemption through love.

I've been pretty fortunate in life to experience some amazing things. I've lived in France, traveled throughout Europe, Australia and New Zealand. I am a mom to an amazing little boy. I'm surrounded by friends and family. And although I love holding a book in my hand, I absolutely adore my ereader, which I've named Ruby. I love to hear from readers so I've made it really easy to find me on the web.

Our authors love to hear from readers. You can find contact information, website details and author profile pages at https://www.totallybound.com/

Home of Erotic Romance